DEATH
DOWN
UNDER

A NOVEL BY DOMINGO A. ROCHA, MD

AN OLD LINE PUBLISHING BOOK

Printed in the United States of America

ISBN-13: 978-0-9845704-1-6
ISBN-10: 0-9845704-1-1

Cover design by Domingo A. Rocha and Tyler Somers

This book is a work of fiction. Any references to real people, events, establishments, organizations, or locales are intended solely to provide a sense of authenticity and are used fictitiously. All other characters, incidents, and dialogue are drawn from the author's imagination and are not to be construed as real.

Old Line Publishing, LLC
P.O. Box 624
Hampstead, MD 21074
Toll-Free Phone: 1-877-866-8820
Toll-Free Fax: 1-877-778-3756
Email: oldlinepublishing@comcast.net
Website: www.oldlinepublishingllc.com

DEDICATION

For:

Helen, Domingo (Sr.), Carolyn, Allie, Holly, and Yum Yum.

ACKNOWLEDGMENTS

Writing a book is a long endeavor that in my case required fortitude and perseverance but also tremendous support from a myriad of people. There is no way to recall everyone that contributed to my being able to write this book. I thank everyone that in one way or another encouraged me.

In particular, I want to thank my mother who correctly thought reading and schooling were the most important thing. Cronin, who made me think it was possible to write again and Dan, whose friendship has been a healing force in my life, and I thank Don and Alex, for changing the direction of my life. Dad, for being an example of a responsible man willing to take risks.

The people listed below directly had a hand in this particular book. They are listed in no particular order. This book would not exist without their help and support. Any mistakes are mine alone.

Kelly, Krista, Anne, and Barb who read my firsts drafts and were able to look past the obvious problems to what was good. Sharon, who encouraged me when I would doubt myself. Lisa, the professional writer who was so encouraging to a novice.

Finally, without the love from my mom, the example of my dad, the unending love of my wife, and the miracle of my two daughters I would never have been able to reach a point where I would have attempted this book.

The one non-acknowledgement is my high school English teacher to whom I showed my first attempt at book writing and whose response was so devastating that I did not write for 12 years.

TABLE OF CONTENTS

CHAPTER ONE

MURDER DOWN UNDER

Presumably, my vacation to New Zealand would relax, refresh and renew my spirits. According to daddy dearest, it would help me obtain closure and revive our closeness once again. Big fat hairy chance. As far as I was concerned, we were done for good. His vicious betrayal of trust far exceeded what could ever be forgiven. Fortunately for me, my resolve was tested that first morning in my hotel room by the unusual event of being woken, by one of the Christchurch's finest, out of a coma-like state while I lay next to a dead male ex-person.

You may well imagine this had many elements of a nasty nightmare and thus I did not respond well. I did not initially understand that the man lying next to me was no longer with the living. My first impression was that two slime balls were trying to entertain themselves at my expense. If I noticed that the man waking me was dressed in a policeman's uniform, I did not notice nor would it have mattered to me. What should have been my first clue, however, was his solemn, courteous manner in conjunction with his gentle expression. So as soon as my brain began functioning sufficiently, I started swinging wildly and viciously. This combined with the unexpectedness of my attack meant that I actually managed to get a few good punches before he dislocated my left thumb while attempting to subdue me. I should have been thankful that they don't routinely carry guns down here, or I might have landed in the morgue next to whoever was next to me in bed.

When I later discovered that the man I had been sleeping with (now cut that out, you know what I mean) was in reality dead and not sleeping, I fainted. Well not completely unconscious fainted, but kind of dizzy, lightheaded, don't-know-what-else-to-do fainted. I could still mostly understand what was happening and what little I had left of my mind was desperately trying to piece the disparate puzzle pieces into any coherent picture whatsoever — particularly focusing on from where the hell did the dead man emerge?

I most certainly had not invited anyone to join me. Had I? I don't drink anymore so I could not have been too drunk to remember. Could someone have overpowered me, dragged me into bed, had his way with me then waited for me to fall asleep so he could do the decent thing and die next to me? No, I don't think so.

While I puzzled over my hopeless situation and still hoping I would wake up from the nightmare, I heard the policeman talking with hotel security. Apparently, the police station received one call about the sounds of fighting in my hotel room. MY ROOM! The hotel reported no such complaints but they sent a security guard upstairs. When their knocks at my door did not elicit a response (what knocks? I couldn't remember anything about last night), security queried the guests in adjoining rooms and they all agreed they'd heard shouting, but it only lasted a short while. No one admitted to calling the police. This morning they received another call. The operator thought it was the same male voice; however, this time he said there was a dead person in the room. They called the room as well as knocked for a while before deciding to use the security guard's passkey.

I was shocked when the policeman mentioned I had been so deeply asleep and breathing so shallow that he believed we were both dead. God, what I do for a vacation.

Once subdued and with my dislocated finger throbbing, I had little choice but to cooperate. Prior to incarcerating me, they kindly had an urgent care clinic check me out. Although none of the eight carpal bones was actually broken, the thumb was dislocated at the MP (metacarpal-pharyngeal) joint and the wrist ligaments were severely strained. The doctor quickly and effortlessly reduced it while my screams were heard back home in Boulder. My instructions were to wear the splint until the swelling came down completely and assured me I would make a complete recovery. My only other physical injury was a nasty cut on the inside of my lip, but since it stopped bleeding, I wouldn't let them touch it. It was left to me to bandage what little was left of my ego and self-respect.

In this respect, I did not help matters that I prefer to sleep with few clothes on. Actually, usually with no clothes on. I insist it is a residue of my father always keeping the temperature too warm in our house. I have vivid memories of long sweltering summers, unable to get out of the heat, jealous of the boys' ability to go topless, but I digress. After being patched up at the clinic, they brought me to this lousy excuse for a cell. Sure, it was clean enough, the mattress was soft enough but the privacy had serious deficiencies. I even had my own cellmate, Louise. She wasn't a talker, but from the little she said and her general disposition, I gather that she belongs incarcerated far more than I do, which is all the more reason my brain was telling me to GET THE HELL OUT OF HERE.

Every time I tried to figure how this all happened, I got a splitting headache. I remembered locking the door. I was exhausted from the fourteen-hour trip and went immediately to bed — alone. I clearly remember I was alone. However, not only did I not wake up alone, I woke up with a corpse (this is were the headache starts). I then struck a policeman — twice. The policeman (in defense I admit) dislocated my thumb, which by the way still throbbed inside the splint. During these events I was completely exposed to the policeman, the hotel manager, a maid and a very young and curious bellboy (this is where the headache becomes splitting). I am at this very moment in a foreign jail for murdering someone I never met while putatively on vacation (this is where it becomes a migraine).

"Miss Prescott?" one of the guards called out.

"Yes?" I answered hopefully, anything to distract me from my thoughts.

"Could you come with us? We would like to ask you some questions."

"Of course!" I stammered. I was more than ready to leave, and besides, Louise and I were not getting along. She was too sullen; she should learn to lighten up. I added, "Although I

14

would prefer answers. At the moment, I have too many unanswered questions of my own."

The guard stopped unlocking the door and took a hard look at me. He decided I was not trying to make fun of him and smiled. "So do we all, miss, so do we all."

He led me past the booking area with which I was now much too familiar. This is where I had been searched (*For what?* I wondered. I literally had had nothing on when they found me) prior to being jailed. We then walked down a hall sparse of decorations and oddly reminiscent of my high school at the end of which we climbed up two floors — four flights of stairs. *Don't they have elevators here?* It truly is wonderful technology, a button and up you go. I decided this might not be the best time to bring this up.

Another interesting discovery is that in New Zealand, and a good part of the world for that matter, the floors are numbered in European fashion. The ground floor is not numbered, the first floor is what we would call the second, etc. So we ended up on their second floor, but we were three stories above the ground (the little things I use to occupy my mind when I want to avoid a headache.) We finally stopped at a door marked "Chief Inspector Yves."

The officer knocked and we heard a friendly voice respond, "I'll be there straight away."

Or maybe I just wanted it to sound friendly. Within five minutes, the door opened to reveal a tall and totally striking man. Not just striking, he was drop-dead gorgeous. He had a full head of gorgeous wavy black hair trimmed perfectly. His mustache was bushy but understated. His eyes were questioning and definitely intense but also happy. That's what I noticed first — happy eyes. That was most unexpected. I had envisioned a combination of grand inquisitor and executioner.

He looked right at me and said, "So this is our sleeping beauty? Come in, please."

CHAPTER TWO

VACATION PLANS

My vacation to the south island of New Zealand began innocently enough while I was taking out the garbage. The garbage was always spilling out onto the sidewalk and the dogs and birds would tear into it through the night. Come tomorrow morning, I would find myself picking up the scattered remains in my work clothes and then smelling my hands during the trip to work. By the time I arrived at my office, my nose would have adjusted and I would be infecting the air with my garbage smell. Not!

I determined to change my Monday-morning pattern. I could not afford a new, larger trash can with a well-fitting lid (actually I could, but I could not allow myself to buy it while my old one remained serviceable, and by the way, how do you throw a trash can away?) So in the spirit of inventiveness, I attached a bungee cord to a handle and sprayed the outside with cheap perfume (very cheap perfume that some idiot I once dated gave me).

As if on cue, Paula, one of the few talkative tenants in my building, came out struggling with her garbage can. "Hi, Yo," she said.

My name is Yolanda. This is much too long for her (and for most people evidently). Because I can't stand my childhood nickname of Yolee, I came up and prefer being called 'Yo.' "Hi, Paula," I replied.

"I'm so tired of going through this trash ritual every Sunday night. I think that in the future some anthropologist will define us by how we handled our trash. And they won't be very impressed," she mused.

I smiled at her observation. Paula has a way with thoughts and is able to put the most different and unlikely thoughts together without the slightest hint of awareness. The thought of my bungee cord being on some display as evidence of the decay of our urban society was funny. I suddenly wished I had bought a new one instead of making do with two old worn cords I found at my dad's house.

With all these thoughts careening through my head, I almost missed it. I was getting ready to go in and continue my Sunday night get-ready-to-work ritual when I saw it. On top of her trash bag, there was a colorful picture of some tropical island: palm trees, deep cobalt blue water, coral reefs and bronze gods pretending to be men. I hesitated while looking at it.

Paula noticed I was staring, "Something wrong...oh, isn't it gorgeous?" she asked. "I was planning to go, but I can't get the time off work. Besides, Al wasn't too thrilled. He said it's too far! Can you believe him? That is the entire point of going away. Men are such bores sometimes."

Despite her comments regarding gender stereotypes, my

mind still wandered down that beautiful beach, the white sand sticking to my toes, the breeze blowing in my...

"Yo! Are you OK? You look kind of dazed."

I quickly recovered and put up a good front. "I have been thinking of going away for vacation. Could I have the brochure?" Not really expecting I would ever go.

Paula made a face, "Well sure, but it is all kinds of nasty, there are coffee grounds all over it."

"That's OK," I assured her and picked it up by the cleanest corner. It couldn't be any more disgusting than the garbage I'd just been picking up. You couldn't get AIDS from paper? Or could you? How about a paper cut? I quickly stopped that train of thought. I could drive myself crazy with all those 'what ifs.' I resolved to ask Dad next time I made a duty call and it would give us something to talk about. Ever since Mom died, we did not talk much and I felt I'd lost two parents that day. Anyway, I fully intended to throw the brochure away as soon as I entered my apartment.

However, upon entering, Nala, my lovable white and orange Maine Coon Cat, was ready and intertwined herself between my legs. I lost my balance trying not to step on her and had to let go of the brochure to catch myself. Now there were coffee grounds scattered throughout the hallway. I walked to the kitchen muttering curses at the gods for making cats so adorable and treacherous at the same time.

But for Nala's behavior, I would not be in my current situation. I believe that blaming the cat is entirely reasonable particularly since I absolutely refuse to take any responsibility whatsoever for this disaster of a vacation. On cleaning the hallway floor, I had a chance to look carefully at the cover without interruption. The place was absolutely gorgeous. The guy lounging on the beach was gorgeous. Could it really be that beautiful down there? Down where? I didn't even know what beach and which mountains the pictures depicted. That is how I wound up devouring the brochure and dreaming of being there (which I discovered depicted the South Island of New Zealand). Although the money wouldn't truly be a problem, I always have to overcome a reluctance of spending any on myself. After years of therapy, we concluded that I am basically insecure and having a fat bank account helps me feel more secure. Duh! Luckily, that's not why I went into therapy and definitely not the only thing I learned from it.

The next evening after a persistently dull day of routine office management, I listened to a message on my machine from Paula. My neighbor, Paula? We were only hallway acquaintances. I could not remember another time she'd called me and I was surprised she knew my number. What could she possibly want with me? Perhaps she wanted to coordinate garbage days? Borrow a bungee cord? Flipped out and is selling Amway (please God, NO!). I fully intended to ignore the call and make her call me back. But the guilt of my Catholic upbringing kept at me, needling me into finally doing the right thing by returning her call. As an aside, I find that many of the Catholics I know enjoy their guilt and find it difficult to function without it. As a former (reformed? recovered? rehabilitated?) Catholic, I no longer like to wallow in guilt but at the same time, I haven't been able to completely rid myself of it either. As with most things, some days are much worse than others. This was one of my susceptible days.

So there I was calling Paula, counting the rings: one, two, dawn of hope she isn't home, three, start composing a message for her machine, four, one more to go before Lord Guilt is assuaged, fi...

"Hello," came Paula's rushed voice.

My hopes dashed; I pleasantly responded, "Hello, this is Yolanda returning your call."

"Hi, Yolanda (not Yo? This could be serious). Excuse me, I was on my treadmill when you called."

Fortunately, I appease the fitness gods on a regular, if not daily, basis. I love to run and I make it a priority to run at least four or five times a week. Therefore, I neither received nor accepted additional guilt.

"I am sorry to bother you but you appeared so interested in that brochure that I thought you would want to hear about the changes."

I said, "Changes to what?" I felt I had missed a briefing. What was she talking about?

"About New Zealand, of course. That trip brochure you were so interested in that you actually touched it. I still can't believe you did that," she said matter-of-factly.

"Oh, yes, I remember now, and it was disgusting but those pictures are unbelievable. I stared at them and imagined being there but I decided the real place couldn't be that beautiful."

"In a way you are right," Paula said, "the brochure you saw doesn't do the place justice. I vacationed there five years, no closer to six years, well maybe it was five years ago and you truly can't capture those mountains and beaches on film..."

"Paula!" I interrupted, "what did you want me to know?" I was getting distracted with the extended reminiscences.

"That's right," she said, sounding embarrassed for

digressing, "I received a call from that travel club president. They had a few people drop out and they need to replace them."

"One more person for what?" beginning to feel that I should have learned to deal with the guilt of not calling. Either I was severely patience impaired or she was unable to get to the point.

"For the vacation trip to New Zealand, Yo, one more person for the trip. You see it is a special discount charter, and to get the good rates you need at least sixty-three people. They have only managed to get sixty. If they don't fill up the airplane they will have to cancel and I might just tell you that Donovan is becoming extremely agitated over this possibility. Now that you mention it, this entire thing came together very quickly and without any warning, which if you ask me is rather odd."

"Ah, now I understand, they are trolling for more people to go to New Zealand, "I said with luscious thoughts of swimming in that bluer than blue water starting to drift through my head. Perhaps that same guy in the picture would be there — Roland? Robert? What would be his name?

Paula interrupted my fantasy, "They have called everyone that they know and they are a bit desperate so they have all agreed to discount these last few tickets. Yo, are you listening? This trip could be an unbelievable steal! I could bash my stupid excuse for a husband for being so damn stubborn. I almost decided to go by myself, but..."

"How much?" I interrupted with a lot more excitement than I expected, "do you think Donovan would charge?"

"Yo, he said they would discount another 20 percent. If you ask me there will never be another great opportunity if you lived as long as my Aunt Marge. Now there is a..."

"Paula, earth to Paula, how much? Like in dollars, US dollars." She finally gave me the name and number of the tour director, Donovan Boers. What kind of name was that? And did I want to go halfway around the world with someone that made me think of wild pigs? I thought not. As the evening wore on, I nearly convinced myself that this vacation was too much too soon when the phone rang. I detected a touch of irony in the ring; do phones know stuff that we don't?

"Hello?" I said.

"Hello, is Ms. [pause] uh, Yolanda Y. Prescott there?"

The voice was deep and slightly hesitant. I did not recognize it. Damn it, a salesman. I hate it when they call, Dad says to simply hang up on them but I can never get myself to do just that. If this one time I'd done as Dad suggested, I would have avoided so much grief.

"Yes that is me," I answered.

"Hello, I am Donovan Boers. Paula gave me your number. Has she discussed with you the amazing vacation opportunity we are offering?"

My God, I thought, *what's up about this trip? Like the tide moving in I can't seem to stop it.* "Actually yes, she has. She said that you needed more people to get some discount?"

"That's right, they absolutely require sixty-three people to board to meet some federal regulation. We are talking to several people and I must admit, we are desperate at this point. It is vitally important to me that we go; my wife and I have been saving for this trip a long time. In fact, I formed this travel club exclusively for this trip." He paused, probably to catch his breath. "You see, if we can get sixty-three passengers, we get...blah, blah, blah...and it is a bargain."

"The trip is for two weeks..."

He was giving me his sales talk and I was catching few of the words. If the talk is not about computers I have trouble focusing for protracted periods of time and anyway, I was dreaming of surfing with the gorgeous dude on the brochure. Donovan had evidently described this adventure hundreds of times before and his voice droned.

"...rooms and tips. All you are responsible for are meals away from the group plus any gifts you buy..."

I quickly broke into his monologue. "The pictures on the brochure, are they actual pictures from there? Not just random pictures you copied from the Web?"

Donovan became excited understanding I was seriously considering it. "They are actual pictures from the area around Christchurch where we will be staying for the beginning of the trip."

I made up my mind. I would finish my current work project this week and put off everything else. I wanted to feel carefree far away from Boulder, and from Dad. Perhaps I would find peace of mind there, the peace of mind I'd lost when Mom died. Still there was the money to consider, "Ok, I know that you need people and time is short so make me a good deal and I'm in."

CHAPTER THREE

NEW ZEALAND

And that is how I found myself headed for an island I'd never seen, or had ever hoped to see. Even though my actual line of business is distinctly non-traditional, I suffer from the same ailments that all self-employed individuals suffer. On those rare occasions when I am not paranoid about not having enough clients, I am complaining about being swamped with work and not being able to have a life.

On this occasion, however, being my own boss worked to my decided advantage. It was much easier than expected; I informed my answering service, put a sign on the door as well as on my web page and, that was it — I was free to go. Perhaps I would find one of those guys on the brochure: Eduard, Austin, or whomever and have my way with them. I have a rich fantasy life.

The trip itself requires little description. That is, unless you like to talk about being stuffed in a too small, too noisy, and too smoky tin can that is recklessly flying six miles above an ocean that never ends and at over ten miles a minute no less! What holds the plane up? These things are heavy and don't bother talking to me about aerodynamics, lift and curvature of the wings — just stuff it. I have heard it all before and you know what? I just don't buy it — not for a second. Sure, if it were made of balsa and cloth I could see it, but these things weigh more that a bloody house! If you ask me, I think that THEY aren't telling all. I think that maybe somehow there is some kind of force field involved. But THEY don't want to tell us because THEY know we will get cancer or something. Well, I am actually not that paranoid but being cooped up for fourteen hours weirds me out.

We arrived without problems. I even started to like Donovan, sort of. The long trip allowed us many opportunities to talk. That is, until his wife (who is a horse of a very different temperament) started interfering. She would not leave us alone. The way she acted you would think that my life's goal was to break up any marriage that was within my reach. Where in the world were we supposed to consummate this relationship? The wing? The closet they call a toilet? The cockpit? At many points along the trip, I wanted to suggest she put a collar with his address and her name (as the owner) on it. That way she wouldn't have to watch so carefully. (I do get nasty after being confined for so long.)

During the flight, I anticipated my two entire weeks of vacation. There were a million things I wanted to do immediately upon landing. We arrived during the morning, two days after we left. I wasn't sure how I felt about losing an entire day of my life simply because I crossed some imaginary line over the Pacific Ocean.

We would stay at a classy ten-story hotel right in the

middle of the city. There were optional excursions every day and some of them actually sounded exciting. Until a week ago, I had known little of New Zealand. Not any of its history, traditions, geography, etc. I was amazed at the number of diverse natural sights to be seen.

Upon signing up for the trip, I raided the local libraries for books on the area. Of course, I did the same with online sources but there is still nothing quite like holding a book in your hands. By the time we departed, I had nearly memorized them all. I was taking this vacation as seriously as I do everything. I told Dad not to even think of lecturing me about being obsessive/compulsive; I was having fun. I found out that New Zealand has it all: mountains, beaches, jungles and even glaciers. In addition, because the settlement of the island happened relatively recently and they consequently have not had centuries of wars to continually destroy what they build, they have a tremendous amount of preserved historical buildings. They also have sheep — lots and lots of sheep. No problems sleeping here.

We landed in Christchurch, the largest city on South Island. New Zealand is composed primarily of two large islands, called the North and South Islands (original blokes, these people). Wellington, the capital, is at the southernmost tip of the North Island and barely twenty-five miles from the nearest shore of the South Island. Through this gap, some of the fiercest continuous winds blow. I planned to check out those winds soon.

Christchurch, on the other hand, is on the east side of South Island. It is a large city with nearly half a million inhabitants. It was founded by carefully chosen CoE (Church of England) members during the mid 1800s and was created in the image of their beloved England, which begs the question, if it was so beloved why did they leave it? They even brought trees and hedges typical of their homeland. It is a modern city now and would be hard to distinguish from many other cities in England. I was intrigued that the US military has a strong presence here, primarily because Christchurch is their staging area for the base at McMurdo, Antarctica. Maybe I could go there for my next vacation — couldn't be any more dangerous than this one.

The first person I met down under was Devin, the assistant hotel manager and was he ever cute. He didn't have quite as much hair as the guy in the brochure and his build was a bit more of the kind that normal humans have, but hey, I wasn't in a position to be picky. Unfortunately, he wasn't all that interested in me so I proceeded to get my room assignment.

After the terribly long trip, I couldn't wait even a minute to walk on the beach. My assigned room wasn't ready but they were able to give me a different one right away. As it turned out, had I waited, I would not be in this mess or in this cell, with miss congeniality, Louise keeping me company — and with severely throbbing wrist to boot. In my defense, back then, I was blissfully ignorant of what was in store for me when I rushed out to the beach.

Paula was right, after all, and I made a mental note to thank her. You could not capture this place on mere film. The brain and retina weren't good enough to do it justice. From the ultramarine blue water to the fine mustard-yellow sand, to the bronze guys sunbathing, it truly was paradise. I managed to slip into my bathing suit in record time to soak up as much of the place as possible. I even deviated from my firm rule to put on my sunscreen before I go out. I simply could not wait to admire the guys sunbathing with their gorgeous undulating chests of theirs.

So, while I applied the cancer screen without once thinking of Mom, I was grateful for the fortunate set of circumstances that allowed me the luxury of this peaceful, relaxing and uncomplicated trip.

CHAPTER FOUR

INSPECTOR YVES

I walked into Inspector Yves' office and noticed he was not alone. The policeman who woke me up and I managed to assault was standing next to a chair.

"Please sit down and make yourself comfortable, Ms. Prescott," Mr. Gorgeous said to me in a pleasing not quite pleading tone. "Thanks, Nate," he called out to the guard who brought me here when he closed the door. "Well, Miss Prescott, I believe we owe you an apology. Wouldn't you agree, Officer Bentley?" There was undisguised force in his question.

"Yes, mum, I mean sir! I am sorry I hurt your wrist. Truth is, you surprised me and I sort of just reacted," he said this formally and with more than a little embarrassment.

I was glad I was not the only one embarrassed. "It's all good," I heard myself say, "it could have happened to anyone. I am confident that you were just defending yourself." (What was I saying? Just minutes ago, I was a ranting lunatic, now I was miss congeniality?). It was nevertheless rewarding to see a blue puffiness around the temple of his right eye. Apparently, I had connected with at least one of my punches.

"I am pleased you feel that way," said the dreamy inspector, "but I was specifically referring to your being placed in custody. They should have treated you as a guest and a material witness, not as the murderer." This was so unexpected that it left me speechless. Did this mean I wouldn't be taken back? I might not get to say goodbye to Louise, how terribly sad.

"My colleagues were not thinking clearly early this morning. I would say that no thinking at all occurred. They felt that since you were in the same room with the deceased...Oh, by the way, did you know the man?"

"Uh...no. I just arrived from the States and I have not had a chance to meet anyone," I said, noticing how subtle his interrogation technique was, and how effective it must be.

"Yes, just as I suspected. To continue, their so-called thinking supposed that you may have been an accomplice in this unfortunate situation. I pointed out to these slow wits that if you had somehow caused this large man's death with not so much as a scratch on him, you would not have then chosen to sleep, much less in the same bed with him for over ten hours!" I must have looked pale because he rose quickly and came over to hold my unhurt wrist while looking intensely at me with those happy brown eyes of his.

"I'm fine," I muttered, not feeling well at all.

"You don't look fine to me," happy blue eyes said. "The department needs to make this up to you. We cannot incarcerate innocent tourists here on this island. Will you let me take you out to lunch? I could suggest an itinerary of out-of-the-way sights that are not in the vacation books."

"Why yes, that would be nice," I said, still not knowing who was doing the talking. It did not sound like me. Normally, I would flee from the police but today I felt different; I did not want to be finished with this man. He projected authority and caring — a powerful combination. So I said, "However, I need to clean myself and take a very long very hot bath, plus I need some time to forget about these last few hours — could we make it dinner?" How brazen of me to force him to buy me dinner.

After a brief barely noticeable hesitation and lifted eyebrows from Officer Bentley, he said, "Yes, of course."

"I do not know where we might go, could you..."

"Don't worry, Miss Prescott, I am exquisitely familiar with every restaurant in this part of South Island. I will pick you up at your hotel around...say, eight o'clock?"

I could not believe this gorgeous blue-eyed man was picking me up for dinner. It was better than a brain-deficient bronzed god from the beach. In my emotional confusion, all I managed was a squeaky, "Yes."

Life was proceeding too fast; I couldn't believe I'd just confirmed a date with a police detective. Can't I ever learn? I castigated myself. I just ended one bloody mess of a relationship with a guy that gives pigs a bad name and eight thousand miles away I jump at the chance to dine with someone I do not know from a lamp post. Even with his dreamy eyes, it just goes to show that Dad is completely right (not that he will ever hear that from these lips). I am completely insane and I cannot adequately control my impulses.

Later, I would think back on this moment and decide that his happy brown eyes had been sufficient reason to go to dinner. And besides, he was undoubtedly paying for what inevitably would be a particularly impressive restaurant considering that the dinner was an apology for the terrible treatment I had received at the station...Oh my God! I completely forgot why I was here. There had been a DEAD person in bed with me this very morning. Waves of nausea immediately rose up and I swayed a bit. I caught myself by touching the wall, and Officer Bentley grabbed my arm (gentler this time) and helped me out.

On leaving his office, I turned back and said just above a whisper, "Excuse me, inspector, but I don't know your name."

He had already started working on the mountain of paperwork on his desk, but looked up to say, "James, James Yves," and promptly went back to work.

On the walk out of the station, I began reeling from the shock of events of this unusual day. Officer Bentley appeared genuinely concerned during the walk downstairs. Could it only be midmorning? I desperately needed to get out quickly. I handle stress better alone without people to worry about. Even as a child, I would need time by myself before accepting comfort from my parents. Though it has caused no small number of problems, I have an uncommonly difficult time tolerating weakness in anyone —especially in yours truly. Pity is best left at the door; I have no tolerance for such emotions.

Therefore, I straightened up, collected myself and used my most professional voice with just a hint of coolness. "Thank you, Officer Bentley, you have been most kind. I feel much better now and will be on my way home, I mean my r...er, I will be on my way. I completely understand why you had no choice but to strain my wrist this morning and please do not give it a second thought. I heal fast."

"Yes, Ma'am, thank you most kindly, Ma'am. Would you like me to have a squad car drop you off at your hotel?"

"NO!" I said much too forcefully, but I recovered quickly. "Since it is not far, I would prefer to walk. The sun and the exercise will be good for me. I can't wait to experience your island."

He looked positively unsure, "It is nearly five miles and a bit confusing to get to..."

I interrupted, "When I tire, I will call the hotel and they will pick me up." He nodded agreement and guided me out of the station and onto the street. I'd not noticed when I was brought (handcuffed) in, but the station was located on a lovely street with well-kept houses and lawns. There were kids, people, cars, birds and a midmorning sun above. I cannot tell you how welcome this was, to feel the warm rays on my skin and face and to breathe the cool fresh air. If I closed my eyes, I could pretend I was back home with none of these worries, and no DEAD person. I wanted my life and peace of mind back! I definitely had plenty of work ahead to regain that peace.

I began walking at an efficient and businesslike pace while I scanned the stores looking for just the right thing. I walked for the best part of an hour, sidestepped a few children, nearly was run over because I could not remember to look right instead of left when I crossed streets (down here they drive on the wrong side of the road). After an hour of pleasant walking, I was desperately lost. I could have found the police station and despite my aversion to do so, I asked for directions twice and was nearly halfway to the hotel, when I spotted what I was searching for. An electronics shop with the Apple logo on it.

Despite the inevitable issues associated with a niche company whose product has barely 10 percent of the market, I prefer them to the commonplace PC. For the novice, either machine will do, but when you have the expertise I do, the superior sophistication of the Mac user interface gives me a significant edge. The store was exactly what I'd expected and identical to dozens of sister stores over the world; equipment everywhere, young, poorly dressed, geeky people behind the counter, older perplexed people in front of the counter.

As an aside, I do not mean anything disparaging by geeky. I mean it only in its descriptive sense without any added insinuations or value judgments. After all, not so long ago, I myself have been described that way.

I talked to a sales 'associate' (I hate PC talk. They are still salesmen no matter how they choose to dress up the title) and talked my way up to the manager. He was thin to near emaciated status and walked in a stilted fashion as if surprised his legs continued to work. He walked up and I noticed he was several inches shorter than my five foot ten. His hair was light brown and combed random fashion. He'd probably just now used his fingers for that purpose. He wore the standard uniform of the hacker elite; a plain well worn and well-wrinkled shirt, partly buttoned, and part of the tail hanging out over his equally wrinkled worn out chino pants. He wore no socks and flopped around in ruined Birkenstocks. I introduced myself and he was cautious and disinterested initially but making sophisticated technical comments, he began to reevaluate me. My knowledge base and comfort with his world finished the process of ingratiating myself. Lastly, we exchanged PC jokes before I came to the point.

I desperately needed a portable Mac, preferably with the latest chip plus a good deal of memory and disc space. I needed it preloaded with specialty software and I wanted to rent it, not buy it. This last issue was the sticking point — as I well knew it would be. He was reluctant for several reasons, not the least of which was my tourist status. We chatted some more and with careful probing discovered that Regis (such a nice name) was struggling with a well-known programming obstacle. (All computer types are working on 'special' software). Without directly saying so, he was attempting to develop a new program that would automate hacking a wide variety of security systems.

You probably already suspect (or fear), it is not difficult for a determined hacker to break his way into any individual computer (If you knew how ridiculously easy it is, you'd freak, so I won't tell you). You hear about it every week.

"...*So and so, a fifteen-year-old high school dropout, just broke into the records of the defense department. No files were breached (a load of bullshit, why break in and not change something, for Pete's sake?) and the security system will be analyzed to figure out how he managed to circumvent the state-of-the-art security systems...*"

What is terribly difficult, however, is automating the process so that the tedious time-swallowing work is already done by the time I...um, I mean he, needs to get involved. To further automate it so that it can do that for a wide variety of systems requires true genius. To further accomplish all of the above and avoid being detected by the extremely talented army of geeks hired, and paid handsomely I might add, by companies to protect their data, well...that requires a true computer guru. Bill Gates is the preeminent one. One of the smartest men I have ever met. I also am one (this is a secret — I will ruin your credit if you even as much as think of telling anyone). Fortunately, there aren't many of us around.

Among my accomplishments, I developed a series of programs in line with the one Regis is trying to develop. I sensed an opportunity and offered to help him in exchange for the use of any of the functioning demos or portables in for repair. I would need it for the two-week duration of my stay on the island. He stared at me with a curious expression. Something between what could you (a girl, and even worse an older person) offer someone as smart as me (this ego thing is normal for computer weenies), and is this person for real?

I reassured him as only another hacker can. I told him about some of the systems I had hacked my way into with just enough detail to convince him I knew my stuff. I demonstrated on his desktop some of my skills entering the medium security hotel network illustrating my room booking. Unfortunately, that reminded me of the dead man once again. I knew he was hooked when he started to take notes. I offered to look over his code and steer him in the right direction. He could then decide if this would merit my getting the laptop.

It took a lot of reassuring, many PC jokes but what won him over were my stories about Bill (Gates of course). Unlike the entire universe outside of Redmond, Washington, he did not feel that Bill was the antichrist. Like most true computer aficionados (hackers to you) he actually admired him. So, when I mentioned I'd actually met the man and spoken to him (many years ago when we were both younger), he nearly drooled on my shoes.

We settled down to serious business. We locked the doors, called for pizza, and demanded no interruptions. I realized immediately that even though he had some skills, he was not going to succeed. He remained stuck with the standard line of attack that thousands upon thousands of hackers have used. Therefore, when I mentioned several new avenues of attack, his eyes grew big with excitement (although he tried to hide it). Then I showed him how to overcome the first of several big hurdles. He gasped. Yup, audibly gasped. There is no higher compliment for a hacker than for a fellow member of the club gasp. It's like winning an Oscar, but without all the fame, glory or money.

Before I knew it, I had my computer with everything I needed and more. He could not have been more helpful. It was the latest in Mac technology, with all the software Microsoft could offer. He could not wait to get back to working on his programming (I didn't mention that he wasn't going to get anywhere without more help. He was ecstatically happy at the moment and that's worth something. Right?)

On the way outside, I realized how late it was. Almost five o'clock! I was going to be late for my...date.

CHAPTER FIVE

DATE NIGHT

I hitched a ride to the hotel without trouble (not difficult for a young, reasonably attractive lady if you are willing to show some leg and look helpless). The manager was so apologetic and helpful that I needn't have worried about where to stay and how to collect my belongings. The police had combed through everything and kept a few things, for which they had dutifully left receipts. They took my vitamin pills, a Swiss Army knife and my passport. The rest of my stuff was already in the hotel's primo deluxe penthouse. I protested that there was no way I could afford such a room for even one night. They insisted, saying they would charge the same rate as my prior room. It also included free room service as well as dining privileges in their five-star restaurant downstairs. If I lacked for anything, I was to call any time.

They seemed genuinely concerned about me and not merely worried about possible litigious consequences. I chose not to bother myself about their motivations, and hurried to my new room to primp for dinner with detective Yves. I left a message with the desk alerting him that I would be late, and for him to please wait a few minutes. Next, I set up my laptop and established a link with my own desktop Mac at my office and while it downloaded some of my unique creative software, I showered and dressed.

Personally, I believe the entire cosmetic and apparel industry is a plot by men to enslave women in the time-consuming chores of make-up, style, accessories, hair and thinness. Men can wake up, comb their hair, pick nearly anything out of their closet (off the floor is more likely) add a tie and they are ready. They could be thirty pounds overweight, have a four o'clock shadow and still no one notices. But, oh my, if a gal is not ten pounds underweight, wearing clothes with matching hose and accessories — plus just the right touch of make-up, everyone and their dog turns and stares.

Although I theoretically and sincerely object to this, I chose to accept current standards so as not to stand out tonight. I put on my regular out-to-dinner-with-a-client ensemble, applied the minimum amount of make-up, and only then did I go over to the laptop. It was only five minutes after six, but I had plenty of work ahead of me before dinner. Besides, it would be good for inspector what's his name to wait for me.

My research proceeded quickly and smoothly. The phone book listed twenty-two Yves in the area. I then accessed the police department directory (it included the entire bloody country) and found five Yves there. Only two lived in the Christchurch metropolitan region and only one with the rank of detective inspector. James Patrick Yves, thirty-six years old. Twenty years with the police force in various capacities. Highly talented, rising through the ranks quickly. Several commendations... "Oh wow, I'm late!" I said to no one. I started the laptop downloading more info while I was away. I desperately wished for more time. I was going into battle unprepared and unarmed. Only when I stopped searching did I realize how hungry I was. I had skipped lunch and had no breakfast. I hoped I would not embarrass myself at dinner by wolfing down the meal.

My dressy ensemble consisted of one slinky, black chiffon dress, which reached to mid-calf, just a touch too big so I looked a tad thinner. (I don't find it credible when Dad and Rick both think I am too skinny), black patent leather heels and I accessorized with a pearl bracelet and necklace. I usually put my hair up, but tonight I did not have the time. Instead, I used a purple hair band with pearls to keep my long black hair under control.

Apart from feeling good about myself, part of the reason of looking good is to distract whomever I am having dinner with. A girl needs an edge from time to time. The outfit I use would be entirely different if I was meeting with a female client (most of my clients are female). In that case, I would dress in a way to accentuate whatever flaws or weaknesses she has. If she is overweight, I emphasize my slimness, if older, then my youth. The only exception is when I know that my client is depressed and feeling badly. Then, I turn on the charm and become sympathetic.

You may think that I am cold, calculating and sick. I will not defend myself beyond this observation. I work in a man's world in a particularly male field. I need to demonstrate quickly that I have the 'cojones' to fix their problem. By the time they come to me, they do not need sweet Betsy from Pike. They want the smartest, shrewdest and definitely toughest person they can find. If I make them a tiny bit nervous and uncomfortable, they like that. After all, they don't want to marry me; as soon as our business is completed, their fondest wish is to never see me again. I am reasonably successful with this approach, and I have always been a fervent believer in sticking with what works.

I remained uncomfortable about my upcoming dinner. I always know a lot more about the person before a formal meeting. Is this James Patrick married? Divorced? Separated? Does he have money troubles? What are his hobbies? Is he a workaholic? Does he enjoy sports? What common interests do we have? How can I use those to my advantage? These are only some of the many questions I could easily answer with but a little more time at my keyboard. With the encumbrance of this GD splint on my wrist (not to mention the pain whenever I tried to use it), and the limited amount of time, I currently had as much information as possible. Bloody hell, I hate going in unprepared.

I hurried down to the lobby in the glass elevator, which allowed me to scope out the situation. Just before the elevator stopped, I saw him and did he look splendid. He stood up and smiled as soon as he saw me exit the elevator. He was absolutely stunning, with a capital H (for hunk). His wavy brown hair was just slightly disheveled for the rough and ready look. I had not appreciated just how tall he was — six foot four, at least. He could have stepped out of a *GQ* cover with his expertly cut suit (my God! It was a Savile Row suit!) What did that cost? I wondered how he could afford such a delicious luxury on a policeman's salary. Perhaps he borrowed it from a relative the exact same size. Yeah, right.

He had a different smile tonight, one I had not seen before. The smile was a mix of cat-with-cream smile and I-know-something-you-don't smile and it left me unsettled. I strode right up to him and said, "Hello, James Patrick, it is a pleasure to see you in these circumstances."

In return, I received a half-raised eyebrow and a widening of the smile. "I see you have been busy, what else do you know about me, pray tell? Tell me which of my men has been playing stoolie and I will have them walking a beat on a glacier."

"Oh, no one told me, I must have heard your name somewhere along my walk home, I can't remember where. I will confide in you that Officer Bentley was completely right about the distance here. I insisted on walking and despite my general fitness, it took longer than expected and I was beat when I arrived. I hope you will excuse my being late."

"You are only seventeen minutes late. Hardly worth mentioning since we Kiwis normally eat late and particularly since you get credit for every minute you waited in that cell downtown."

"Shhh...not so loud," as I looked around, "do you want everyone to think I am a criminal?"

"And an extremely lovely one at that. When I first saw you, I didn't recognize you, Miss Prescott. You are devastatingly beautiful this evening."

I blushed, I actually blushed at this obvious but so effective flattery. I hate this about myself in particular and women in general. Give us a little praise about our looks, or give us flowers, and no matter how a big a jerk you are, we just melt and become brainless morons. Yuck. It was not going as planned, I was supposed to be putting him off balance; instead, I was back on my heels and calling for reinforcements. "I'm famished, will you take care of that?"

"Of course, Miss Prescott."

"Yolanda, my name is Yolanda, and I would prefer that you would use my first name. However," I added coyly, "if you can handle it, you can use my nickname 'Yo.' Most men in my country find this particular abbreviation exceedingly difficult to use. They tell me it feels like they are hailing a taxi or something." At this he laughed, not a small polite laugh and not a huge belly laugh, but a sincere, deep hearty and surprisingly proper laugh.

"You Americans are an odd lot. I think I will choose 'Yolanda,' but only because I think it a most beautiful name and I want that added opportunity to use it. I have not heard it before, is it North American?"

This guy was absolutely shameless with his flattery, nevertheless I found it appealing. "You are almost right, it is Hispanic or you could say Mexican. My family was born in the Southwestern US, but our ancestors came from Mexico. You have probably already surmised my father had a thing about the letter Y and he made sure I had two initials with it. You might notice that they are used differently in each name. In my first name it is used as a consonant and in my middle name it is used as a vowel —thanks, Dad."

"Sounds like a fun guy your dad, I should think I would like to meet him." I could not help but smile — there was little chance of that. He lives eight thousand miles away and is married to his work.

"He can be a lot of fun...if you don't have to live with

him...day in and day out, one new thing after another. I don't know how my mother put up with him for all those years."

After a short pause, he said with clear disbelief, "The name Prescott is Hispanic? Sounds more British to me."

"Actually, you are now noticing one of our family skeletons," I said brightly.

"I am so sorry if..."

"Not to worry, it doesn't bother me at all, but it bothers most of my family. Nearly half a century later and they still carry it as a badge of shame."

"I don't mean to pry."

"It's not prying, James, I think it adds character and interest to my family, but my dad and I are alone in that perception. You see, when my grandma was just sixteen, she worked for a family named Prescott who were very proper and very British. She had an affair with their oldest son and, as you can guess, she became pregnant. Well, this was not all that unusual in those times. What was different was that these two teenagers decided to get married. Neither family liked it. His family disowned him, and although her family took them in, they were treated like the embarrassment they were."

"And your father was that child?"

"Exactly, James, how perceptive. But the story gets much better. They were actually very much in love and completely devoted to each other for their entire lives. They made a good home for Dad and even when they left the confines of the family house, they continued to see them so that we would have roots.

"How about your mother, how does she feel about it?"

This question must have caused me to become pale or

something, because he clearly noticed there was a problem.

"Is she no longer married to him?" he asked with reservation and after seeing my reaction, immediately retreated, "I'm so sorry, Yolanda. This is personal business, I think my training and my job crept into our dinner."

"That's OK, I murmured with my accustomed sadness. It's been over three years since she died yet I still feel like it just happened." I noticed his surprise at this and I pressed on. "I remember when I received the phone call from Dad. I was in college then and when I heard his voice, he was more serious than at any other time. I remember thinking this was going to be one of his reverse psychology stunts, and I was getting prepped for it when he whispered half choking with tears that I needed to come home right away." The memory still caused me to tear up. I always do on retelling this story. "He then told me that Mom was dying and she was calling for me."

"Yolanda, I am so very sorry, please forgive..."

"It's OK, James, it has been a long time but it refuses to heal up."

At this point, he became noticeably more reserved and his words more guarded; he transformed into a different person, "I can empathize with that, I thought your parents divorced, please forgive my intrusion. Also please call me 'JP.' I much prefer it to my given names."

I stared at him before speaking, "Two letters, huh? I think I now know why you found my nickname so funny."

After a wink and a pause, "Now you know. Shall we eat? Since it is so late and the restaurant here in your hotel is so good, I suggest we eat here."

"Of course, you are the chief," I said with just the slightest touch of coyness. I noticed I was relaxed and comfortable in his company and I did not have any trouble with his taking my arm in his.

CHAPTER SIX

FALLING TO PIECES

I followed him toward the dining room, which was pleasantly elegant — when someone called my name, "Yolanda, over here."

I turned to my right and saw the culprit standing and waving like a loon. With the tragic events of last night and the aftermath this morning, I had completely forgotten that I'd arrived as part of a charter. I winced internally and hoped my eyes hadn't done a roll, well...actually, I hoped it showed enough so they would leave me alone. Donovan Boers, the travel club president, was the lunatic waving and motioning for us to join them.

"Are you all right? And where have you been? We called and eventually went to your room where we saw it was sealed off by the police. Their only comment was that you went to the hospital."

"It's OK, Donovan. I am fine, it's just a flesh wound." I hoped the old joke would distract him but he seemed on a mission to unearth every detail of my misadventure.

"That arm doesn't look too fine to me," he said with serious disbelief. "How did it happen? Was anyone else involved?" He was clearly getting all worked up and I wondered what he meant by the 'anyone else' comment. I decided it meant nothing.

"Really, Donovan, I am perfectly well. I was clumsy and had a small tumble when I got out of my bed in the night and sprained my wrist. But as you can plainly see, it's all fixed up and I am walking and feeling normal. Oh, excuse me, this is Chief Inspector Yves of the New Zealand constabulary. James, these are the members of our tour." I introduced the people whose names I remembered and faked the rest.

"Won't you join us?" Donovan asked, despite it being overwhelmingly obvious that there was not enough room at their table and that we were dressed for a date.

However, I was ready for that gambit. "No, please continue with your meal, as you can see I have gone to extraordinary lengths to arrange a date with this dashing detective and I won't share him."

If JP was startled, he did not show it; in fact, he seemed quite pleased about the situation. Donovan, however, was initially taken aback, then he understood and reluctantly acquiesced. He had a disappointed expression probably reflecting that he wouldn't get the inside story behind the police tape, but he quickly recovered his composure.

We left and asked the hostess to seat us as far as possible from their table. When the hostess left, JP cleared his throat and said, "So you arranged this date?" His tone was playful, his face full of mirth.

"Absolutely, JP, you cannot fully appreciate how hard it

was to get that dead body into my bed, much less sleep next to him and to make sure it happened in your district. I also had to bribe Officer Bentley to throw me into the cell so you would feel sorry for me and ask me out." At this point, we both burst out laughing. I had not laughed that freely in over three years.

The waiter had been discrete and did not disturb our moment. We noticed him and waved him over. JP, in a practiced manner, proceeded to order a wine, appetizers and dinner. My tension must have been obvious because he asked in a hushed tone if there was a problem. I could not think of anything to say except to be blunt with the truth, "I don't drink wine anymore, JP, it makes me crazy." He paused for only a second as if reevaluating me before revising his order to make it two virgin Piña Coladas (my favorite, how could he know?).

When the waiter left and we were alone again, he gently asked, "How long have you been in recovery?"

I was surprised at his deduction — but only for a moment, it wasn't rocket science. I only managed to say a tremulous "nine years."

"At your young age? I am quite impressed. I have known many people in recovery and always enjoy their company." He then caught himself and again apologized. "I keep intruding into your personal life, Yolanda, please excuse me once again. My colleagues say I never stop working and I suppose they are right." He sat there embarrassed and anxious, playing with his salad fork while awaiting my response.

It took me several deep breaths to respond, "JP," I said with more assurance than I felt, "you indeed have your detective radar on and your accuracy is unsettling. Around you, I feel a neon sign over my head is broadcasting my secrets. I suspect you can't turn it off anymore than I can turn off my problem with alcohol. But let's both of us give it a try and keep going. I would very much like to forget this day and have some fun during my vacation."

"Of course, Yolanda. Thank you for being so understanding."

Our appetizers arrived and we proceeded with small talk. I was chatting more than he was, but I needed it more and he was a great listener: attentive, focused, with just the right comments at exactly the right moments. He found out I was an only daughter (only child actually). That I had been catered to by my parents and grandparents and that I'd developed my alcoholism during my senior year in high school. Only after a horrific car wreck in which I survived unscathed but seriously injured two people did I enter rehab. During that rehab, I unwillingly but finally dealt with the guilt and attempted to resume my life. I obtained my GED and entered a small liberal arts college far away from home. There I obtained a new lease on life and flourished for nearly four years, but for reasons that I did not share with JP, I never graduated.

I discovered JP had one daughter, Michelle Elizabeth, twelve years old, but likes to think of herself as much older. She is clearly his pride and joy and the only subject about which he chatted without reticence. Michelle is bright, precocious and heavily into computers. Up to present, she has shown little interest in either boys or sports. He admitted that despite the stress and abnormal hours, he loves his job despite abhorring the paperwork associated with it (he swore me to secrecy). I suggested that if they did not suspect as much, they would have him analyzed by a psychiatrist. In all, we were having a good time, enjoying a fine meal and most importantly, I had forgotten how this date materialized.

"These are great onion rings!" I said.

JP smiled, "Not onion rings — fried squid, calamari," looking at me for a reaction.

"I don't care, they are delicious. I wonder if I can find them back home?" We continued the food discussion about the overcooked potatoes and peas (just like the bloody Brits). However, the roast lamb main course had been moist and tender with several subtle flavors, none of which was mint.

After we finished the Crème Brulee we'd chosen for dessert and while we waited for the coffee, his demeanor transformed and he was suddenly the inspector once again. "If you're interested, I have some information on the victim."

He should have known better than to tell me and I should not have succumbed to temptation. "Who was he?" I said with unexpected intensity.

"His name is…was Peter Osbourne, a businessman from the United States. Your backyard actually, his home office is in San Francisco. He flew over just three days ago. He works…um worked for a big multinational corporation, Soltex."

"The oil company?" I blurted.

"Well, yes, but Soltex is much more than an oil company, they have their hands in many different enterprises. I haven't been able to find out exactly what he was working on or if he was simply on vacation. Interestingly, he was using an alias, Roger Wilson, and we should be getting a warrant this evening. That way we can search his hotel room. Perhaps then we will obtain useful information."

"You need a warrant to search a dead man's hotel room?"

"That is an interesting point, Yolanda, and if he had used his real name we would not, but since the alias is relatively common here, we are treading carefully so we don't enter the wrong room. At least then everything is proper and above board. We would look inept indeed if we not only entered the wrong person's room and it was discovered that we did not have the authority to do so. I don't know what your press is like in the States but our press would surely enjoy roasting us."

"Yeah, that sounds the same as the media back home."

"We are pretty sure we have the right room and I have a stakeout in place just in case any of his friends, or his enemies, decide to pay a visit." He was so calm about it, which both intrigued and comforted me.

I had to ask the unstated question, the one thing he had failed to mention. "And what did he die of?" I croaked timidly.

He looked at me for just a moment and decided to tell me. "We are not entirely sure; his body had no obvious marks, no gunshot or knife wounds, no blows to the head or elsewhere, no signs of struggle or strangulation. They did find one tiny, fresh puncture wound on the nape of his neck that the pathologist assures me happened peri-mortem. By the way, peri-mortem is…"

I interrupted, "I know what peri-mortem means, it happened at the time of death," I said, suddenly not feeling well.

"That's good. The puncture would have been missed if there had been a more obvious explanation. We suspect some kind of lethal injection."

I became quite anxious, my hands were suddenly clammy and I was sure my face was pale. This time he failed to notice. He droned on, "The timing of his death was in the early hours. He had been dead for many hours prior to the discovery." He grimaced and became even more serious. "Yolanda, I am confident you have already surmised that it would have been so easy to inject you too. Please feel reassured that whomever killed poor Mr. Osbourne — chose not to. I don't believe you are in any danger. I suspect there was a falling out among his conspirators and you were just an innocent bystander."

Under the table, I began nervously rubbing my wrist. I was struggling emotionally with this information. It turned out to be the ultimate TMI. I was now in the all-too-familiar situation of wishing not to know now what I didn't know then. Fortunately, the waiter brought our after-dinner coffee. I absolutely love coffee; it is my one remaining 'addiction.' Fortunately, it is legal and does not play games with my mind. I took a long sip and tried to calm my heart. A movie began playing in my head. In the movie, I saw Dad receiving a phone call from the New Zealand police telling him his only daughter was dead from poison simply for being at the wrong place at the wrong time. And I haven't yet forgiven him for Mom's death.

It was a while before he told me the last of it. "Yolanda, there is something else that I need to tell you, and it will be difficult to hear."

Despite my efforts to steel myself for anything, I was startled by the amount of anxiety that flowed over and through me. The fear of the unknown remains my worst foe. A gnawing sensation started just underneath my breastbone and grew inexorably in intensity and scope. Within seconds, I felt my chest would cave in. In the distance of my mind, the subtle desire for a drink began. I was desperate and I used one of my biggest weapons. I allowed my anger to come to my rescue, "And what is that?" I barked. "Is this why you invited me to this extremely expensive restaurant? To soften me up for the third degree?"

I could have gone on in this vein for some time, but he gently touched my hand and I calmed down. "Yes, I did know this when I asked you to lunch but it wasn't the reason I asked you. I wanted to get to know you better first. You have no family here and no support system within eight thousand miles. I decided to be careful. But then.."

"But what?" I screamed.

"But you are far more mature and confident than most people your age. Further, when I found out you were in a recovery program…"

"What in hell does that have to do with it?" I was still just barely in control.

"That means that you have a built-in support system here that is stronger than most people's regular support system. Further, you handled the other news so well that I thought you would rather know now, contrary to what our police psychologist says."

"Psychologist, support system, what is it you are trying to tell me?" I was choking back tears of both anger and fear, hoping the anger would win because fear would bring the alcohol back.

"Yolanda, you were also injected. In your case, instead of a poison, he used a drug named Versed. It causes you to forget the recent past." This was so unexpected I was dumbfounded. I had to consciously focus on continuing to breathe normally to help disguise my feelings of utter revulsion and invasion. I wanted to crawl out of my skin.

JP persisted with the horrible story, "You probably saw or heard something but only briefly."

"Why briefly?"

He proceeded to explain how Versed works. Apparently, the medicine not only sedates you but also interferes with the placing of memory into long-term storage. When given, the previous five to ten minutes prior to the injection cannot be stored into permanent memory and therefore cannot be remembered. I had evidently seen or heard something last night. JP repeatedly emphasized they had expended significant efforts not to hurt me. All they wanted was for me not to remember something identifying, undoubtedly someone's face. I now recalled that during my brief stay at the hospital, the nurse came back to redraw my blood, claiming the blood lab dropped the first vial. Now I knew they were double-checking the results.

Furthermore the doctors were adamant there was no way of recovering the memory because it had never been laid down as a memory in the first place. There was no memory to recover. Much as in computers we initially put our experiences on volatile memory like RAM, and only the significant events are placed in long-term memory, the disk drive. The brain cannot store or access everything that happens and it needs five to ten minutes to decide what experiences are important enough to store. This explains why if a person is distracted, we will forget something that has just happened, or why we do not remember how we obtained a small cut or bruise. The brain perceives it, but if we are too busy or intensely focused on our current activity, the event won't be placed into long-term memory.

I knew I owed my life to the effectiveness of this drug; nevertheless, I suddenly felt absolutely exhausted. I was done with this discussion and at the same time I hated the idea of being alone, at least not yet. So I changed the subject, "JP, you now know everything about me and I know hardly anything about you."

"There isn't much to know," he said defensively (or so I thought) and he started again on his favorite subject, "for starters, Michele is nearly thirteen years old. Her birthday is in two weeks (the day I leave for home, in fact). She likes to play the flute and is quite good if you will take a proud father's word for it."

"Of course." He was now warming up to his subject.

"Her favorite subject in school is computers (at this I smiled) of which I know little I am afraid. I have a difficult time with all of the commands, acronyms and peripherals."

I laughed and it felt good.

"Did I say something amusing?"

"No you did not, but my life is computers and more to the point you were steering the discussion away from anything personal."

He smiled. "You caught me," he admitted, "and I thought I was being subtle. You have remarkable talents; what is it you do when you are not in this part of the world?"

I would not be distracted, "What is your wife like?" ignoring his question.

"I'd rather not talk about her if you don't mind," he said this with a undisguised defensiveness to his manner.

I jumped to my feet furiously, "I do very much mind, Mr.

Chief Inspector. In the past twenty-four hours, I have woken up with a corpse next to me, had my wrist nearly broken by your goon of a police officer, been thrown in jail, and just now discover I was injected with a drug to forget things. I could have been raped and wouldn't even know it! Finally, when I ask a simple question about your wife you clam up!" I was just warming up and the anger felt wonderful.

"What is your problem, are you trying to seduce me? And you don't want to mess it up? Just what am I supposed to think?" I gave him no chance to answer. I did not want an answer, I wanted to get the hell out of here and leave this lousy island. "I will tell you what I think. I think you are playing stupid mind games. You are not what or who you propose to be. I absolutely do not ever want to see you again. DO-YOU-UNDERSTAND?" I was at the top of my voice by this time and I realized that everyone was staring at me. Even worse, several of my traveling companions were coming over. JP was starting to say something when I turned and left, nearly falling over the chair.

"Are you OK?" asked Donovan as I nearly bowled him over in my hurry to leave.

"Get out of my f#$%* way! I am just bloody fine!"

CHAPTER SEVEN

HELP ARRIVES

I stormed out of the dining room and quickly turned down a hallway and out of view. If he chose to follow, I did not want him to find me. What I most needed now was time alone. Time to calm down, and time to get help. I was right at the ragged edge of control and I was close to having that first drink, just to calm the nerves. Part of me desperately wanted that drink and I could already hear my rationalizations: 'You woke up with a corpse, for Pete's sake, the police are out to get you, yada, yada, yada.' I nevertheless did not want to revisit the hell I lived while I was drinking. I opened my purse and found the names and numbers I'd obtained from my regional intergroup before I left Boulder for this miserable excuse of a vacation.

For those of you not familiar with the structure of AA (Alcoholics Anonymous; not so anonymous in my case), there is an intergroup in each area, which among other things, has listings of meetings and contact people from all over the world. So, if you find yourself traveling, it is almost impossible to be out of touch with someone in the program. I noticed that even Russia and China have them now.

I have been in the program over nine years, but I had a relapse when Mom died and I have only been sober for three. I had been sure I would never need these contacts, but my sponsor insisted. How could Sallie have known how desperately I would need them?

After locating my room, I locked it and threw the chain. I then blocked it with a dresser that with all the adrenalin flowing through my veins I had no problem manhandling into place. (To keep people out, or to keep me in? I didn't know.) I tried three numbers before I found someone home. "Hello, I am calling for Michael," I stammered.

"Just a minute," said a tired female voice. I overheard, "Mike, it's someone from the program asking for you," pause, "no, I did not get the name."

"Hello, this is Michael," he said with some trace of impatience in his voice. I choked up and stared to sob. I related a little of the story. He quickly understood and became much more understanding. He wanted my name and location. After I told him, he instructed me to stay put and absolutely not to go to the bar. He would be over in fifteen minutes. He reminded me I could hold on for that long and to only focus on one minute at a time.

Although at the time it seemed like several hours, Michael arrived in just over the fifteen minutes he promised. It took me some effort to free myself. The dresser seemed a lot heavier now. I had a difficult time moving it and actually had to take out the drawers to get it out of the way.

You may be surprised that I not only opened the door for

a complete stranger but that I was in a hurry to so. To understand, you need to appreciate that my recovery was in jeopardy and without that, I have no life worth living. So if Michael could not help me, well, nothing else would matter.

I don't need to go into the gory details, but suffice it to say that he has been in the program for twenty-eight years and has been through this kind of thing before. He had been slightly delayed because he had brought along another friend of Bill (how people in AA refer to themselves), Kathy. The relief that he had been so thoughtful to consider that I might need a female presence was tremendous. Kathy only had six months in the program. She was there to provide comfort for me and to learn how to stay sober herself. I had been in her shoes many times and knew that she felt far more uncomfortable with the situation than either Michael or me.

It would be easy to believe I had been lucky to get him, but in the program, most of us do not believe in coincidence. Most of us believe they are miracles in which our higher power remains anonymous. By calling for help, I had done my part of asking for HP's intervention. By having Michael the only one available, HP had intervened on my behalf. Michael and Kathy listened to the events of the previous day and to their credit accepted it all at face value, even as incredible as it sounded.

Michael was aware that the drug they had given me is related to Valium and that these drugs are dangerous to us alcoholics since they cross react with the alcohol receptors in our brain. Kathy became more comfortable as we stayed up and talked for hours. The urge to drink lessened as it had on many prior occasions. I vaguely remember Kathy tucking me into bed before they left. Michael left his cell number, Kathy's number and the number of other members that would be glad to help.

I startled awake late the next morning. I could not immediately tell what part of the previous day had been real and what had been a dream. It took several minutes and the pain in my left wrist to convince me that the truly strange stuff had been real and the commonplace events had been a dream. Miraculously and predictably, my craving for a drink was gone, banished by the efforts of last night.

My wrist throbbed, my mouth was parched and I needed to pee in a bad way. I jumped out of bed, stopped in fear when I saw I was in pajamas (yes, I do own one pair), but relaxed when I remembered Kathy putting me to bed. I almost did not make it to the bathroom in time. While I sat there, I began to formulate a plan of action.

CHAPTER EIGHT

RICK

Richard is my best friend. He is balding, pot-bellied, irreverent (my favorite quality) and whip smart; not only school and test smart but intuitive and practical smart. When I am trying to make something that is quite simple into something difficult, he quickly slices to the core of the matter and makes it easy again.

When I first moved into an apartment on my own, a conflict began with the upstairs neighbor. Not only did he play his stereo so loud I could not hear my music, but he also played it late into the night and I could not sleep. This guy, George, was big, sweaty with long skinny legs and would not listen to reason. He stated that it was his constitutionally given right to play his music when and as loud as he chose. He added that if I didn't like it I could move to a different building. I began by enlisting my neighbors, the police, and the landlord, but my apartment was the only one affected and I did not receive much support. The process was going to take forever. I was actually going to cave and considered moving as the most expeditious solution to the problem, when Rick suggested, "Why don't you turn the tables on him?"

"What do you mean?" I asked, a smile forming because I knew this was going to be good.

"It occurs to me that if his life were to be turned upside down he might move." Rick started pacing as he thought. "He is predictable, that is good...he starts his stereo around seven in the evening. What if you could arrange for only his power to fail around that time?"

I was beginning to like it so I played my part, "And how would I do that, oh wise Jedi master?" He beamed, he lapped up this kind of flattery. He was a formidable opponent (as city hall found to their dismay last December).

"First, find out what kind of fuses this building takes; they should be downstairs. We will obtain several and I will show you how to blow them. On a periodic but frequent basis, and only in the early evening — before he usually turns his stereo on — you will carefully replace his functioning one with a blown one. You will have to exert care to make it seem that the fuse is blowing not that it is being replaced — I will show you how. Then after he has paid for an electrician a couple of times and the circuits are certified as working nominally, these sudden fuse failures will cease and we will go to step two."

I was laughing so hard I started hiccupping. It was beautiful.

"You know what the real beauty of doing this is, don't you?"

I was not sure what he was getting at, "Sure, that I start

getting back at the son of a bitch."

"No, Yolanda, revenge is not our mission, if you choose that path you will inevitably drink again. Maybe not today or tomorrow, but someday. In that direction lies the dark side of the force Obi Wan Kenobi would put it. "

I sobered up, "OK, wise ass, if it isn't about getting even what is the beauty of it?"

"Yolanda (he absolutely refuses to call me Yo), you may continue with your laughter, I enjoy hearing it, but you must have your priorities straight. The beauty of it is that while you are trying to permanently correct a difficult situation, your problem is immediately solved. Without power, he cannot blast the music all night long, and then time is on your side, not his. Your sleep and rest will no longer be disturbed and you can concentrate on your work and perhaps even find a date..."

I had heard this story before, "Stop right there! I do not want another man in my life. I have had enough to last me for three reincarnations." We proceeded to have the same argument for a few minutes before I returned to the subject at hand. "What is step two?"

Richard paused and looked at me with his feline grin; he was enjoying himself immensely. "We need to arrange to cut only his power in different less detectable ways so that he gets the same problem but without the fuse blowing; I think that will drive him absolutely stark-raving mad."

Of course, Rick was right. One trip to Boulder's building records office yielded the electrical plans for the building. As suspected, the building's wiring was bundled so that his power lines traveled next to mine. We cut a small easily repairable hole in my wall, which gave us access to his main electrical feed. We proceeded to cut and splice heavy-duty switches into his lines, patched the hole and we were in the electrical power disruption business. The next evening, we began turning his electricity off and on in an unpredictable and infuriating manner. When he most wanted to use it, we flipped the switch, then when he was ready to sleep, we would restore it. The electrician came three times in one week, and each time the circuits came on just as he arrived. Besides getting sleep and being able to relax, my spirits soared because I stopped being a victim. In the end, I made the idiot upstairs a deal. I told him a friend of mine was a genius with electrical things and he could come by and have a look, but only if he would play his music softer and not after ten. He readily agreed and of course my 'friend' fixed the problem.

Rick lives alone, unless his daughter Allie is visiting. He'd been married a long time ago, but as things go these days, they split. Allie visits on an irregular basis. He doesn't care much about money and believes that money was the root cause of his divorce. He lives frugally, works when he needs to, and in general seems to indulge in whatever interests him at the moment.

I remember when he 'found' water coloring. He started because Allie's art class was doing so and to his surprise, it became an outlet of expression he never suspected. He promptly went to the artists' corner downtown and found one of the 'struggling artists' you see selling prints. He chose a watercolorist whose style was appealing and he charmed him. He had no money to pay for lessons, but Rick has rare skills with which he barters. He will help them solve some life problem with which they struggle in vain. In his particular case, he was losing a fight with the city bureaucracy. He made a deal, if Rick could make his headache with the city go away, he would gladly teach Rick and throw in the supplies. This guy didn't have a clue about dealing with difficult people or bureaucracies but he knew his art. When Rick was done with his end of the deal, the artist was so happy he could not be more helpful. Rick, in turn, learned (for free, mind you) about transparent versus opaque colors, color wheels, spatial perspective versus linear perspective, color tone and value, as well as numerous other things. You should see his paintings! Not sales worthy but adequate for decorating his apartment.

The first thing on my action plan was to contact Rick. I did not call because I was not confident the telephones were secure. I probably could have rewritten my custom scrambling program in a short time, that is, if I had the use of both hands. This bloody splint was getting on my nerves.

I dialed up my home desktop (you just never know when you might need access to a protected database). I could now actually work exactly as if I was at my home computer using the laptop simply as a 'dumb' terminal. I thoroughly filled Rick in on the events of the first thirty-six hours of my vacation (longer if you start counting when the plane left, but I never count transportation). I have learned not to leave anything out because Rick says his mind works best with all the tiny details in place. By the time I finished, I'd typed five full pages.

I laid out my basic plan highlighting the parts that needed help. I set up a time to ichat. I could only hope that he would check his machine before then. I gave him until six in the evening my time. That would put him about bedtime the day before. Whoa! This time thing is confusing. Anyway, that is what my pocket travel guide says. I now had seven hours to get as much information as possible before 'talking' to Rick.

When I finally looked away from my screen, I noticed that my phone message light was blinking. I did not want to talk to anyone but eventually my curiosity overcame by better sense. I was ready to ignore it if from JP, only to find it was Donovan wanting to check on my well-being. Apparently, I'd missed another of the scheduled events and they were all concerned, specially considering last night (he left that hanging, to see if I would feel the need to clarify last night's events — I was not about to oblige).

I needed to leave him a message to stop. I called the front desk and was amused to discover he had the room directly below mine and relieved that he was seen leaving the hotel. Therefore, I was able to leave him a long-winded message on his voicemail detailing how well I felt, and I'd decided to spend the rest of my vacation on my own; checking out the sights, laying on the beach and avoiding that utter cad of a detective (I cringed just thinking of him). Hopefully, that would finally stop Donovan's persistent nosiness.

The six hours before I chatted with Rick were filled with the usual activities of web searches: chasing dead ends, collecting bits of information here, finding clues of where to look next somewhere else. Time is always the enemy and huge amounts are wasted waiting for downloads. Luckily, the files of interest were the human resource (personnel) files and they are not nearly as tightly protected as the financial and research files and are not very large. It amuses me that it is readily possible for nearly anyone with computer experience to enter human resource databases with almost entire impunity. The reason is partly that so many people need to use them on a regular basis. The other reason, and the most significant, is that most companies do not consider these files as 'sensitive.' I managed to disguise my inquiries so that even if their security people noticed the break-in, they would have a difficult time tracing me. I'll tell you how another time. Maybe.

At this point, I must make something clear. I do search restricted computers regularly. To be completely frank, I do this for a living. It is scary how much I can learn about a person or a company or a government agency without ever leaving the comfort of my office. As it so happens, there is a tremendous market for my skills even after you eliminate slime balls, people out for revenge, etc. What I want to make clear is that I do not alter the databases in which I sneak a peek. I do not, if at all possible, download anything from them. That is the line I draw for myself; a peek into the window but no breaking and entering, if you will excuse the analogy.

My clients are mostly women looking for their slime ball, deadbeat ex-husbands, and parents looking for runaways. Although I once had an amnesiac who wanted to check out his life before going to the police for help (he was OK). So now you know.

I know, I know — I live at the ragged edge of mainstream society and fairly deep into the gray zone of legality. Nevertheless, there is an unmet need for my skills, and as long as I can live with my conscience (I do have one), feel useful and occasionally help someone, I will continue to support myself in this manner. Someday, the statutes will catch up with the current technology and I will probably be in trouble. Hopefully, by then, I will have another marketable skill or will have married a millionaire. Until then, however, I need to make a living just like you and everyone else, but your brother-in-law that mooches…but I digress.

By the time I was ready for a break, I knew who this Peter Osbourne fellow was, a vague idea of why he was in New Zealand and no idea whatsoever as to why or how he ended up dead in my bed. Actually, for a second I had just the glimmer of an idea but it was too silly to write down as a possibility. I began wondering why inspector Yves had not checked on my well-being. Not that I wanted him to, you understand, but I expected him to and he was not behaving according to plan.

With only twelve minutes before my preset time to talk to Rick, I showered in the hottest water I could stand. I felt refreshed and hungry. After rummaging through my bags, I snacked on one of the chocolate-chip granola bars I keep everywhere. At six, I logged on, switched on the scrambler software and dialed his number. His modem picked up routinely and I waited for a response.

"Yolanda, are you OK? Your message was not clear on how you are doing." I could feel a tear slide down my cheek. How I wished he was here in the same room.

"I am just fine. I have a heavy splint on my left wrist that slows me down but otherwise I am just as physically fit as I was when you dropped me off at the airport."

Rick asked how I was doing emotionally.

"I am much better now," I told him about Michael. Then I switched the subject. "What time is it over there? I am quite confused."

"It is only four hours ahead of you so it is ten in the evening. But, Yolanda, it is your yesterday."

I had to pause with tears streaming down my face, reflecting on what I would do differently if I could actually go back to yesterday.

Rick continued, "I have some of the information you wanted."

It was hard not being able to talk freely like on the telephone. I would have to finish a thought before he could reply. When there is a large amount of information to exchange, the delays can be maddening.

However, slowly, we proceeded to exchange our information. Even though he had only looked at his e-mail ninety minutes before our set time, he'd accomplished a great deal. He had been able to verify some of my discoveries and had some of his typically ingenious ideas on how to proceed further, if I wanted to.

"Do you want me to fly over?" Rick asked sincerely.

Yes! Yes! I wanted to scream. "No, do not come over here. It is clear that it was indeed all an accident. I was at the right place at the wrong time and they were at the wrong place at the right time. I am just trying to find out enough so I can get closure to this insane day. I will then resume my vacation."

"I still think that I could use a South Pacific vacation myself. I could be there in less than forty-eight hours."

"Richard, listen to me," I insisted "I am feeling better, I have Michael if I get in trouble and by the time you get here I will be on the beach, a drink in one hand and hopefully some bronze god on the other. You will be the third wheel so stay home. I will keep you posted on how things proceed."

"OK, but call if you need anything."

"Say hi to Allie for me. Is she still with you?"

"Yes, she is and I will. Her mother is gone on one of her junkets again so I have her for an extended period. I always hope she will forget to come back and I can keep her permanently. But I think she comes back just to spite me."

"It's OK, Rick, we have been through this before. Enjoy her stay. I will be in touch." With that, we disconnected. We'd 'talked' for two hours and twelve minutes! It passed in a blink and now it was already past my dinnertime.

When I started searching, I tried to find everything I could about this former live person I had 'slept' with. Both Rick and I found out much and confirmed each other's findings. He had done it by telephone. He is so smooth and disarming that he usually can obtain far more information from people than they realize they are giving. However, I had to trudge the ether waves in my search to flush out this corpse (Brrr...I still get the shudders if I think about it too much).

Mr. Peter Nathaniel Osbourne born September 15th, 1950, in Okinawa, Japan. Father a senior NCO and "lifer" in the US Navy. Peter traveled widely as a child and apparently even more as an adult. Out of high school he enlisted in the army (what did his dad think of this?). He volunteered for duty in Vietnam at about the height of the war. Let's see...Tet was in early '68 and he was seventeen so he must have known about it when he enlisted. What does that say about him? Did he want to be John Wayne? Was he trying to better his dad? Or did he have a dark side that needed the carnage? All of the above?

I could not get exact postings during the war but his many and varied movements indicated that he was either CIA or in one of the two greatest oxymorons of our time, 'Military Intelligence.' The other one, if you care, is 'Medical Science' and infuriates my father. This Osbourne fellow stayed in the army through the end of the war and then received a general discharge instead of an honorable discharge. That means something happened. It either could not have been very bad or they couldn't pin it on him because in that case he would have been dishonorably discharged. Still, it couldn't have been something minor, which the army typically ignores within its ranks. Particularly since he'd become an officer during his tour. I had asked Rick to look into what kind of offenses would be typical. I had little hope of finding out the exact incident. It probably was in a paper file and not online.

After the war, his trail was harder to follow. I didn't even have a city for a starting point because he did not have a home town. He could have moved abroad since he seemed to be at ease with several languages. He could speak some Arabic (hint of a Middle East posting, maybe pre-Khomeini Iran) and Vietnamese. I picked up his trail again after his employment with Soltex in 1989. It was hard to figure out his exact job description. His title was executive assistant to the COO/International Division. Had he gone to business school after the war? Where else had he worked to get so high up in a multinational corporation? He didn't seem the secretarial type, perhaps a translator. He would be able to talk with the Saudis who produce the oil and with the Vietnamese who are an emerging county rife with possibilities for investment.

This was all just pure conjecture and I needed to refocus on what I actually knew so I could get this over with and get back to my vacation. Back? I hadn't even started it! His salary was $105,345/year (not bad). I could easily get by on half that much and have lots left over. But the interesting part was that he was paid in Pounds Sterling (England), not in dollars. Was there some lien against his earnings in the US? He was listed as being single. Divorced? Child support payments? Tax evasion?

The one great bit of info that Rick 'seduced' from one of the secretaries was that Peter Osbourne was tacitly on vacation in the Middle East! We are as far from there as one can get. People are of course entitled to change their minds or even lie to their staff so they cannot be reached. But this type of man did not care what anyone thought of him and could tell anyone who interrupted him to go to hell.

Our information stream ran dry at this point. Of course, a lot more questions sprung up than were answered, but then I was not attempting to write his bio, just to find out enough so I could let go of him. There were some interesting further inquiries that I could pursue, but found what I needed. The police would finish the job, and I would eventually read about it in the paper. After some more reflection and a whole bunch of snacks, I decided I did have enough and I chose to let go of him. I promptly sent Rick a message to stop any more inquiries and to resume his life. I didn't now care if I ran into Inspector Yves or any of the police force. I was putting this ridiculous event into the past and I was going forward with my life. One day at a time — just like the program says.

Since the room service was on the house, I ordered my dinner. They did not have my favorite food, Mexican (they didn't even know what a taco was). So I ordered a hamburger with mushrooms and bacon with a side of fries. And, of course, the requisite diet soda. Although I don't have to watch my weight (I know, now you hate me), why tempt fate?

In addition, I eat so little sugar that the regular sodas taste too sweet.

The food was just as good as you can imagine. I wasn't able to finish the burger or the fries. I tossed the latter but saved the burger for a snack if I got hungry later. I surfed the Net on local websites and found loads more stuff about New Zealand of which I had not been aware. Suddenly, I had a real dilemma. I probably did not have enough time to do everything I wanted to. There were tropical beaches, impenetrable rain forests, a desert, all kinds of water sports. There was a skydiving competition next week, all kinds of festivals and historical sites.

During the research, I became interested in the history of the island. It was rather unique in that the natives and the 'invaders' — that is, the British — seemed to have been able to live together in reasonable harmony. Not at all like my ancestors and the Spanish. The latter felt that anything not nailed down was not only theirs but put there by God just for them. Fortunately, before I could get upset by these ancient injustices done to my forbears, sleep and fatigue overcame me. I fell asleep with thoughts of beaches and adventure.

CHAPTER NINE

NEW BEGINNINGS

When I awoke, I decided what I would do first. I had arrived on a Tuesday (local time) and now it was Friday. It was time for a new beginning and I settled on a day at the beach soaking up some rays, putting on my RAY-BANS, swimsuit and sun block (not necessarily in that order).

I truly enjoy a day at the beach and have outgrown the need to prove it to everyone by turning lobster red. And even though I am naturally a bit darker than most of the Anglos that turn themselves into lobsters every summer, I can still burn if I don't watch it. Further, I think my dad's admonitions about the evils and dangers of skin cancer may have taken effect. I felt he worried more about the sun than about my driving. As far back as I can remember, he was preoccupied with sun exposure; and as it turned out, for good reason. So, after carefully covering myself (sun block requires fifteen minutes to work), donning my favorite swimsuit (not too tight), putting on my shades (I look great in them), and packing my beach bag with reading material, I unblocked the door and rushed on out to the beach.

It was still a weekday, leaving the beach to tourists and beach bums with their attendant bunnies. I suppose that even down here most people have to work to get by. It did not take long to find a spot near enough to the lifeguard to see and be seen, but not so close that it would seem intrusive. The water was a remarkably transparent ultramarine blue with occasional highlights of teal and cobalt. There was hardly any wind and the white caps were conspicuous by their absence.

A few preteen kids were playing in and out of the water and I began with my most recent reading acquisition. It was a highly interesting story about how a scoundrel with pretensions to the Chinese throne and his sidekick hatch a scheme to net themselves close to a million dollars. The plot was excellent, the characters extremely real with lots of little hints and nefarious twists that I knew the author would sort out in the end (now why couldn't I write like that?) I was lost in the world the author had created, when a shadow closed in over my book and me.

For a second, I felt that a cloud had drifted in front of the sun but then my brain connected that I had heard the squeak of flip-flops walking in sand just prior to the shadow appearing and I was startled when I realized there was someone looming over me.

I could not believe it. I even told myself it just wasn't possible. I may even have rubbed my eyes to be sure. It was JP. He had a neutral/sheepish look on his face. I was more shocked and stunned than scared or angry. Then I realized he was dressed for the beach. A t-shirt with Opus the penguin on the front, swim trunks, hairy legs that showed some age but were still quite attractive (attractive! what was I saying?) and flip-flops, red ones I think.

"Hello, Yolanda."

"Uh, hello, inspector," I managed after a short pause. "I am surprised to see you here, after Wednesday night and all." A direct approach is best.

"Yes, I can understand how you would be angry with me. I was not at my best that evening. I came to apologize once again and see if we could put it behind us."

"In swim trunks?" I asked in disbelief.

"That was indeed a problem," he admitted. "By the time I was able to come over, you were already at the beach. I felt that my suit would be too inappropriate and would bring far more attention to us than you would appreciate. But I wanted to get it o…that is, I wanted to be prompt in my apology. If it helps, you can think of this outfit as a disguise rather than beach wear." He said all this with a hint of a smirk. It was at this point that I started noticing little things.

My father always said that if you don't look for things you will never find them and that the only way to notice what is going on around you is to look for them. After a lifetime of living with him, I developed his habit of being aware of details, small, large, subtle, obvious. It did not matter, my dad saw them all. His work profited immensely from this type of scrutiny and it reinforced his habit even more. It made my adolescence a living hell (actually, only when I was trying to get away with something, which unfortunately was most of the time). He would notice mood, excitement, clothes, timing, whatever. Damn him if he couldn't usually figure out what I was up to.

What I was noticing here was the incongruousness of his

clothing. The swim trunks had never been in water, the flip-flops were new, his skin was the whitest shade of pale and had not seen direct intense sunlight probably since he was born, if then. "You haven't been to a beach in years, have you?" I demanded.

"Actually no, I haven't."

I cut him off, "In fact, you didn't even have any of your 'disguise' before you bought it today, did you?" My tone was becoming a bit demanding if not shrill.

"So you noticed," his sheepishness becoming more acute as he studied his clothing. "I confess, that aside from the skin and hair, I pretty much had to buy everything."

"You don't even have sun block on!" I admonished.

"No I don't, is that important?"

"You goddamn well better believe it is, you bloody idiot."

I rummaged in my pack and found my bottle. "Get down here and sit before we have to peel that skin off you." My tone must have been commanding because he did just as I said. "How long have you been out in this blazing sun? Don't you know that you can burn in fifteen minutes if you are not used to it? Particularly as pale as you are. You Anglos are all alike." I started putting gobs of sun block over his ears and nose and began working on his face.

"Well, I..."

"Don't give me any of your bloody excuses; I will not be responsible for you needing intensive-care burn treatment. From now on, if you are coming to see me, wear all the required apparel. Sun block is every bit as important as those trunks you are wearing. Probably more so." By the time I was done with his face, neck and shoulders, I'd calmed down and realized I was touching him. I grabbed the bottle and nearly threw it at him, "Here, now you know how to apply it, put it on your arms and legs and don't miss any spots. It will still take a good five minutes to get any real protection. Here, I'll stand and shade you while you finish. Then you can go since I accept your apology and will be glad to get this entire mess behind us."

His entire manner had changed during this outburst of mine (God, was my father ever familiar with my outbursts). He was more relaxed, more confident, much less cautious. It caught me off guard. What had happened to cause such a change?

"What is an 'Anglo'?" he asked with his smirk returning.

"You are," a smirk of my own forming, "all you palefaces; anyone that came from the old country and took over the North American continent like it was theirs already. Never mind my ancestors had been there for millennia." I quickly stopped what was quickly turning into a familiar diatribe and waited for a response.

"I want to thank you for your help. Apparently, I have a lot to learn about going to the beach. I do, however, want to get on with my..."

"And that's another thing, how in blazes did you know I was on the beach anyway? I did not tell anyone." My anger was flaring up again. "Are you having me tailed?" as I quickly scanned the area.

"He isn't there anymore and I wouldn't call it being tailed," JP said calmly.

"So what would you call it, 'protective custody'?" my sarcasm evident.

"You were so upset I just wanted to make sure you would be all right. I had one of the hotel people keep an eye on your movements." I was so, so…hell, I didn't know what I felt, but I did not like it."

JP broke the silence with a loud and formal voice. "Yolanda, I am sorry for Wednesday night. I had not intended to upset you. Please forgive me for making what was already a difficult day for you much worse." It sounded a bit rehearsed but the emotion behind it was genuine and my mood and demeanor changed.

"Thank you JP, I truly appreciate your apology. Last night I was much more upset and fragile than even I realized."

There followed a long and uncomfortable silence. He had made himself vulnerable by apologizing and I had too by accepting and we did not have the kind of relationship (did we have any relationship at all?) that would let us respond to this situation. We both listened to the sounds of the beach, the surf building, the seagulls making their incessant racket while they searched for scraps, and the few kids running about…

"I am truly sorry," he said with much less formality and much more emotion.

"I know," I stammered as I broke into tears.

I find it a great relief to cry; however, I won't tolerate it being perceived as a weakness. When a man needs a release and punches a hole in the wall, no one views it as anything but a sign of strength. He doesn't hurt anyone and is able to express his frustration in what is generally considered a socially acceptable way (as opposed to punching whomever was upsetting him.) But NOOOO, when a woman vents or releases some frustration by crying, all the clichés of our culture come out as to how 'the little lady cannot handle herself' or 'see, they are the weaker sex.' Nevertheless, I needed the release and could not, at this moment, worry about what others might think.

JP immediately stood up and held me. I had not appreciated how much taller he was. I am just a whisker over 5'10" but this time I did not have my heels on. He towered over me — perhaps 6'4" or 5." Despite his size, JP was gentle. Gentle enough that I found myself able to let go of my remaining reserve, and let my inner-self vent itself dry. After what seemed like hours, I felt much better and I pulled away. I found a towel to dry my face.

"I suppose you think I am falling apart," I said it more as a statement than a question.

"No, Yolanda, I think you have been trying to hold in more than anyone is capable of and the dam just broke." He paused. "I have a young daughter who tries very hard to be as 'tough' as her dad and every once in a while she too has to vent."

I was seriously taken aback by this odd mixture of sensitive hard-nosed police detective. I may have seriously misjudged him. "What a lousy vacation! Even when I try to put it all behind me by coming to the beach, it comes right up and smacks me in the head."

"No, Yo, it is truly over. In addition to the apology, I came to tell you that we found out who killed Mr. Osbourne." He let that hang while I tried to recover and close my mouth.

"Already?" it was all that I could manage to say. I was more than impressed; I was astonished. Back in the States, I would have been surprised if they caught him at all, much less within forty-eight hours! JP now had his happy eyes back with a Cheshire Cat smile I had not seen before. He was obviously immensely proud of his accomplishment, as well he should. I found myself bursting with curiosity. "Who was it? Did he confess? Why did he kill him? And why for God's sakes did he do it in my room?"

"Easy, Yolanda, I will tell you all I know. First, why don't we get out of this cat's toilet and find ourselves a nice shady spot to have a cool, refreshing drink?"

"I can't stand it!" I screamed, "Tell me, and NOW!" But I was not mad, just excited.

"All right, Yolanda, but let's at least start walking to that shady spot. I don't want to turn into that lobster you mentioned awhile back."

I gathered my stuff and hurriedly shoved it into my beach bag. To hell with orderliness. To my surprise, I found myself handing the bag over to him so he could carry it for me. It made it easier keeping up with him.

"We have been lucky in our investigation," he said modestly.

"I would say so."

"First of all, we circulated pictures of Mr. Osbourne."

"The dead guy I slept with?"

"Right," he gave me a curious look but I just smiled back and he relaxed. "One of the maids recalled seeing him that night. He was with another man, a tall lanky fellow, and they both acted lost and were roaming around. In fact, she would have called the manager except they were dressed in nice suits and expensive shoes. Also, they always nodded at her when they passed by her. They were memorable because the hotel has mostly tourists and they were clearly business types."

JP pointed to a small coffee shop that had several outdoor tables, some with shade. The shop had a sign: 'The

Long White Cloud.' We ambled our way there.

"We then obtained confirmation from a few of the other staff. It is clear they had been hanging about for a few days. We obtained the search warrant I told you about and were able to enter his hotel room and discovered he had arrived with a fellow who called himself Rogers, uh…Marcus Rogers."

"Seems like an odd name," I observed.

"Yes, we think it is an alias." Think? Did he say think? I thought they had caught the guy? Still, I allowed him to continue and enjoy his moment.

After ordering two tall, ice-cold lemonades and a couple of scones (a type of pastry, quite sweet and luscious), he proceeded. "We placed an all-out alert for this Marcus person, Uh…I think you Yanks call it an all-points bulletin."

"Yes, that's right."

"We also searched his room but it was mostly empty. We checked the airports and that's where we got lucky. The clerk at the desk of Qantas clearly remembers a man coming into the terminal early yesterday morning. He was nervous and excited and kept asking if the plane would be on time. He gave the name of Marc Roberts."

"Same initials," I exclaimed.

"Precisely, we figure he came in under his Rogers alias and had all the papers to support that identity. However, when we entered Osbourne's room, he must have panicked and needed to leave in a hurry. He did not have time to get new papers and since the first flight did not leave for several hours, he could not be sure we would not be waiting for a Mr. Rogers."

At this, I giggled and asked. "So how did you catch him?"

JP looked surprised, "Catch him? I don't...Oh! No, Yolanda, we have not caught him, at least not yet, but we know who he is. I am sorry if I led you to believe that we had him in custody."

I realized my mistake. "No, JP, it was my assumption. You said you knew who the killer was and I assumed that meant you had him, in custody, please proceed." However, with that revelation, my energy level had noticeably dropped.

Prior to resuming his story, he cut a scone in half and lathered it with butter and jam. He then started to talk with his mouth full. I let the *faux pas* pass without mention. After all, I wasn't his mother and I might in the past have done something like that once or twice.

"We called the reservations office and were able to locate the actual gent that took the reservation. I am afraid that we did have to wake the poor chap, since he does work the last shift."

"What did he say?"

"It was such a strange call he remembered it well and had told several of his pals. According to the reservations computer, he received the call at 2:38 AM and the person was frantic. The agent had to calm him down several times so he could understand him. He didn't seem to know where he wanted to go. He kept trying different cities such as Hong Kong, Tokyo, Singapore and Los Angeles, but those flights leave in the late afternoon or evening and every time he kept saying 'it was too late.' He finally asked what was the earliest flight out of the f@#$% island, his emphasis, Yolanda."

I nodded in understanding.

"To anywhere that he could make connections." It turns out that the earliest flight out of the airport every day is a commuter flight to Sidney and that's the flight he left on. He would not reserve any further connection. He insisted he would make it when he arrived at the Sidney airport." JP paused to munch on a scone and sipped his drink. I was reeling from all of the information that I failed to prod him on.

He eventually resumed. "We called the authorities at Sidney but because of the early morning hour, they couldn't get their act together in time. Bloody 'roos," he murmured under his breath. "By the time they arrived at the airport, he was gone." JP stopped like he was finished.

"Yes, yes and where did he go?" I was screaming.

He just smiled and pretended that he had not realized he hadn't told me. "He caught a flight to the States, Los Angeles to be precise. It should have landed just an hour or so ago. The police will be waiting, and I expect a call any minute now. "We are working with your national police; I believe you call them the FBI."

"Yes we do, but only when we absolutely have to." I laughed at my own joke. It took him a moment or two to get it and then he only laughed out of politeness. "Excuse my humor, James, it is juvenile, but it is the only humor I have."

He just nodded and continued to eat his scone.

CHAPTER TEN

CHRISTCHURCH

Astonishingly, with the emotional history we carried, JP and I began a comfortable if not friendly discussion regarding the island and its attractions. I estimated his skin would be spared a major shedding episode. When he stood up and excused himself, I consciously reevaluated him. He had a tall, slim, muscular frame that allowed for a long easy stride. He exuded a rare sense of comfort, which I found so appealing and attractive. I could better appreciate these traits now probably because I was freed up from my problems. (Thank God it was all over!) He was a sensitive man and quite extraordinary as a policeman, or maybe down here policemen were all like this.

He wore no wedding band but his ring finger showed a faint ring mark. Recently divorced? Separated? On the make? My cynicism fueled suspicions and required effort to suppress. He looked to be about forty-one or forty-two from the wrinkles on his face, but I knew him to be thirty-seven, on his next birthday. Like my dad always says, "It's not the age but the mileage that's of importance." His hair was thinning at the edges, but still plentiful of a nice dark brown. He combed it precisely with the part on his left. Did that mean he was right handed? Or was that irrelevant? I continued for another five minutes with this kind of reverie before I snapped out of it. I attempted to pay but the waiter assured me that it had been taken care of. When? I had not seen him pay. I left a tip anyway; it allowed me a small sense of independence.

On the way to my room, I toyed with the idea of going for an exploratory walk of the city. Or maybe I would find out what the group was doing and go with them. I liked the idea of being with other people so I called up to Donovan's room but there was no answer and I left a message. I looked about and recognized one of my fellow travelers. I walked up to her and fumbled for her name.

"Hello, I am with the group."

"Oh yes, my dear Yolanda, you are the poor darling that had that nasty run-in with a dead person. I just cannot imagine such a thing. I think I would just die with fright. Even thinking about it gives me the willies. This is worse than…"

I was sure I was about to die from this conversation. I interrupted, "Do you know what is on the schedule for today?"

"My name is Margarette, with an 'e' at the end; so many people leave that out, you know."

"Margarette, yes, but have you…"

"I have been trying all morning to find that darling man that is running this show, but none of us have seen him all day. He did leave a message to go on without him, but we thought he might be back by now."

I was now a bit more interested. "Back from where?"

"From wherever it was that he had to flit off to so suddenly. One night he is talking all about what we are going to do the next day and then he left this message that he had to take care of something. I personally think he found a lady friend, but then I am such a romantic."

"Yes," I nodded, wondering what Mrs. Boers would think of that notion. I desperately felt the need to extricate myself before I took root. "Thank you so much for your help, but I have to run to my room and change."

"But I haven't even told you what is on the agenda!"

"I think I will just create my own agenda and maybe find a gent of my own."

She giggled and smiled, "Maybe you will make up with that dashing detective fellow; have a good time." And with that, I made my escape.

If that exchange was an example of what I would have to endure, by traveling with the group, I would rather repeat yesterday. Then again, maybe not, but it would be a close call.

I learned something though, and I was intrigued by Donovan's sudden disappearance.

The non-logical part of my brain was insisting something was odd. I felt a tendril of an idea gnawing at my mind and I started at the beginning: he organizes the tour, makes sure it is full, plans all the activities and reservations and starts participating with everything until...? What happened to change his plans so suddenly? Does he know anyone here? Family? Did he get a message from home that some emergency came up? Why the secrecy? What about that clutchy wife of his? Now that I thought about it, I did not see her at the table Wednesday night. My interest was now definitely peaked. I walked over to the desk and inquired. A young man probably no more than eighteen was behind the desk. "Has Mr. Boers, uh...Donovan Boers returned?"

"No ma'am, I don't think so, let me check." He looked at the computer screen for a minute. "He hasn't picked up his messages yet," he said politely.

"Were you here when he left?" I persisted.

"No, ma'am, but I have been on duty to record the messages from your group. He must have a dozen or more and some of them are not very...well...nice." Good grief, now everyone was getting pissed off. I reminded myself I was on vacation and regardless how interesting this all was, I had things to do and even better things to discover than this mini-drama. I turned to go but before I went two steps, he volunteered more information.

"Ma'am? If you want to talk with him, Chet is in the back room." He looked hopeful; I was missing something.

"Chet? I don't know any Chet, wh...?

"You know, the guy that saw Mr. Boers leave the hotel."

"Oh...I understand." Before I could demur, he left and called out, "Chet, this lady guest would like to hear your story 'bout that gent who left in such a hurry."

"Great, tell her I'll be right there, I just need to take a leak."

He turned to tell me but realized I must have heard it all and started turning red.

"It's all right, I too sometimes have to 'take a leak'." That embarrassed him further and I couldn't resist having some fun. "I just hope he remembers to wash his hands."

"Yes, Mum. I mean, ma'am. I mean, he will remember, I mean he always does, not that I am always with him..."

I took him off the hook, "Thank you so much for your help. Please feel free to go on with your work."

"Thank you, ma'am," and he left. Good thing too, I was getting tired of all of this 'ma'am' stuff. I was only twenty-eight, for God's sake, you would think I was ready for retirement acres or something.

Chet came out in the one minute he promised. He was short, thin and looked younger than he must have been. He had a wide-open smile and was bounding with the kind of energy that sort of reminded me of Tigger the tiger.

"Hello, Ms. Prescott, I am Chet."

"How in blazes do you know my name?" I inquired firmly.

"Everyone knows who you are, ma'am. You are the lady who had that dead bloke in her bed all night long and then had a nasty fight with the nice police detective."

I should have expected that, but it caught me off guard. I made a mental note to think about changing hotels, or cities for that matter.

"Do you want to hear about Mr. Boers?" he asked hopefully.

"Yes, unless it will take a long time," I replied.

"No problem, ma'am, it isn't a long story but it sure was weird." He looked around to make sure no one else was there and then conspiratorially he started in a low tone. "You see, I knew Mr. Donovan, he was so friendly and talkative. At about lunch time, I received a call for him. I knew he was in the dining area so I go and tell him. He took the call at the courtesy phone over there," pointing to a standard black phone on a table next to a teal couch.

"I noticed that he was on the phone for over twenty minutes. At some point, he started yelling into the phone and then would catch himself."

"Yelling what?" I asked.

"Well, I ..."

"I can take it. I probably have heard worse." That prospect seemed to disturb him for a second.

"OK, ma'am, the only parts I distinctly heard were, 'I don't f@#$% believe it!' and 'Those assholes!' Sorry, ma'am."

"That's perfectly all right, I am quite familiar with those terms, please continue."

"He then slammed the phone down and nearly ran out of the lobby."

"Is that all?" I sounded disappointed. The build up had been overdone.

"Oh no, ma'am, while he was on the telephone I received a telegram from the United States, which was urgent. I was waiting for him to finish so I could hand it over. I called him but he didn't seem to notice. I figured he was still thinking about his troubles so I ran after him."

"When I stopped him you would have thought the devil himself was inside the man. I hardly recognized him. I gave him the telegram and he exploded. For a second there I was afraid for my safety. He yelled he wasn't going to let them get away with it and they could shove their corporate policy."

"Are those the exact words he used?"

"No, ma'am, he added a lot of those colorful words he used before." He began to blush. I couldn't decide if he was personally uncomfortable with the words or because I being a woman would be mortally injured by hearing them. "What kind of adjectives did he use?

After a short pause to reevaluate me, he resumed his discourse. "...he particularly liked panty-ass, but his favorite seemed to be the phrase 'lower than whale shit'."

At this I laughed. I had not heard that one before but the image was a particularly good one. I thanked Chet and excused myself. This was strange and I had a good amount of thinking to do. Being on vacation, however, I decided to do it while I toured the city of Christchurch. I was determined to get on with my life and if it indeed turned out, I was not the only one having an unpleasantness occur to them, so much the better.

I started on my sightseeing adventure immediately. I dashed upstairs to my room intent on changing quickly, making a pit stop and dashing out just as quickly. Then I saw the blinking light on the phone. I cursed loudly for all the good it did. I would not pick it up, or so I kept telling myself. Of course, I eventually gave in and to my amazement, it was from JP. What in blazes did he want now? I wrote down the number but I did not call him back. If it was important, I had no illusions about his ability to locate me.

I decided to start at Cathedral Square. It is a truly magnificent gothic church. It is huge, even by today's standards, and sits amid modern buildings, cars and people. I cannot adequately describe it but I know it took almost fifty years to complete and it is a monument to how Anglican these settlers were. To devote so much of their time and energy on a project of this magnitude clearly makes a statement about their priorities. This is even more remarkable when you consider the hardships they had. (There were no Wal-Marts or supermarkets around the corner.)

The Avon River winds its way around and through the city on its way to the Pacific. It looked in pristine condition, unlike some of the rivers I've seen in US cities, and I decided to walk along its path as much as possible. It has grassy banks that were being used as picnic areas and in some places they even had paddle boats available. One local person must have noticed my map and stopped to talk. She told me some of the history surrounding the river but emphasized the beauty of the botanical gardens through which the river flowed. It was located in the west end of the city, and at least according to her, it should not be missed.

The architecture varied greatly, but is predominantly Victorian in style. So many of the streets had English names that at times I could believe I was back in England. Later, I would find out that the settlers were so adamantly Anglican that they brought with them the trees and hedges with which they were familiar. I also discovered that many considered Christchurch more English than any town in England.

Although I always found the British people friendly enough, I found the New Zealanders (Kiwis in local terminology) just as friendly but more alive and more energetic. Sometime during my walk, I let go of all the past and was aware of only the current moment. I like being in the present moment. No concerns beside what was happening right now. The child running down the street yelling for his chums to slow down. The black Labrador checking me over before following his master. The sudden breeze that caught my hair but cooled me off. Many and varied were my observations before my stomach made its presence known. I then noticed that several hours had passed — in such a short span of time.

I stopped at a coffee shop that served food. I had a steaming cup of Colombian Supremo with cream and NutraSweet. Rick says I don't actually like coffee or I wouldn't smother it with so much stuff. I, however, find coffee one of life's great joys. It ranks way up there with air conditioning and indoor plumbing. While snacking on calamari (I'd developed a taste for them) and a tuna salad, I had an impulse. I called the number JP had left not knowing what I would say. If he was even there.

After the third ring, I heard a young voice say, "Hello, Yves residence." She said it with that self-assurance of youth that is so unique. It says, "I am alive and there is nothing that is not possible. Hurry up because my time is precious and I can't spare a single minute." Which is why, I believe, kids in general resent having to go to sleep.

"Hello, Michele?"

"Yes, this is Michele, who is this?" her voice curious and suspicious.

"This is Yolanda, I have heard many things about you..."

"DAADDDYYYY," she yelled without bothering to cover the mouthpiece. After a short pause, JP came to the phone."

"Hi, JP, it's Yolanda returning your call."

"Yes, of course, thank you for calling. I hope you are well and enjoying your vacation?"

"JP, I hope you did not call just to see how I am doing, but if so, I will tell you. I am at a delightful coffee shop with a wonderful view of the Avon. I have just finished a huge plate of calamari and I am on my third cup of delicious Colombian."

"That's great. You certainly sound like you are finding your way around well enough." There was a pause that I was determined not to fill. He had called me after all.

"Yolanda, are you still there?"

"Yes, I'm still here."

"What I called about was...well tomorrow is Saturday."

"Indeed it is, JP."

"And, Michele and I go on daytrips every Saturday, perhaps you would be interested in joining us?" He had finally blurted out the reason for calling. The invite, although not anticipated, was not surprising after our pleasant last encounter at the beach and coffee shop. Personally, I was thrilled not to see the island alone without Margarette 'with an e'." I viewed this as a private tour of the island. While I understood that Michele's presence was absolutely essential to my acceptance, I hoped she wouldn't be one of those whinny kids that you couldn't please. Do they have MAPs (Mexican-American Princesses) down here? What would they call them, NZP? Kiwi Princesses?

I answered trying not to show excessive excitement, "I would love to, JP. Thank you so much for asking."

His tone brightened, "Wonderful, it's going to be a glorious sunny day, what do you say we get off to an early start? Say seven AM? At your hotel?"

I gulped, I had hoped to sleep in. "As long as you are driving, and I don't have to be fully awake, I will be ready."

"I will bring a thermos of my best coffee; you will love it, I guarantee it."

Was this the same man that was stumbling over the invitation? "What should I wear?" I asked.

"Cool summer clothes but throw a swim suit into your bag, we may decide to take a dip in the lake."

"OK, JP, I will see you and Michele at seven and again, thanks a lot."

"You're welcome, see you at seven." He hung up.

I sat there holding the phone thinking, *What in heaven am I getting myself into?*

CHAPTER ELEVEN

JP AND MICHELE

I surprised myself and woke early without need for the alarm. I felt alive, full of energy and ready to explore the country. I chose not to ponder about any hidden meanings JP's invitation might entail and proceeded to pack. I wanted to pack light, but I did not know what I might need. I decided since they were the hosts, I would let them worry about anything I didn't bring. I waited only six minutes before I saw a late-model Land Rover pull up to the hotel. I wasn't paying much attention to the people inside until I recognized JP walking toward me in decidedly casual wear. He wore a loose flannel shirt with well-worn jeans and docksiders without socks. It was not the same man with whom I'd agreed to sightsee. I was getting a bad feeling when a bubbly, dark-haired girl shouted, "But daaaddyyy, do I haaave to gooo? Like, I have so many things to do, and there is no cell phone signal and..."

"Stop it, Michele," JP said in a tone probably more stern

than he intended. "It has been decided and that is the last I will hear of it." I was most definitely feeling some bad karma. Why was JP dragging his daughter along? Did he invent this trip with her just as a way to invite me to come? Most importantly, how did I feel about that? "Hi, JP, you look so... different."

"Thanks, Yolanda, when I am off duty I choose comfort. Particularly since we may be gone a long time. [If only I had known how long it would actually be.] How's that wrist of yours? You don't have the hospital's splint on anymore."

"The hotel concierge found me a canvas one. It is commonly used for carpal tunnel syndrome but it is so much more comfortable that I decided to chance it; as long as I don't hit any more policemen, it should be adequate." He smirked at my comment. He was opening the passenger side door when I insisted that Michele could stay there; I would prefer the back seat. "That way I can view out of either side of the car." JP looked at me unsure, but Michele was clearly re-evaluating me.

We took off and after ramping onto Rt. 1, JP handed me a thermos of coffee. "This is my special blend. A friend of mine is a coffee grower on Java and sends a pound periodically. He even named it after me, *JP's Roast*." He then clarified some things. "Michele doesn't like to go on these outings."

"Oh, dad." Michele sounded mortified.

"She would much prefer to be at home behind that blasted computer of hers or on the phone with her friends."

"Dad, that is enough!" That last statement was said through bared teeth and with enough venom to kill anyone but a parent.

I could remember only too well being embarrassed by my

father in front of strangers. JP either didn't hear or ignored her comments and continued, "So, I insist on an outdoors trip twice a month whether we need it or not." Michele, in desperation, started fidgeting with the radio.

I dove into their family dynamics without fear, "I can understand Michele's perspective; I am quite attached to my computer also." This brought an abrupt change in Michele's radio tuning. "In fact, it took a significant amount of emotional effort for me to leave it at home."

"What kind of computer do you have?" she asked tentatively. I'd hoped her curiosity would win out. When she wasn't whining or angry, she had a melodious voice. She should be in a choir.

"I am partial to the Macintosh operating system..." She smiled and turned even more to face me.

"Now the two of you will have to refrain..."

We ignored him. "I have the latest quad processor that runs at nearly a GHZ. I set it up with three Gigs of RAM, fire wire, usb2 and more software than you can imagine — it really screams."

"Wow, do you think I could see it? Dad here won't buy me a new one and mine is already three years old."

"Three years?" I said surprised. "That's older than this car."

"Ouch," JP said.

"Have you told him how computers are obsolete in eighteen to twenty-four months?"

"Till I am exhausted."

Now that she had an ally, Michele was warming to her subject. "But he refuses to understand."

We chatted about our mutual interest and when we were

on firm footing, I said, "I will talk to your dad about the utility of non-obsolete computers — but not now, I have traveled eight thousand miles to see this beautiful country of yours. Do you think you could tell me about it? By the way, JP, you are right, your coffee is wonderful, you will have to introduce me to your source."

Michele's entire demeanor changed and she proceeded to be a wonderful tour guide. She would go on and on about all the fascinating things (with her own interpretation thrown in at no extra charge) regarding the history of New Zealand. Even JP seemed amazed at the scope and depth of information flowing from his daughter. Every once in a while, I caught him looking in awe at her. When she saw it she said, "We are studying history at school, Dad."

New Zealand was one of the last (relatively) uninhabited habitable lands found by the sea-faring nations of the nineteenth century. It caused a huge stir in the adventurous set and it proceeded to get a large number of arrivals within a short span. There were some 'land wars' with the natives, but by the standards already set by the colonialists of the sixteenth and seventeenth centuries, these were mild if notable at all.

After an hour-and-a-half on route one, we turned right onto route seventy-nine and followed the signs for Lake Tekapo. The air was chillier but still comfortable. This special lake had been carved by glaciers and it had a wonderful location where we could eat while looking at the mountains. I was in for a real treat. It was supposedly one of the most photographed sites on the entire South Island and as I was finding out from Michele's travelogue, it was one of her absolutely most favorite places to go. She would repeatedly state with the utter conviction of youth that it would be where she would live when she graduated. I was not quite sure if she was talking about high school or college.

The signpost said Burke's Pass. I momentarily wondered who this Burke person was and what he had done to get this pass named after him. Probably something dangerous and uncomfortable. The pass was a gateway to the Southern Alps (as they are called), which were ahead of us and growing with every kilometer. I have never seen the Swiss version, but the southern version is, to state a cliché, breathtaking.

I found myself having to remember to breathe as I gazed at the snow-covered peaks that seemed to climb forever. The view released a flood of memories from storage. Some pleasant and some not so pleasant. I automatically started repeating the serenity prayer to help me. "...serenity to accept...things...cannot change...courage to change...things I can...wisdom to know the difference." It always helps. It frees me to focus on the precise moment of time I am currently inhabiting. I am thus better able to resist being overwhelmed by the past.

Since I am at least a few minutes from falling completely apart, I can indulge myself and explain what happened to my mother and why a pall still exists between Dad and me. Excuse me if I pause from time to time, or if I break out into tears. This story remains painful.

Three years ago I was in my last year of college (at Kalamazoo College, a wonderful little school located in the lower part of Michigan's mitten). I was majoring in Computer Science (what else) and actually was having the time of my life. I had remained sober for over five years by then. I'd made my amends and paid off just about everyone to whom I owed money. My life was finally coming together and every day was full of wonderfully exciting things to do and fun people with which to do them. That is when I got The Call (I always refer to it that way).

I was on the Quad basking in the first semi-warm days of spring when a sophomore named Royal Alsworth ran up and told me I had a phone call and to hurry because it was important. (He had no idea how that call would change my life.) It was from Dad. He needed me to fly home as fast as absolutely possible. Mom was dying.

This is the point of the story at which I tend to fall apart. I can recall the shock and stupefaction of the exact moment when he uttered those words, "Mom is dying."

The three years since her death have enabled me to scab over this wound. It doesn't bother me until someone picks at it and opens it once more. I remember yelling, "What are you talking about, Dad? She was fine at start of semester." I went on ranting, "What kind of sick joke is this?"

All he would say was, "Please come home now." He would explain when I got there. I stormed around for a while trying to get a hold of myself. I called my sponsor and she helped me get ready and inform everyone at the college. When I arrived at the airport, we had just missed the first flight with connections to the west coast. The next one did not leave for three hours. That bloody, bloody plane; how my life would have changed if I had made it.

Dad picked me up at the airport. He looked horrible. I had never seen him look that way, as if something had sucked out his life energy. He held me for such a long time and it took me only a few seconds to realize I had not arrived in time. Mom had died ninety minutes earlier.

I don't remember much of the following few days. My aunts made the arrangements, my dad needed me close, and I still expected my mother to walk in at any minute. Of course, in time, I found out that Mom had noticed a small black mole on her shoulder; around the time I was leaving for fall term. She had it biopsied and it had been the worst — malignant melanoma. She absolutely insisted I not be notified. She was determined to beat it, and further, she would not disrupt my life when I had fought so hard to get it back. She would tell me after graduation. (I never did manage to go back and graduate.)

She had received chemo and radiation and for a short while did well. She then started to lose weight and energy. She developed the complications of pneumonia and eventually liver and kidney failure. That was when she asked for me. I can still hear her asking for me in her last few moments, wanting to hold my hand. If only I had gone straight for the airport, I would have made it. This is the point at which I usually lose it, so please bear with me.

After a few weeks, the recriminations started. Why did Dad not call me sooner? Didn't he know that it would take time for me to get home? It has left a permanent barrier between us. We no longer talk about it (God knows we have spoken enough about it) and it prevents us from being as close as we once were. I cannot get past the fact that he should have bloody known what was happening. He is a bloody doctor, for Pete's sake. And he keeps saying he was both respecting Mom's wishes and was much too close to the situation to make those kind of judgments.

There is a reason for this digression. It is my Mom's absolute love of the mountains. In her case, it was the Rocky

Mountains just outside of Boulder, Colorado. Each winter we would go there to toboggan and she would be mesmerized by their harsh grandeur and permanent beauty. Now, my current surroundings, half a world away, stirred up this inner dragon. I knew that I would have to find some time to myself to remember her and to pray for help.

"Yo, are you all right?" JP asked, bringing me back to the present.

"Yes, I'm fine, why?" (As you well know, 'fine' can mean anything from ecstasy to complete and utter depravity, which is why I like to use it.)

"No reason, except that 'roo-in-the-headlights daze you have been wearing. Or maybe that you haven't said anything for over a quarter of an hour."

"Oh, I'm sorry," I said, trying to sound cheerful.

"What's wrong, Yo?" This comment came from Michele, in a surprisingly sensitive and concerned tone.

"The mountains are wonderful, but they reminded me of something sad, that's all."

Michele said, "Sounds awful, what was it?"

"Mich, please respect her privacy," JP said this in a hushed tone that I was intended to overhear.

I was torn. I did not want to open my deepest, rawest wound to strangers; people I hardly knew. Still, I felt some indefinable sense of safety with them. In addition, Michele and I had just developed the rudiments of rapport and I knew if I clammed up now she might not venture out again. "Michele, you are unusually intuitive, it is very painful."

JP cut in, "Yolanda, you don't have to say any..."

"I know, JP, and thanks, but my reluctance is more that I have only just met the two of you and it is not your duty to listen to my problems."

Michelle added, "But, Yo, I want to hear it, really, I will listen quietly and be respectful." JP glared at her, more in surprise than anger.

After a minute of uncomfortable silence, JP said, "Yo, I don't know what you should do. I have a suggestion, however. We will be at the lake in just a few minutes. Why don't we discuss what we will or will not do over lunch while we are gazing at the lake and the mountains? Personally, I find the spirit of nature to be a help in these matters."

I was again surprised by how sensitive this policeman could be. Had I sensed this part of him? Is that why I accepted his invitation? "That sounds like a plan, JP, particularly since I'm famished." With that, we resumed our prior conversation as if nothing at all had happened.

CHAPTER TWELVE

LAKE TEKAPO

We arrived within minutes and the location was indeed spectacular. Lake Tekapo is a long skinny lake and it is the deepest of blue. I think the color is called ultramarine. The end was lost out of sight in the foothills of the mountains. It was calm and the reflection of the mountains captured me. The illusion of twin mountain peaks created by the mirror effect is hard to dispel. Michele said the lake has a large amount of suspended minerals that give it not only its color but also its high reflectivity. Lake Tekapo is obviously in New Zealand's eighth-grade curriculum.

JP drove directly to a restaurant with its tables overlooking the lake. We walked in and were seated promptly at one of the front-row tables. It gave us the most commanding view of the lake possible.

Wherever I had seen JP, he had been able to command such a high level of service and attention that I found it unnerving. People wanted to please him. At work, that was only to be expected, but at the restaurant? The coffee shop? After reflecting, I decided that the truly discomforting thought was that I too wanted to please him. I was not sure why.

"I would recommend the seafood. It is good anywhere on the island but here they excel at it," JP advised.

"That sounds awesome, why don't you order for me, make it small and light without any green things in it."

"You don't eat vegetables?" Michele said with surprise.

"I am sorry, Michele, but I am a poor role model when it comes to a balanced diet. Personally, I feel that vegetables are not only highly overrated, they are now obsolete considering we have vitamin pills."

"Yolanda, please don't encourage her. I have a hard enough time getting her to eat anything but jam, burgers and fries," JP said in a half-mocking tone.

"Don't mind me, I am just a tourist." (I didn't add that I had been raised almost exclusively on PB and burgers with an occasional side order of fries.) We all laughed and chatted while waiting for the food. JP had ordered me steamed jumbo shrimp (another oxymoron) with a delightful buttery sauce. It was followed by a big bowl of seafood chowder, which included the largest scallops I had ever seen. Michelle ate her fish and chips with ketchup as the vegetable.

I felt safe and I was able to relax. Even my trapezious (shoulder) muscles were letting go of their unending nervous spastic vigil. While we were finishing and waiting for our coffee, I asked, "Is there a place I could go and be alone for a short while without much distraction?"

Michele must have been anxiously waiting for this. She quickly blurted, "There is the chapel of the Good Shepherd. It is famous and it was designed so you could see the mountains from inside. It's only a few minutes' walk from here. Do you want me to show it to you?"

"That is nice of you, Michele, but I think I will need to be alone. If you are still interested, I would like to tell you what upset me on the drive here."

"Sure," was Michele's ready reply. (If only either of us had known the tremendous impact this would have on all of us for the next few days — possibly for the rest of our lives.)

JP added, "If you are confident you want to share it with us, I also would like to hear it."

I almost changed my mind, but their sincerity overcame my natural reticence to share my pain. "The mountains are similar to the ones around Boulder where I grew up."

"The Cascades," Michele blurted out.

"No, those are much further north. They are on the west coast of Washington State. The ones to which I am referring are the Rocky Mountains. My mother loved those mountains and the mountains here reminded me of her. I spent some of my happiest times as a child there."

Had I been more observant, I might have noticed JP's anxiety building up. "I had not expected to be reminded of her and I was caught by surprise. I still have not been able to reconcile myself with her death..."

Michele suddenly began sobbing uncontrollably and was having a hard time catching her breath. JP went quickly to her side and held her. I sat there dumbfounded, not knowing what had happened. "What! What? What did I say?"

JP looked up with a most dreadful look.

For a moment, I thought he was going to cry. He looked in pain. Initially, I could not identify the emotion and then I got it! Grief. He was showing enormous grief. That's when he cleared it up for me.

"She lost her mother just this past year." It took me several moments for this revelation to sink in and to feel all the implications. My equanimity was shaken deeply and Lord Guilt was trying to use this for an unscheduled cameo appearance.

I had thought JP to be divorced, or at least separated. It had not occurred to me that he might be a widower. The obvious pain Michele was showing was so similar to what I was feeling that without thinking, I joined the two of them and I cried right along with them.

Eventually, I was able to whisper to Michele, "I'm so sorry for bringing this up. I just didn't know..." It was quickly becoming obvious (to me anyway) that JP seemed to be at a loss as to how to handle his daughter's feelings of loss and abandonment. He did not know how to comfort his mourning daughter. His own pain was probably getting in the way. In a flash of insight, I finally realized that in the same way, my dad's pain had gotten in the way three years ago.

I stood up and held out my hand to Michele, "Please join me at the chapel, we will pray for both our mothers." To this day, I do not know why she reached out for my hand and came with me. But she did and we left her dad to deal privately with his own grief (I now understood his reluctance to talk about his wife during our brief dinner).

She valiantly tried to stifle her sobs and sequester the enormous pain she had been feeling for the last year. I just as firmly encouraged her to let it all out and to hold nothing back.

When we arrived, the chapel was empty. We had this beautiful serene structure to ourselves. It seemed to free her up and her crying intensified. I held her the way I had wanted to be held three years ago, close and tight. I talked to her the way I would have wanted someone to talk to me so many years ago. She eventually let go of the struggle for control and wept completely. Later, she told me the circumstances of her mother's death. A drunk driver had crossed the centerline and crashed directly into her car. (A violent shudder ran through me. But for the grace of God...) She had died at the scene. Her father had not let her see the body and she could not forgive him for that. She still dreamed that her mother was still alive and would come home soon. She said that she knew differently but she couldn't let go of the dream.

I began sharing similar feelings about my loss and in this way, she was comforting me. We stayed in that chapel for what seemed hours, crying, talking and eventually becoming quiet with our own personal prayers for our mothers.

By helping this twelve-year-old orphan mourn her mother, I was able to start the healing of my own three-year-old wound. It had taken a trip around the world and a corpse in my bed to jumpstart the process. No wonder my sponsor says there are no coincidences, just miracles where God remains anonymous. It felt good that on returning home I would (hopefully) be able to forgive my dad and eliminate the barrier that had kept us apart for so long.

Right now, however, I had to concentrate on a hurt little girl who was trying to come to terms with insanity. What did she know about drunks? Or death? Or mourning? Or forgiveness? "Michele, you have to forgive yourself," I said firmly. I was on solid ground here. "You had nothing whatsoever to do with this."

She looked at me with tears rolling out of her eyes and

her how-did-you-know look.

"There is nothing you did or did not do that caused this. You could not have prevented it."

"But Yo, she was late picking me up; if it wasn't for me, she would not have been on that road."

"I know, I know. But it still remains true that your mother... what was her name?"

"Melinda."

"She would not have traded you for fifty extra years. The joy you brought into her life went well beyond her survival. She gave you life and wants you to live it fully."

"How do you know? You never even met her!" she demanded.

"I don't need to meet her to understand her. I see her every time I look at you."

With this, she again started to cry but there was a note of relief in it that hadn't been there before.

We found ourselves walking the lakeshore and occasionally skipping rocks. Her father had taught her well. We both noticed JP at the same time. He must have been shadowing us for some time, not wanting to interrupt. We both waved him over and Michele ran to him. He was a mess but was struggling to hide it.

I overheard him ask in a quavering voice, "How are you, Mich?"

"I am so sad, Daddy, I miss Mommy so much."

"Me too, Mich." They held each other for a long time. I started to feel intrusive and I made a move to leave.

Michele saw me and said, "Don't leave, Yo, please don't leave." She turned and asked her father, "Yo says it was not my fault that Mommy died."

"Mich, where in the world did you ever get that idea?" JP said alarmed and shocked. "Well, Mommy was coming to pick me..."

"My dear Mich, you had absolutely nothing to do with her...accident..."

I quickly interjected, "You two need time alone, I won't go far."

I walked away from the built-up areas, in no particular direction. I took in the water, the birds and those mountains. I began reflecting on how good I felt; how the events of the past few hours had freed my soul. How I wished Dad were here — and Rick too. I wanted to put the unresolved hurt to bed and free up the rest of my life.

Within a few minutes, I saw what was either a large house or a lodge of some sort and made for it. I was thirsty and hoped I could get a soda or at least a glass of water. I was almost upon it when I saw several people coming out. They were dressed too formally for the setting. All the men were in suits and the lone woman was in a severely cut suit jacket and skirt. In the bright light, it looked Navy, but I suppose it could just as well been black. She looked vaguely familiar and then I recognized her. It was Donovan's wife. Donovan was there too — in a suit. This did not make any sense.

Chet's story came to me and I had just started to get out of sight when they both saw me. The initial shock in Donovan's face gave way to a dark and menacing look that stopped me cold. They both looked around to see if I was alone. That action made it plain to me that I should not hang around any longer. I turned around and picked up my pace. I noticed over my shoulder that they were hurrying the other men into the cars. I had seen their faces clearly and although two of them looked familiar, I had no idea who they were. *What the hell*, I told myself, I could use the exercise and I decided to break into a jog just at the time that Donovan began moving in my direction. I looked again and they were both running after me. My mind was still trying to figure it out. What had I stumbled onto? My mind considered stopping to ask them, but the reply from deep inside my lizard brain was almost immediate — ***I don't think so***.

Fortunately, I love to run and since I had expected some walking, I was wearing my running shoes. I quickly decided to use them properly. I sprinted up to my fast long-distance running speed (seven-minute mile pace) and after getting comfortable at that speed, I checked their progress. It was obvious that they had not expected me to run so well; they were just barely gaining on me. I was no longer worried. I could see they were both at a flat-out run and would not be able to sustain it.

With the security of my running ability, my anxiety gave way to mischievousness. I knew they would not be able to catch me and I was pissed that they were after me. So I slowed slightly and started to act as if I was running out of breath. They took heart in my simulated exhaustion and persisted running way too fast (and inefficient too, arms flailing, short strides, etc.), I let them get within twenty feet and then increased my pace but made it look like I was going to collapse at any moment.

This caused them to try for the quick catch and went to an all-out sprint. It was what I wanted them to do. What they would be able to do with me, if they did catch up, was a mystery, since they were both in such a high oxygen debt already that they would be lucky to remain standing up.

As soon as I could see they were all used up, with their lungs and legs screaming fire at them, I started my six-minute mile pace and smiled back at them. It stopped them cold. They were so tired their hate almost did not get through. I waved in my most solicitous manner and made my way back to the chapel.

By the time I arrived and found both of them, still by the shoreline and talking, I had done a significant amount of thinking and planning. It would be best to leave here as soon as possible. The Boers would catch their breath and go back to get their car and might come after me quickly. After my taunting, this was rather more likely than not. I did not know for sure that they meant me ill, but their looks and actions did not bode well. I decided that if we did need to meet, it should be on my terms.

I ran up to JP and Michele only moderately out of breath. "JP, Michele, we have to get out of here, NOW!"

"What...?"

"I don't have time to explain, you have to trust me. Give me your keys."

He started to take them out of his pocket. "What is the matter, Yo?" JP said with a trace of alarm.

"I will explain it when we are on our way. You two start walking to the car, I will run up ahead and drive it back this way." With that, I snatched the keys out of his hand and took off.

I told myself this was just another one of the cross-country races I enjoy so much. I set a pace and slowly kept stepping it up. As I neared the car, I slowed enough to arrive without needing any time to catch my breath. Of course, I lost a few seconds because I ran to the wrong side of the car (bloody limeys), but I finally got it started and picked them up. They were actually running. I must have transmitted my urgency to them better than I had realized.

I told JP he had to drive and Michele had to be in the passenger's seat. I laid down in the back out of sight. "Is there more than one way off the mountain?" I asked.

"Not really, that is, not for regular cars, there is a dirt road for..."

"That's great, please let's get going and see if you can catch a car that left about fifteen minutes ago. It is a black Mercedes, one of the big ones, I don't know the model."

"Do you have the plate number?" JP's policeman's instincts were clearly evident now.

"I'm sorry, JP, but I was too far away and it wasn't important at the time." JP reflected for a moment and added, "There is no doubt as to which way they went. There is only one road and if you go south, there simply isn't any city of any size that would support a car like that for hundreds of miles. Therefore, we go north and we have until the fork at Rtes. 8 and 79. They either have to go to Timaru or to Christchurch. I would bet on the latter, it is much bigger."

Once we were on our way, I filled them in. The experience had felt endless while it was occurring; however, it took surprisingly little time to relate the events. Michele would add an occasional gasp. JP had a hard time understanding why I felt so sure that they were after me. Michele had understood immediately but it took a few minutes for JP to process it through his policeman's filter. When I further described Donovan's expressions in detail, JP became serious.

"Do you think this has anything to do with Mr. Osbourne's death?"

"I have been wondering the same thing."

CHAPTER THIRTEEN

CHASE DOWN THE MOUNTAIN

JP drove professionally fast, no squealing tires, no turns out of control. He planned ahead and focused more on keeping speed up on turns and curves than on speeding up on the flat stretches. (You lose more time on the slow part of your trip because you spend more time at a slow speed.)

JP signaled his intentions to pass and rarely had to touch the brakes. I was impressed with his driving skills. During this race down the mountain, I would occasionally check on Michele. Each time I checked she appeared to be having the time of her life. She was, after all, on a high-speed chase after bad guys with her father the police detective.

I kept looking for the Mercedes, but also looked back to ensure we weren't surprised by Donovan.

"This is so exciting, my friends at school will not believe this," Michele commented.

I looked at JP, but his hands were full with the slow traffic navigating the twists and turns down the mountain. "Michele,"

I said, "I don't think it would be a good idea to mention this to anyone. At least not for a while."

"Why not?" she said with just a hint of a pout.

"We still don't know what is going on. And..." I was explaining when she interrupted me.

"Oh, I get it, they don't know that Daddy and I know and we have an advantage on them that we shouldn't give away," she said this triumphantly.

I was so surprised that I blurted out, "Bloody right."

"It is a shame I can't say anything though."

"Cheer up; someday you will be able to write it up for a class project."

"Like Nancy Drew?"

"Exactly." That seemed to please her and we continued our vigil.

JP threw us a curve ball, "I will have to stop at the next filling station, our petrol is low."

"How low?" I inquired, not wanting to give up even a second of time. I desperately needed to know who those people were.

"The warning light just came on," JP said.

"Damn, damn, damn," I said before I let it go and focused on what we could do, "at least let's get it done fast. I will pump while you pay. We'll get the minimum we need.

How many miles to the gallon does this monster get?" I inquired.

JP answered, "I haven't the foggiest. Over here we calculate consumption in liters per one hundred kilometers, and the Rover takes fourteen liters per hundred in the city."

"OK, OK, let me figure this out, sixty-two miles to a hundred kilometers, and four liters to a gallon, so you get something under eighteen mpg. I figure if we don't find them in the next forty or so miles, we won't find them at all, so we need three gallons, or in your language twelve liters minimum."

JP countered, "That is a bit tight; let's get twenty so we can find another station or if we do find them we have enough to follow them."

"Good point, JP, you pay while I pump. By the way, how much is gas down here?"

"It fluctuates around NZ$1.70 to NZ$1.80 per liter," JP said without any real concern. It took me a few moments to convert to dollars and then to gallons.

"That's almost four bloody dollars a gallon!" I exclaimed.

"Is that bad?" asked Michele.

"I don't know if it is bad, it's just that I am used to about two dollars a gallon."

"What?" It was JP's turn to be surprised.

Within minutes, a road sign indicated that the next filling station was only four kilometers ahead. JP spotted it quickly and slowed down to pull in. I sat up ready to jump out and pump when I screamed, "They're right here. I can't bloody believe it. They are right here." I dove onto the seat and wished myself invisible.

Michele said, "Oh, Daddy, what are we going to do? I'm scared."

"First, we are not going to panic, from Yolanda's story these people may not even recognize her or suspect that they are being followed. Michele, grab the blanket from the bag and cover Yo with it. I will still pay but you will need to pump instead of Yolanda. Second is a change in plans. Mich, keep pumping until it is full or I tell you to stop. I will attempt to discover what I can and delay them if possible. Yolanda, you will have to be very still and quiet. It is a small station."

"No problem from me. I am doing my best imitation of a floor mat. I only wanted their bloody plates for Christ sakes, I didn't want to meet them for tea and crumpets. I don't bloody believe this."

While I lay on the floor with Michele's blanket over me, I kept muttering various invocations to myself. After a few minutes, this sudden impulse to sneak a look blossomed inside me. I was fighting the impulse when the back door opened and someone began rummaging in the car.

In a whisper I heard, "Yolanda, it's me, JP. It's important that you do not show your face. These people are in fact after you and we have to keep you hidden. Please don't try to peek."

(How did he know?) The door closed and he was gone. "After me?" I said to myself. I couldn't make sense of it. How did this get out of control so fast? One minute I am walking along a lake and the next I am being hunted by...I didn't know who wanted me. Men in suits in a Mercedes. If this was New York, I would think the mob, but here in New Zealand? Get real. But why? Who was I to them? What had I done or seen? My only exposure to these men, of which I was aware, was by the lake. So it had to be that I saw them — with the Boers. I was one of the few people on the entire island that could identify Donovan and that bitchy wife of his. Were they not supposed to be seen together? We were back to the first question: who were they? I had to get to my powerbook and delve deeper into things. I had to contact Rick; he would know what to do. Would I be able to leave the country or would they be watching at all the airports?

My reverie was cut short when I heard the pump stop and Michele replace the gas cap. Within seconds, she was back in the car.

"Hi, Yo, are you OK?"

"I'm fine but you should not talk right now. We can't have someone see you talking to yourself."

"Oh, yeah." I heard her turn on the radio.

"Now people will think I am singing along with the music."

"You are a smart lady, Michele. What is going on? I am dying of curiosity."

"Daddy started talking with the attendant. One of the men is on the pay phone and Daddy is doing his best to overhear him without being too obvious."

"What about the other guy?"

"He just finished pumping gas and is buying chocolates. He is kind of fat."

"Is your dad coming back?"

"No, he is dawdling, looking at snacks, I hope he buys something, all this excitement made me hungry."

Kids are amazing; their sense of propriety is just not the same. The last thing I wanted was food. A drink, well that is a different story.

"Here he comes."

"Who? Who is coming?" I could feel my pulse racing and the sweat starting to drench me.

The door opened, JP was back, "Ladies, it is time we left."

With that, he started the Rover and we left. I held my breath for as long as I could and did not come up for at least two minutes. Even then, I came out slowly. I think maybe I was expecting a firing squad. I looked out in all directions before I faced JP and said, "Let's have it, and don't leave anything out."

"We have to get off the main roads and figure this out. It just does not make sense. Yolanda, look at the map and find a place off the beaten path not too far from here."

It did not take long to find a place. "There are two ski resorts not far from here that have to be fairly vacant since this is the off season. They are Fox Peak and Mt. Dobson."

"Right, that's good. I have been to Fox Peak, I had forgotten it was nearby. It has hotels and cabins and it is remote — excellent. Give me directions and we'll go over everything and figure out what in hell we are going to do next." I saw Michele stare at him. It was the first time I had heard him swear and it may have been the first time for her also. This did not bode well for my vacation. I fell into a trance looking at the scenery and wondered when I would talk to my father again so I could set things right between us.

When we arrived at the ski resort, it was not as abandoned as I had expected. It was not exactly bustling, but we did not stand out either. JP went to one of the ritziest inns and while we waited in the car, he rented us a room. It was a cottage on the backside of the lodge, not far from the office but not in direct view — actually, perfect. We had a view of the approach to the mountain and the lodgings were sumptuous. I hoped I would not have to pay for it. Later, when I knew how much trouble I was in, I would not care.

As soon as we were in the room, Michele and I both cornered JP and forced him to talk. In another setting, it might have been comical. Here, however, he had two scared women who wanted to know.

"It is hard to know where to start. It simply does not make sense."

"Try us," I insisted.

"OK, the best I can make out of it is that the Boers called them on the car phone and told them about you. They stopped to call someone on a landline, either because they were worried about security or because the reception was poor. By the way, we were extremely lucky to see them there."

"Lucky?" I said with disbelief.

"Yes, they were headed to an airport in Timaru. We would not have caught up to them on the way to Christchurch. Anyway, when I first approached the phone area, I heard them clearly mentioning your name. Right down to the middle initial. When he started describing you, I went back to the car to make sure you would not show your face."

"Good thing too, thanks."

Without acknowledgment, he continued. "When I went back he was telling someone it was vital they find you, but that it had to go through proper channels. He told them to contact the Christchurch police department detective division. That's my division. I was about to leave when he mentioned my name."

"He recognized you?" I was becoming unglued; I was losing my only ally.

"At first I thought so too, but when I turned around he was facing the other way, thank goodness. He apparently was just repeating the name the person on the other end was giving him."

"So they are going to call you to tell you to find me?" I said with concern rising.

"It sounds that way."

"And then what?" A little anger was creeping into my

voice (or was it fear?).

"Yolanda, I am afraid they are going to try to frame you, in order to get you out of the way."

I sat aghast. "You have to be kidding. I just can't believe any of this. We were just going on a sightseeing vacation. I did not sign up for the cloak-and-dagger tour." I started storming around the room muttering to myself.

"Yolanda, I have not told you the worst yet."

"Worse than some Mafia types using their cronies in the police department to set me up for a fall? This I have to hear."

He looked at me and for a second it appeared as if he was hurt by my outburst, but after a few seconds of thought, he chose to ignore it. "It took me a while but I finally figured out why they were so familiar; particularly, the fat one. He was chowing down the chocolates pretty fast. He must have been nervous. When I saw him address the clerk, he became calmer and then it hit me. Please sit down, Yolanda."

"I will bloody stand if I want to, go ahead with his name, there is no way I will know him."

"You are right, Yolanda, you won't know him. He is the Finance Secretary for New Zealand. The other guy was easy to recognize; I had the general idea. He is the Foreign Secretary for New Zealand."

With those words, all my bluster vanished and I staggered. Michele came over and held my hand. "Daddy, you can't let them take Yo away, I won't let you."

I was still speechless. There was no mob, no crazy person with a weird vendetta against me, it was just the entire government of New Zealand that was after me; and the man they had picked to find me was sitting right there, within two arm lengths.

I actually thought of making a run for it. But even if I was able to get the keys to the Rover, there was no plan that would keep me free for more than a few hours tops. I had no money, no knowledge of the country and spoke with an accent. I would stand out almost anywhere. There was no way for me to get lost and stay lost. I was trapped up here.

Had I been in either Madrid or London where my family visited often, or in the vicinity of Boulder, Colorado (my home base in the States) — then, I could have gone underground in a way that would make most moles envious. With a computer and a phone link, I could have remained hidden for weeks. In fact, once upon a time I'd done just that.

A few years ago, I gained access to several credit cards and charged the small 'necessities' of life on a rotating basis. It's not all that hard — you call in the order and tell them the 'nanny' will pick it up and show up in a nanny disguise. They never remember the details. It is important to pick cards that charged many things monthly and that had large purchase amounts. Then I would be able to bury my small purchases in there without anyone noticing. You can order food or clothing, etc. from the same store that the card owner had used. This way when they looked at the statement they would have to remember how many times they had gone to that store. It did limit what could be bought, but if you are trying to hide, that is a small price to pay. To this day they would never have found out if I hadn't told them and made amends.

I slumped into a chair and JP must have read my mind. "No one is taking Yolanda anywhere. Listen up, you two, we have to work this out and come up with a plan."

"So you are not going to turn me in?" I said hopefully.

"Honestly, Yolanda, if the head of law enforcement on the

island called me up and told me the story, which I will hear tomorrow, I would have a hard time believing your version. Fortunately for both of us, I actually witnessed that you did not do anything of any significance, and was also witness to the sensitivity and depth of your character. Neither Michele or I will ever forget what you did for us today."

With that reminder, Michele came and sat next to me, holding my arm. JP continued, "I will not be party to any miscarriage of justice. Further, I am going to make every effort to get to the bottom of why two of my country's leading politicians are meeting with foreigners in a remote area and scared to death that a beautiful young lady saw them."

I found tears running down my face and without a word, walked over to him and hugged him. "Thanks," I whispered. Then in a more playful voice, "for the 'beautiful' part."

We settled down to business. First, we sent Michele for food and other essentials. She objected but we convinced her she was the only one who no one would remember and she had to help out with the jobs she was most suited for. When she came back, she took over the note taking. This allowed us to focus on strategy.

First, we had to make sure no one would find me until I was ready (if ever). Therefore, I could not go back to my hotel or to Christchurch for that matter. He felt this room would be safe indefinitely. No one had seen me come here and would remain safe as long as I did not go out. My opinion was that it was much too close to where I encountered the Boers. With all the resources the government could muster, a sweep of the general area would nab me in no time. Also, there was no way to pay for things without being traced. I had brought no cash with me. JP waved that consideration aside. We finally agreed this place would be safe for at least one perhaps even two days.

He then put cash on the table, "You can pay me back later."

There was NZ$482 (for you English majors that is about $200 US and some change). I dutifully wrote out an IOU on the hotel stationary and made him take it. I needed to hold onto my pride and my delusion of independence.

We only had a few hours before JP was called into the case. If he tried he could probably avoid being called for another six to twelve hours. More than that, and they would call his deputy, who in JP's words, was a good chap but a bit rigid with protocol. I did not think rigid would be the best option under the circumstances.

Michele and JP would go directly to my hotel room and get everything I needed. I made a list, but JP slashed it — we had to be inconspicuous. We settled on the essentials. Primarily my laptop, but also a few personal things and one change of clothes. It had to be easy to carry so I asked them to get me a backpack.

I gave the list to Michele.

"Me?" she squealed.

"If you wouldn't mind. I think that your dad would attract too much attention, and if they saw him going into my room... I think it would all be over."

"I am not entirely comfortable with this," JP said.

"I'll be OK, Daddy. Just in and out like a professional. No one notices a kid anyway. Even if they do, we are all generic, you have told me as much." He finally agreed because descriptions of kids were less than useless; apparently, adults do not place any importance on them and do not notice them.

"You can let her off a block away. She can leave by the loading dock and you can pick her up behind the hotel. If she is only carrying a small beach bag and is dressed appropriately, no one will give her a second look." He looked as if I was trying to tell him his business. We settled on the plan but I had to give up all my personal stuff, just my computer and one change of clothes. He would then overnight the package to me and avoid having to drive back. I could then start doing my thing. 'My thing,' as I call it, was to find out as much as possible about the Boers and any possible connection they might have with the government. (As well as contact Rick and make plans to get me off this bloody island.)

JP would then go home and get the message we knew would be there. That's when he would find out what they were attempting to pin on me. Michele would be the intermediary. We traded email addresses. Her messages could be in normal speech, because my mailbox was fairly well encrypted. It was also abroad. My messages back to her would have to be coded in case anyone was snooping. As unlikely as I considered that possibility, my paranoid tendencies were erupting.

"Snooping on my daughter?" shouted JP.

"You just never know," I said with concern. "They could have someone like me poking around, trying to find some trace, and people may have seen me leaving the hotel with you."

"Damn, I forgot about that. I will have to come up with a story to cover that."

Michele and I went over our 'code.' I would be her pen pal

from the States. When I said I had done something it would mean I was planning to do so. The timing would be backwards; if I said I had done it two days ago, I would be doing it in two days, etc. She caught on quick and seemed excited by the intrigue.

We ate cold-cut sandwiches, which they call cold meat sandwiches with salad; the salad being the lettuce and tomato in the sandwich. We washed it down with a fruit drink I had never before had 'orange passion fruit.' I decided I could stand not having it again. They had to leave before I was ready. Not only was the sun going down, making the sense of isolation worse, I had in some totally unexpected way bonded with this young lady.

For one of the few times in my adult life, I did not look forward to being alone. I gave her a hug just before she left. This time it was me crying and her giving me support.

"We won't be long, you'll see, Yo. My dad is the best detective on the entire island and he will have this figured out in no time. Then we can spend some more time together, you know, and chat a while."

"I would like that, Michele, thanks. Now get going and be careful, I don't know what I would do if I didn't have both of you to help me out of this mess.

CHAPTER FOURTEEN

ON THE RUN

I now had loads of time and not much to do. I am not fond of TV for either entertainment or news. I find it way too passive as well as boring and predictable. I had asked Michele to get me some books from the paperback rack. I steeled myself to see what kind of books a twelve-year-old preadolescent girl would pick for me. The first two novels, "A Night to Remember," and "The Prince from Slovania" were the typical romance trash I should have expected and warned against, but the other two were far more my speed. "The Hot Zone" and "Briarpatch."

I was too keyed up to read but could look forward to reading later. Right now, I wanted to get out of here. I needed to move, to breathe fresh air, to see people and experience normalcy, which is why I had her buy me a few special things prior to leaving. Hair coloring (Auburn), headbands, make-up, cheap sunglasses and a scarf. With these I was able to effect a reasonable disguise, particularly if I didn't do anything to bring undue attention to myself.

I strolled around the small town trying to feel as normal and carefree as the people I saw. I used some of the money for more supplies and I investigated what transportation options were open to me (not many, the extended thumb being the most promising).

I noticed a group of college age kids milling about, probably on tour. But most important, I renewed my confidence. I felt I could once again keep going, on my own if need be. Several questions came to me. Could I trust JP? Sure, he seemed sincere enough. He did also have personal knowledge that, whatever the charges they were trumping up, I was innocent.

Yet, he was human, and a lot of pressure can be brought forth by big shots in the government. It would also be a huge feather in his cap if he caught me quickly. After much back and forth, I decided that he could be trusted, at least for a while. After all we had been through, he would at the very least involuntarily telegraph his intentions and I would get some warning. Therefore, I went to question number two. How could I get myself out of this place? There had to be more options, it did not bode well being so dependent on others.

After a thorough reconnaissance, I concluded that my only two options were to steal a car or to convince someone to ferry me to a larger city. The theft idea was promising. It is not necessary to explain how I have some knowledge in this field, but the actual theft posed no problem. The trouble was that it added credibility to whatever story was being cooked up. It would make any denials on my part so much weaker. Also, if the owner reported it too soon, there would not be enough time to get to a transportation hub before the alarm went out. In an island country like this with few crossing roads (mountains after all), I would be spotted quickly. And of course the stakes I was playing for were alarmingly high.

The other option was safer. By acting quickly, no one would have started looking for me. I might be remembered later but by then would be long gone with several changes in transportation behind me. This option, however, had one sticking point. It was harder to find and I wasn't willing to walk down the road thumbing. That was way too visible and asking for trouble. I would have to mingle, meet possible targets and then turn on the charm and convince them to take me with them. It would be a high exposure solution. If I couldn't find anyone, I could always go back to plan A.

Once off this mountain (hopefully with my computer), it would be my turn. I could and would trash whomever was doing this to me. His credit was nothing. The gloves were off; I was ready to totally destroy them. I would start with his personal history. Deleting a driver's license is always a good start followed up with a phony marriage certificate, one that predates his current one. A copy of this accidentally forwarded to the newspaper is a good touch. His work files would be history. If there was any outside access at all to them, he might as well pretend they burned up for all the use they would do him. If any of his records were confidential, well then heaven help him because it would not take me long to figure out who would most like that information.

I was cooking now, my pace had picked up. I was talking to myself and was psyched. I almost felt sorry for those two poor sods — almost. It was going to be fun twisting their tiny insignificant lives into such knots they would never be able to verify anything and they might as well start their entire lives over. I decided to wait on calling Rick because he might talk me out of it and I was enjoying myself way too much.

I returned to my cottage unnoticed and to my surprise fell right off to sleep. It was the sleep of a woman planning revenge, deep and sweet. I awoke the next morning with the muscle aches and body heaviness that made it hard to get out of bed. I cursed myself for not having the forethought to buy coffee. I stomped around and eventually settled into a stretching and calisthenics routine learned in high school. It helped wake me and eventually took the kinks out of the far reaches of my body.

After a quick shower, I put on the generic grey shorts and light blue shirt bought last night. My now auburn hair and dark complexion would not allow me to pass for a native so that idea was a total nonstarter. Neither could I duplicate their accent or their idiomatic expressions but needed to blend in, so I bought touristy stuff although not excessively loud or unusual. The familiar 'I visited New Zealand' or 'I saw a Kiwi walk around,' etc. I wanted to look exactly like one of the 2.2 million tourists that visit yearly. In that way, becoming invisible to the locals and it was them I feared. After all, they were the eyes and ears that the authorities would recruit to assist in locating me. If I became one of the continuous blur of tourists they endure all season long, it would give me added mobility. I would not have to remain in this bolt hole desperately hoping to be rescued by JP, a man whose motivations were unknown to me.

I felt absolutely helpless without my tools. With them, I was larger than life, able to effect great changes on nearly a global level (or so I claimed). It was a weapon greater than any previously invented. Anyone in the developed world could be reached with my laptop and it could cause more enduring carnage than a bomb in their house.

Have you ever considered what your life would be transformed into with a perpetually expired driver's license, erroneous warrants for your arrest, inconsistent balances on all your bank accounts, mortgages? If you have achieved high position in government or industry, consider the repercussions of these problems being leaked to your employer or to the news media, specially done with complete false verification.

I can create so many new SSNs for one person as to make it nearly impossible to file taxes or to attribute withholdings to the right account. All of this just barely grazes the surface. When I breach your business computer system, every report, proposal and research you slaved over for your life are at my mercy. I would not dream of deleting them for that lets you off the hook much too easily. They would be altered in a manner that would not be immediately obvious. My tampering alters any conclusions and eventually drives you stark-raving mad.

By using a laptop computer and channeling my efforts through unprotected computers, no one could track me down. I can violate your life with near impunity. Lucky for you and the rest of humanity, there is a rub. The problem with my doing all or any of these things is my wish to remain sober. This, in effect, does not allow me to do any of them. The emotions that result out of the dark side of computer society are full of self-loathing and paranoia. They lead to a myriad of self-destruction behaviors (in my case, alcohol). All that notwithstanding, I was now in a self-defense mode and fairly desperate. So I would do what was necessary to survive. Rick would be sure to keep me sane — it would be so easy and delightfully fun to allow myself loss of control. However, before any of that became a worry, I needed my laptop.

I was eating a cold breakfast of Frosted Flakes right out of the box and on a whim I turned on the TV searching for news. There had been a satellite dish on the roof and figured international news would be available. I could catch up with whatever was happening back home. The news channel was recapping the world news. Nothing new, the republicans were making elephant droppings of themselves and the democrats were remaining the asses they usually were (I am not especially political). Then the station switched to local news. The lead story was the death of a tourist by drowning in Lake Tekapo. I dropped the box of Flakes as my heart shifted up to second gear on its way to third.

When they showed the photo of Mrs. Boers (Donovan's wife), my heart skipped third and fourth gear and went right into overdrive. I could not move or breathe for the longest time. They interviewed Donovan with the solemn face of mourning we learn early on — no tears allowed. The reporter was stating the Christchurch police were on the case and they planned a press conference for noon today. Chief Inspector James Patrick Yves was in charge of the investigation. There was also speculation that an extensive regional search for a fellow tourist was underway and an arrest was imminent.

I started shaking in helplessness and rage. Betrayal was bad enough, but I had the further pain of misjudging him terribly. That's why they are called MEN (Morally Emaciated Neanderthals). I was in deeper Kimshi than ever and there was no time for plan B — it was time for plan A. It took me a few moments to collect the essential things. I checked the time and it was five minutes before ten. I must have slept late, damn it. The police were probably on their way to collect me at this very minute. The news station must have jumped the gun and given me a small head start. I opened the door and was rushing out; there was a young man walking briskly to my door. Stifling a scream by biting down on my tongue, I realized it was already too late.

In my defeat, it took me time to realize there was only this one person. He wore an unusual uniform that was reminiscent of the brown UPS uniforms back home. Hope springs eternal, maybe there was still a chance. I attempted and failed to act casual and all I could manage to say was 'hello' in a loud and tense voice.

"Good morning, ma'am, this is an urgent package for a Miss Yves, Miss Michele Yves. It will require your signature."

I said, "OK," as he handed me his pen. I had the presence of mind to verify the name of the sender, M. Yves. I was barely able to sign because of how much my hand was shaking. My mind was swimming from all of the implications.

"Thank you, ma'am."

What is it with this ma'am shit anyway? "You're welcome," regaining some of my voice.

"There is a message that goes along with the package. He read from a note, "'You are to proceed to the pre-arranged meeting place as soon as possible.' She said that she left instructions in the package."

With that, he left in the same hurry of all delivery people. Everything they delivered was urgent, at least until it arrived.

I needed time to unravel this turn of events. However,

leaving this cottage had become the first priority, particularly after that cryptic message. What prearranged meeting place? We did not talk of that, or did we? Just holding it revealed the package to be my laptop. The adrenaline surge that rushed through me from the moment he handed it over was doing its magic. I felt secure, confident, in control. The fact that none of those feelings had any basis in reality was completely irrelevant. As my father used to say when he was losing an argument, "Don't clutter up the issue with facts."

How I missed him and wanted him right here with me. He would make it all better; he would stop the madness. I also wanted to begin working immediately on the problem and further needed to send a letter to dad and Rick...But first I had to locate a safe place. JP, or Michele, whoever sent the message, implied that I should not remain here any longer; and by 'here' it was obvious she (or he) meant the entire Tekapo/Fox Peak resort region.

I walked briskly to the lobby of the resort and set up the powerbook. No one new me here. JP paid in advance and as far as anyone knew, I was part of the college tour that was still hanging around. The battery was fully charged but there was a prominent plug and used it to conserve the battery. To my surprise, there was a spare battery in the package. They must have taken the time to get one. Did Michele have one at home? Did they have to buy one? It did not look new.

It sounds paranoid, but one of the first things I did while waiting for it to boot up was to check the entire package from top to bottom for electronic gizmos: bugs, homing devices, the lot. Remember — just because I am paranoid doesn't mean people aren't out to get me. And in this particular case, people were truly out to get me. I just didn't know for sure which ones and how many.

There was nothing hidden as far as I could tell. It was the same case I had borrowed a lifetime ago from that sweet young guy. Now what was his name? I couldn't remember but it would come to me. The computer itself was working normally and there was no sign of tampering. Besides the backpack, however, there was nothing else in the case — no personals, no clothes, no note, no nothing.

When it was ready, I checked the directory for files arranged by date in reverse chronological order. There was one file created yesterday afternoon. Michele must have done it immediately on arrival. The file was password protected. The name of the file was 'LakeWalk'; I did not know the password. Up to this moment, I had been in such a frenzy that it took me a few moments to realize they expected me to guess. The title must be a clue. To my chagrin, it took me over five minutes to figure it out; truly embarrassingly slow. Through a few tricks of mine, I was able to tell that it was a six-character word. Within seconds, I had it: 'Chapel.' There was a long message.

"Dear Michele, we arrived well and had a productive trip. Unfortunately, the cell phone kept me busier than we would have liked and I was not able to fully enjoy the trip. I will also have to work this weekend and hope that won't effect you in any way. You will probably be worried about me but I am fine. Excuse me while we turn off the TV, there is such inane stuff on it these days. I think you will find more interesting sightseeing at the other places we talked about. You have probably seen everything of consequence there anyway. I left home just a few minutes ago and am writing this on my way to work. Wish I could have been of more help; feel free to go in whichever direction seems most promising. Remember to write. Take good care of yourself and don't talk to strangers. Love, your dad."

I wiped tears while deciphering the message. He was warning me and telling me to leave immediately. Apparently, anywhere was better than here. He was risking his career by doing this and now knew he would give me as much time as possible. The rest of the message was fairly clear. He'd been called on his cell and placed in charge of the investigation; they expected him to begin immediately and work through the weekend. The note also explained the news conference and in fact he may have been the person delaying it until noon. I looked at my watch — God, that was only ninety-three minutes away. It was time to get the hell out of here. His comment about TV implied that stories on the TV should not be believed and lastly his comment on the time told me how long it should take me to leave: "...a few minutes..."

I sat back and while packing the laptop, I looked around and started to plan. There was no choice, I had to take chances and walked to where a group of coeds were talking and interrupted. I used my sweet semi-helpless injured voice. "Excuse me, girls, sorry to interrupt." They looked at me with blank faces. They were not hostile but not overly friendly either; after all, I had intruded into their space.

Fortunately, I look younger than my age. I purposely dressed young and my hair was in a ponytail. I appeared only a couple of years older than them, and was still part of their world but none of them said anything.

"My boyfriend brought me here but we had a horrid fight and he abandoned me on this mountain. I need to go somewhere I can get transport." I paused and made a show of holding myself together. "Are any of you leaving soon?"

One of them got up and came to me. Pointing to my wrist she said, "Did he do that to you?" I acted embarrassed and that opened her up. "It's OK, there are jerks everywhere. We have all had our share of them, haven't we, girls?"

She then introduced herself, "My name is Maggie, over there are Stephanie, Janice and Jessica. We are students at Christchurch Academy on a field trip. I have never been du...abandoned in a place like this, but you are better off without him."

The rest of them picked up her lead. "We will help you get off this mountain. What's your name?"

"Yvonne," I said.

"OK, Yvonne, when and where do you need to go?"

"Anywhere, it doesn't matter as long as there is a bus that will take me to an airport. I just want to go back home to Seattle." After dabbing at a few tears and stifling a sob I continued, "If it's possible, I desperately need to leave here immediately and as you can see all my stuff is already packed." This was the telling moment. Up to this point, they were buying the story; after all, it was hitting them where they lived, boyfriends, splitting up, feelings of abandonment. But, and here was the big but, would they accept the urgency I was insisting on? And if they did would they be able to accommodate me? I encouraged them further with more tears without bothering to dab them. I just let them run down my face standing there shivering. My act seemed to be working; Janice stood up and held me while the other girls clucked nearby.

Many people may feel that this was cold, calculated and conniving. And actually it is exactly that, but I was desperate and the feelings were genuine, even if they weren't about this imagined boyfriend. More importantly, I desperately needed their help to avoid being incarcerated on trumped-up charges.

The girls were not leaving until tomorrow in the bus that brought them and they had no control over the schedule. They mentioned that joining them on the bus would be no problem whatsoever but within a few minutes of discussion they remembered a guy that mentioned he was leaving today. They did not personally know him well, but he seemed nice enough and he might let me tag along. I said that would be great and asked where I could find him.

"He has a Beetle, you know a VW, and it was still in the parking lot when we walked in."

I fought to overcome the intense urge to sprint and catch him before he left, but it would not be in character. I allowed them to lead me, however agonizingly slowly, to the parking lot. Stephanie carried my backpack. I held onto the computer; I could not bear to part with it for even a second.

We found the car at once and it caused me to groan inwardly. It was a faded hunter green Volkswagen with a red right front quarter panel. The interior was worn and the stuffing poked out everywhere. I was surprised it would even start much less convey me to safety. There was a young guy placing bags in the back seat.

Jennifer introduced me to him, "Hello, Kevin, this is Yvonne. She needs a ride off the mountain today and we thought you might let her tag along with you."

He looked me over and we shook hands; neither one of us used a firm grip. "Where are you going, Yvonne? Let me warn you, I'm not going to a big city but for the gold mines on the south part of the island. I want to see what they were like and perhaps work them. Perhaps I was born too early. I always saw myself as one of the adventurers..."

Interrupting his fantasy with my best imitation of meekness I said, "Hello, Kevin, if you don't mind me tagging along, that destination sounds good. (I had no idea if that was good or not, but he was my ticket off this mountain.)

He was shorter than me and exceedingly thin (in Spain we would have called him 'fideo,' which is 'vermicelli' in English). I understood why Jennifer wasn't worried about my going with him. I could overpower him, not the other way around. "I don't have much luggage so I wouldn't be taking any space at all and will help pay for gas and..."

He interrupted, suspicions aroused, "Is there something I should know?" he asked the four girls looking them over carefully. I must have looked too anxious and besides, the story was odd.

"Nothing whatsoever, why do you ask?" offered Jennifer, unconvincingly.

I stepped forward and said, "Yes there is, Kevin, my boyfriend just abandoned me here and I absolutely have to leave this place." I looked straight in the eyes and let him see my tear-strewn face before looking down. "I wouldn't get in the way and will be quiet. I won't bore you with my troubles..."

Kevin relented, "OK, OK, I have room and could certainly use the gas money. But here are my rules; I choose the radio station, drive and certainly don't appreciate comments about my driving; you pay for all the gas and we buy our own food. In return, I will drop you anywhere within one hour of my intended course. Deal?" He put out his hand.

I smiled at him, grabbing his hand in both of mine and said, "Deal, can we leave now?"

"I wasn't planning to leave for a couple of hours."

I took a moment as if considering his schedule and made a counterproposal. "If we leave right now I will buy all the food." This grabbed his attention. My guess that money was of primary importance to him was right on the mark. He readily agreed and turned to the girls feeling genuinely thankful. I'd lied to them and felt bad about it so I hugged them one after the other and thanked them profusely.

By the time I opened the passenger's side door of the Beetle, Kevin finished tying his luggage to the roof. It looked like it would tip over around the first turn and I inwardly crossed myself. Jessica gave him my backpack and Kevin shoved it into the back seat.

Suspecting he was going to do likewise with my computer, I volunteered, "I'll carry it."

"Great then, we are ready but we do need to fill up the tank first," looking at me for a reaction. He wanted to verify I had money or was just bluffing.

"Here," handing him a NZ$50 bill, "I don't know how far these gold mines are but this should take us most of the way, when that runs out just let me know."

"Great!" he said with newfound enthusiasm. "Let's go."

My next immediate objective was obtaining a map of the island. To plan my escape, I had to know where we were headed. Gold mines! Where in New Zealand were the gold mines? I asked him, "Kevin, do you have a map? I can help navigate and am actually quite good at it."

He looked over at me briefly. "That's good news because I was planning to take the main roads instead of the more direct back roads. I don't understand maps, specially when driving. My mother says I have never been spatially oriented.

But my dad disagrees and says I have always been a space cadet." He looked over for effect. Once I knew he was joking, I relaxed and laughed politely.

"Take a look after we catch Route eight at Kimbel on the way to Lake Tekapo. There is a small road that leads straight to Lake Benmore and then winds around the lake and catches Route 83 at Otematata."

It only took a minute to orient myself, "Yeah, I see it. But the map's legend shows it as a tertiary road, which doesn't sound good. Perhaps we shouldn't take it." We argued for a while, my point being that it would be inadvisable to become stranded off a main road and his point that it would eliminate many miles from the trip.

Throughout our discussion, I noticed, to my relief, that he drove very carefully. Actually, he drove in a manner that would normally cause me to weep. He was slow, methodical, signaling way before he had any intention of turning. He would accelerate at an agonizing pace and hardly ever needed to use the brake. It finally dawned on me he was doing his utmost to conserve gas. His entire driving style was to increase mileage and care for his car. I finally won the argument when I reminded him that I planned to pay for all of the gas on the trip and that the main roads would not be as likely to cause a breakdown. Soon after deciding our route, he started making trouble for me.

I started feeling better; in fact, much better. Every mile behind us eased my breathing and heart rate. My chest no longer felt like it would implode from the stress. I had expected the police to show at any second and now could plan further than the next few minutes. Even if someone saw me now, I was no longer a lone person, but part of a couple, which made recognition significantly more difficult.

I was comforted by Kevin being a sight more nonconforming than me. Attention would naturally first settle on him. How much time did I have before the search began in earnest? I had to stay with Kevin until another method of transport became readily available. If a nationwide hunt was indeed starting, I would have to remain at least one step ahead of the wolves.

This meant that by the time Kevin was found and told all to the police, I would need to have already finished the next leg of the journey. In this way, there would be hope of eluding the search. I studied the map over carefully and kept saying interesting things like, "Wow, there are a lot of gold mines in New Zealand!" or, "We will travel nearby Mount Aspiring." He would then run a monologue about the comment that I barely paid attention to.

Route 8 would not have a useful place for me until at least Cromwell nearly two hundred kilometers to the southwest. The way he drove that could take over three hours not including time for lunch. Although Cromwell itself was a small town, it was close enough to Queenstown and Frankton that there was bound to have local bus service or at least enough traffic to hitch a ride.

My next question: where did I want to end up and how many legs should it take? I needed to find a bolt hole and fire up the trusty old powerbook. I desperately wanted to reach Rick and Dad and decided on risking only one more leg for my trip after which I would drop out of sight.

"Are you going as far as Cromwell?" I said casually.

"Cromwell? Where is that? If that is on our way, I don't remember seeing it."

"It is at the junction with route six and you either go right to Queenstown or left for Alexandra."

"Then we must be going through it because we are headed for Queenstown. That is the heart of the south part of the island. There are many museums there devoted to the gold rush of the '60s. Tomorrow's plan is to visit actual mining sites."

"Could you drop me off at Cromwell, I need to go in the other direction. I'll go past Alexandra to Dunedin; they have an airport there. I will spend a couple of days on the beach trying to get myself together before I return home." He readily agreed and because it wasn't out of his way, he actually started to feel bad about making me pay for all the gas. I told him that while my ex-boyfriend was getting ready to maroon me at the resort, I liberated his money out of his wallet. This accomplished two objectives: it gave him a believable reason for my needing to leave quickly, and it would make him think twice before pegging me as a victim.

The way he started making trouble was by insisting on playing the bloody radio. When the announcer was on, I would distract him by asking numerous questions, hardly listening to the answer, trying to come up with another question. While a song was playing, I would relax, until the announcer came on again. It was past noon already and there should be a news flash any moment. When we reached Lake Pukaki, it was one o'clock and I suggested we eat lunch.

If we dawdled while we ate, any reports would be over by the time we resumed our trip. Despite my encouragement, he ate only a small sandwich, which he gobbled down. I took my sweet time in the ladies room and insisted on buying supplies for the road. I subtly turned the radio off while he filled the tank.

Despite all of my efforts, the inevitable happened about forty kilometers from my destination. The announcer started with the latest on a breaking story. "Tourist dead at Lake Tekapo, poli..."

I leaped into action, "Let me find you some music," and spun the dial.

"No, I wanted to hear that, turn it back!" he bellowed.

"What did you say, I didn't quite catch that?" pretending ignorance.

"The story about the tourist, turn it back to the station!" he insisted.

My ignorance continued, "Nothing about a tourist, are you sure?"

"Yes, it said there was a dead tourist; hurry up and tune it in."

"OK, if you are sure," fiddling with the dial in both directions, avoiding the station.

"Uhm...forgot which station it was, do you know the station number?" I knew it by heart since they broadcast it every bloody fifteen minutes since we left Fox Peak.

"1098 AM, quickly!" He was clearly anxious to hear the story.

I took my time fumbling with the knob, then found the station but went past it. This was actually fun although I worried Kevin would have a stroke from the frustration. He wanted desperately to tune it himself but he would not allow himself to take his eyes off the road. This was turning out easier than feared. Finally, not being able to stall any longer, the station tuned. There clearly was still talk going on about the story, so in a loud voice I said, "Is this the station, Kevin? Do you think this is it or should I keep searching?"

"Yes, yes, this is it, please be quiet, I want to hear it."

"... and that was inspector Yves of the Christchurch police department. Now to more of your favorite tunes..."

"Damn, it probably won't be on for another hour."

I pretended to be hurt and started sniffling. "Sorry, Kevin, I just wanted to help, you have been so good to me and I thought you wanted music and..." This clearly caught him by surprise.

His mood changed, "It's OK, Yvonne. I don't know why I made such a big fuss anyway because we will still be driving in an hour, won't we?"

Actually, not really, I said to myself. I fully expected to be long gone in an hour, but there was no reason to disabuse him of his notion.

I sat back and closed my eyes; I needed to concentrate. The TV announcer said that Donovan's wife was dead with the implication that it was not an accident or of natural causes. How and why? Was she actually dead like Osbourne was, or was it simply a way of getting the police to chase after me? Wouldn't they need a body (besides mine, of course)? If she indeed was dead, why would they be looking after me? What connection existed between Mrs. Boers and myself — only Donovan and the so-called vacation tour. These questions kept running through my head without any resolution. Eventually I let it go; I just did not have enough information to even begin unraveling the puzzle.

With that behind me, I continued my planning. Kevin would drop me off in about twenty minutes. Then, sometime later when the bloody radio station repeated the news, it would become crystal clear why I had not let him listen to the news report. He would by then be thirty or forty minutes away and in the mountains between Cromwell and Queenstown. Would the station reach him? Would they give only a sound bite with no details? How quickly could he go to a police station and report that he had just dropped off the suspected fugitive?

I decided it would probably take him another twenty minutes to even get to a town much less find the police. Then he would have to convince them he wasn't a flake; on a Saturday no less. I probably had two hours minimum before they would be searching the entire area of Cromwell for me.

I planned to use the time well. I needed a method of transportation that would not be detected easily or quickly. I let my mind go blank like Rick taught me, which allowed the creative part of the brain, the right hemisphere, to take over and within a minute it came to me. Rick was crystal clear on this method of problem solving.

"Yolanda, you have to let the right brain work. It is the creative side and it will put things together without effort if you get the logical left brain out of the way."

He was absolutely right. The plan was nearly perfect. It would give me at least a thirty-six hour head start, perhaps even more. Only the larger problem of finding a place to 'drop out of sight' remained.

I would let my right brain work on that, after leaving Kevin behind. Right now, my main concern was that I would miss my opportunity at Cromwell, forget my pack in the car or not find the situation I needed. Letting my gaze drift outside my focus was on not missing the signs for Cromwell. I wanted desperately to talk to someone I trusted; either Rick, Dad, or

Michele, still not sure about JP. Being the focal point of a nationwide search was already wearing me down and I had to remind myself that it had barely started; if I couldn't handle this much stress I might as well turn myself in at the nearest police station.

I hated to admit it, but I was enjoying this. After all, I knew I had not done anything wrong, so there was the conviction that eventually truth would prevail. Maybe it would need a little help from yours truly and some of my friends, but in the end truth would prevail. I did not have the same delusions that justice would prevail. So, I was 'The Fugitive' fleeing from the law while at the same time trying to find my 'one armed man.' As the notion played in my mind, I liked it: the excitement, the drama and finally the vindication. I hoped I would not have to make a jump from a high dam to escape.

"Cromwell coming right up," Kevin commented.

"Thanks, I must have been daydreaming because I completely missed the sign." Daydreams could be dangerous.

"Did you want me to find any place in particular, perhaps the bus station?" He asked and I paused to consider, "It is a beautiful day and could use the walk. Drop me anywhere that passes for the downtown area; I will find my way."

After another short pause, I added, "And you can be on your way to find your fortune in gold."

"I wish," said Kevin with a laugh, "the only gold in these parts any more is in the jewelry stores. This trip is about doing research for my college thesis. I am studying what life was like back in the 1860s, particularly in the frontier towns."

"Eighteen-sixties! I thought you were actually going to prospect for gold and you led me to believe that."

"I may have, its fun having people reach that conclusion; it makes me appear adventurous. Here you are, downtown Cromwell." I seriously doubted anything would make Kevin appear adventurous but held my tongue.

I looked out and saw what could pass for an abandoned hamlet. Fortunately, a few stores were open, and there was a little traffic. I stepped out after grabbing both my backpack and my computer. No need risking Kevin taking off as soon as I stepped out. (I sound paranoid and cynical but, well, uhmm...OK, so I am paranoid and cynical — what's it to you, anyway?)

I set my belongings on the sidewalk and just before I closed the door, I leaned in and thanked him profusely. I used my most sincere tone, which wasn't hard since he had rescued me from a tough situation. Leaning in on the seat, I gave him a kiss. Not just a peck on the cheek but a nice soft kiss on the lips. It only lasted a moment, and it did catch him by surprise. It gave me just enough time to turn the radio off and spin the dial. With any luck, he might just forget about the bloody radio altogether.

CHAPTER FIFTEEN

HIDING

I took a deep breath and scouted my surroundings. I quickly located two businesses of the type I was looking for. The buildings were old without obvious loading access. I concluded there must be a service alley behind the row of shops. Before I could verify this, I needed to quench my thirst and ambled to the bar at the end of the block.

On entering, I nearly choked on the smoke that permeated the place and would have turned around but I was on a mission and time was not on my side. The place had several small tables in an orderly pattern and was more of a saloon than a bar. I sat down and signaled to the waiter.

The bartender quickly strode over. I guessed he was the owner of the place. He was in his early forties, hadn't shaved in days, and walked with the swagger of someone comfortable in his own skin and in his own life. He fixed me with a look that said he may not have seen everything but he had just about heard everything.

"What will it be, young lady?" he spoke heartily.

Now here was a guy after my heart; no 'ma'am' within earshot. "Just a tall, cold orange juice, please."

"We don't sell orange juice; this establishment is a bar not a fruit stand," he said without rancor or annoyance, just stating a fact, like reporting the weather.

"No problem, I'll just have a tall, ice-cold screwdriver but hold the vodka," I smiled pleasantly at him as I said it.

He looked me over a second time, but this time his gaze lingered on my eyes as opposed to the curves of my body. I felt he was looking for sarcasm and finding none, he smiled broadly and laughed like I had gotten one over on him. "You're all right, miss, and with a good sense of humor no less — one virgin screwdriver coming up."

He returned with the drink and I noticed it had exactly one ice cube. Was there an ice shortage or an ice embargo? I decided to let it slide and inquired, "I need to get to Dunedin, is there bus or train service?"

"Yes, miss, leaves every morning and evening."

"Which one, train or bus?" I inquired.

"Bus, there are no trains in the mountains, too many trestles to build."

Information was hard to come by in this joint. "Where would I catch this bus?" I prodded.

"Not too far, just down Main Street for three blocks and a left on King's Street, and you'll see the station. Looks like bus stations all the world over." The guy didn't look like he had been further than twenty kilometers from this town in his lifetime, but today was not the time to pursue that thought.

"Looks that bad?" I said with a smile.

"Yes, indeed, young miss, you do have a fine sense of

humor. That screwdriver will be two dollars."

I drained the rest of my drink, chewed on the ice cube and left a dollar tip. He nodded at me and I made my way out. I noticed it was already four-thirty and I hurried to the station. The next bus to Dunedin did not leave until six. It wasn't perfect but I could make it work. I purchased the ticket to Dunedin. I was informed there was plenty of room on the bus, but I informed her I wanted to be sure of getting a window seat. The ticket agent said it was open seating, but I insisted that I would like to reserve a window seat. She eventually pacified me by informing me there were twenty-four window seats and only thirty tickets sold, many of those couples. She knew there would be openings.

I walked back to the business area where Kevin dropped me and I found the alley behind the shops. To my delight, I quickly found exactly what I was looking for. The delivery trucks for several businesses were parked there without any fences or gates. There was a choice of a florist's delivery truck, an electronics repair van and a hearse associated with the funeral home.

I chose the last one for several reasons. It was the least likely to attract attention on a weekend (I recently discovered that people die at the most inopportune times and places). Also, I would not feel as bad about borrowing it for a while. The other two would definitively have schedules on Monday, but the funeral van might be inactive for weeks and they might even have a backup vehicle. Even if they didn't, it wasn't like there was a spoilage issue to contend with. Their client would wait patiently.

I checked the doors of the hearse, but they were all locked. I rummaged in the nearby garbage cans for a while and in the florist's trash, I found wire; the type they use for arrangements. It took me only seven minutes to open the door (I am out of practice). I then used some broken glass to scrape the insulation off the ignition wire and start the engine. I looked around and seeing no one, I quickly and quietly found my way to Route 8 toward Dunedin. I was careful to blend in with traffic and suppress my normal driving tendencies. I did not need any further attention from the authorities.

When my heart rate dropped below the car's rpms, I concentrated on my next hurdle; I needed to fill up the gas tank. Luckily, the tank was still a quarter full. How big was the tank? I had no idea how far I could go, or for that matter if the gauge was working. I looked for the largest and busiest station and pulled into a truck stop just outside of Cromwell. It had the new type of pump that lets you pay with a credit card at the pump. I used one of the trucks as a shield from the clerk and quickly used my VISA card. I filled the tank up to the brim. It took fifty-one liters and cost almost NZ$100. The only good thing was that I was conserving my cash. When I finished I headed the way I'd come and started looking for signs to route 6A for Queenstown.

Queenstown would definitely be the better place to hide. I left the trail for the police to follow because they are happier following clues. The questions at the bar, the struggle with the ticket agent and now the credit card on the road to Dunedin should keep them fairly happy and on the wrong road.

Please don't get me wrong. It's not that I think policemen are dense; it's that they generally encounter people that are not bright (that's why they get caught). They were undoubtedly now thinking I was an amateur (which technically I am) and would be expecting me to make these mistakes. Once they figured out that I was leading them on, they would not underestimate me again. I would then have to give them better and more subtle clues.

For now, I was content that I had obliterated my trail. The hearse would in all likelihood not be missed for days, and by then I would have left it behind. Given the number of problems with which the police have to concern themselves, it would not surprise me if it took a long time to connect me with the van's disappearance.

I picked Queenstown because it had four methods of escape: car, plane (large airport for all the sightseeing scenic flights), boat (Lake Wakatipu is long with many coves to hide in), and finally foot (there were several climbable mountains around Queenstown that during this time of year would be easy to navigate). When I reached Queenstown, I was pleasantly surprised because it was bigger than the map intimated. I would have an easier time dropping out of sight than I had expected. I found an inconspicuous place to park, made my way to the back of the hearse, curled up on the floor and cried for a long time. I had been on edge for over twenty-four hours and this was my first time I could release the built-up tension.

By the time I was ready to look for a nice cozy hideaway, it was already seven-twenty in the evening. Fortunately, at these latitudes and at high season, sunset was at least an hour or two away. I drove around the city trying to get a feel for what was available. I went over the requirements: one, absolute security, that meant no one seeing me go in and no one being around to see that I was in there; two, a phone line that no one was monitoring closely; three, a way of detecting unwelcome visitors; and four, a couple of ways of escape.

I already figured I would need to change locations. My first bolt hole would need to work only for a day. I would use that time to find the second safe house, which, with planning, should last much longer. I would then move from time to time, depending on how close the hounds were getting.

My ego insisted that with an adequate supply of money and as long as my nerve did not fail, I could keep this up indefinitely. But my brain knew better; those feelings were a delusion and in reality, the time pressure was intense. No one could hold up alone for any extended period of time. I would either start making too many mistakes and they would find me, or the cravings for a drink would begin and they would surely find me.

With a renewed sense of urgency, I scoured the business district. What I needed was an office building that was not well secured and offered a shielded entry point. It would have to be shielded by other buildings or trees, etc. It took more time than expected and there were several false starts. One building was perfectly hidden but well locked up and another had open windows on the top floors but no way to get to them. Finally, an old brick house, which had been remodeled into offices, had it all.

On the backside there was a window ten feet up that was open (I didn't see an air conditioner so I figured they were trying to keep it cool). There was a large live oak that shielded that part of the house. Between the old brick work and some big vines, there were enough places for my hands and toes to climb up. I wrote down the address and was careful about remembering where this house was. I did not want to lose my way and have to reacquire it again.

I now had the luxury of shopping for supplies and located a convenience store similar to the ones that are ubiquitous in the U.S. I loaded up on everything I might need: food, toiletries, string, envelopes and stamps, etc. Before going back, I drove around the neighborhood for another hour, familiarizing myself with the area. I took notes and felt I knew the immediate area as well as anyone. What I did not know were the traffic patterns, which road gets blocked up in the morning, which one is frequented by the police, etc., but that could not be helped.

It was now dark enough to drive to my house (I did feel somewhat proprietary) and hid the van (sounds better than hearse) in the back. I used the roof as a ladder and would require only a couple of footholds to reach the window. Having some rock-wall climbing experience, I felt this would not be a problem. Alas, my left wrist refused to cooperate. As soon as my left hand needed to hold my weight with it, I almost fell and had to stifle a scream. The pain shot through my entire arm and into my core. Panic struck for just a few seconds because I did not have the time or daylight to find another place. It would also be unlikely to find another one any easier to enter than this one. Studying the window more closely, I needed only two steps to reach the window ledge. I liberated the passenger's seat from the van and used it as a stepping stool and was able to reach the window. It opened fully easily enough (they must use it regularly for ventilation) and I was inside.

The first thing I did was to look for alarm wiring. There was none visible from the outside and once inside there was none on the window. There weren't any alarms anywhere on the top floor. Crime must be slow down under.

I pulled up my pack and computer (by tying them to the end of the string), and fervently started to look for a phone line to tap into. The window was at the end of a hallway from which several doors led to a variety of offices. Not all of the offices were unlocked so I did not have access to the entire building. There was an attorney, a draftsman, a surveyor and a private investigator. All those doors were locked. Down the stairs, there was what seemed to be a waiting area with a secretary's desk. It had a typical layout: copier, fax, computer (an IBM clone) and, of course, a twenty-button phone. The offices undoubtedly used a common receptionist/secretary to save on expenses.

I checked out the front door and it too had no alarm. The back door was just down the hallway and to my relief, the dead bolt could be opened from the inside without a key. In case it was necessary to leave in a hurry, all I had to do was flip the lock and jump into the van. Despite desperately wanting to start working, I took a few minutes to back the van in and restore the seat to its proper place. I then set my stuff on the floor behind the secretary's desk and used everything available to block the window. Still, I turned on no lights. The light of the screen would be sufficient.

There were so many things to access first that I froze. Eventually, after a deep cleansing breath, I prioritized. After accessing my father's checking account, I wired funds to a local Western Union office; one down and all night to go. A quick email to Dad explained the fund transfer and an email to Rick told him that I was currently OK, but in trouble and would be in touch soon — could he please stay close to home. My last note went to Michele thanking her for the warning and the computer. I remarked I was having a good time and wanted to see the sights including the famous lover's leap (in Dunedin, of course). Only then did I hack into the police computer system. It was harder than I expected.

They must have only recently computerized and thus had the most recent security systems. After gaining access, I found the log-in file for grand theft auto in the Otago region. There were no reports of a mortuary hearse being reported stolen, nor was there mention of anyone named Kevin reporting the transport of a fugitive — dangerous or otherwise. I smiled to myself; maybe the kiss did work after all, or maybe he just didn't give a damn. Either way, it appeared that I was in the clear. Finally, the Queenstown police department computer did not reveal any alarms or reports of any kind about a B&E on this street.

Now to the real work. First in line was writing a program that would search these three sites on a continuing basis for any new reports. If the report had any of the key words I gave it such as my name, Kevin, auto theft, or burglary, it would cut into whatever screen was open, otherwise it would just alert me that something new had been inputted. Once it was working, my neck and shoulder muscles relaxed. I knew that at the very least I would get adequate warning.

My mailbox had many letters from Rick. On reading them they were all the same; please call, there is important news. Each successive letter became more frantic. Guilt flared inside me even knowing I could not have contacted him any sooner. The computer dialed with my scrambler, connected and called him but there was no response. Let's see, it is four hours later but yesterday. That would be Saturday about two in the morning. So Rick is asleep and his computer is off and that is why he isn't responding. Knowing his schedule and his tendency to sleep in on Saturday, I would have to wait over six hours for him to log on. My stomach chose that moment to inform me I had not eaten anything since lunch. Munching on peanuts and cookies, my thoughts drifted back to my first encounter with Rick five years ago next month.

He was a guest lecturer on ethics and morality in modern society. He struck a nerve with me because of my interest in poking around others peoples' computers. So I went up to him after the lecture and posited that in fact the morality of the average hacker was far superior to that of the average person. Whether it was my brilliant arguments or something else, I will never know; this prompted an invitation to lunch with him and discuss it further.

Rick is older than me by about twelve years and is not particularly handsome. He has a bushy, unkempt beard that hides facial scars. He was also balding and could benefit from losing forty pounds or more. We talked for hours at lunch. It was not his arguments that made him stand out, but stand out he did. When we were talking, I could almost read his mind. Something like what I imagine identical twins feel like. So in time, Rick became the older brother/confidant I never had. We would happily talk about anything: grades, boyfriends, my fights with my parents, even my mother's death. He frequently insisted I forgive my father. This one subject has caused some of our worst fights.

He has wonderfully funny stories. When in 'Nam during the war, doing some of that spook stuff, he was in a plane that had been hit and caught fire. Not wanting to jump, he started an argument with the pilot. Rick felt that the airport was only a few minutes away and that it would be better if they landed instead of bailing out. Apparently, this went on for a while.

Then Rick gets this grin, "Do you know how I knew my argument was a lost cause?"

"How?" I asked.

"The pilot jumped out and left me behind in the plane. Even then I couldn't jump until the flames were right at my behind." At this point, he bursts into laughter. I missed that. Another ti…"

FLASH! New file being created by Queenstown police.

The file was about someone's dog barking late keeping the neighbors up. This broke my reverie and I reverted to searching seriously regarding my current predicament, scanning the online newspaper stories to get the latest news but was not prepared for what appeared.

The radio had been right. There was a dead tourist in Lake Tepako. Furthermore, I was involved up to my eyebrows. Mrs. Donovan was dead, and they were searching for me in connection with her death. I sat still for a long time and could even feel my heart beating. I stubbornly refused to believe the first newspaper but was unfortunately able to verify it quickly. She was alive the last time I saw her and this was utter nonsense. What in the world were they up to? I finally had to let it go and went on to something else.

Although the name was easy enough, the search required patience and perseverance. There weren't many Boers in the US (the wonder of it is that there were any at all) and when I put in an approximate age and location, it narrowed the search significantly. The problem was that Donovan had nothing on file, and I mean nada, zip, zilch. As if he had been dropped on earth by alien practical jokers. Yes, he had a driver's license and a birth certificate. But there were no citations, bank accounts, credit cards, library cards, land holdings, marriage certificate — in short, any of the stuff that makes us real in the US of the 90s and 00s. Most disturbing, there was no SSN as far as I could tell (how did he obtain a passport?).

This pointed in only one direction: his name was an alias. A more complicated process than just choosing any old name; there had to be backup documents. He needed a passport to get here; this took time, money and heavy-duty planning. It is also illegal, as in big-time illegal. It was not the equivalent of hacking into a protected database when if caught might get you a suspended sentence and a fine. It meant significant jail time. It might even be jail time with 'Bubba.' Not a prospect anyone should take lightly. There had to be an extremely important reason for him (them?) to assume these risks and go through all of this trouble.

I looked up Donovan's poor dead wife and not surprisingly discovered a similar trail. Here I was luckier because her driver's license application was recent; in fact, just one month prior to leaving. She put as the reason for application 'name change' and she placed her real maiden name and telephone number. The number was not the one Paula had given me. It was from a different state altogether, with a 212 area code. I noted it down and researched her 'maiden name.'

The search engine hit on someone immediately. I had an address outside of Houston, TX, with a person about her age. I accessed her photo from the DMV and lo and behold, it was Mrs. Boers herself, although now, it was a Tracy Smith who worked for Levox International. On a hunch, I broke into their personnel files. They had unusually high security indeed and it took skill and effort to make an effective search. Once inside, I searched for any employees matching Donovan's general description. Since he is white, middle-aged and with no clear distinguishing characteristics (besides his intense hatred for me), there was a large group of files to pick from. The search further limited by first names starting with D and still there were over a hundred. I tried for an hour to limit it further without any luck.

I was going to give up on this approach when it occurred to me to search for employees that had significant personnel problems. It brought it down to thirteen and then I started downloading the personnel photos from the most senior person on down, which is when I found him. The second file down was David Street, VP of international acquisitions. Apparently, he could not consistently control of his temper. There were several reprimands dating as far back as ten years. Most dealt with verbal assaults against other VPs, but one was with a superior. I wondered what made him so special that they put up with his less than stellar behavior.

I began to feel ill. There were too many people with alternate identities. First Marcus Rogers turns out to be Marc Roberts, then Donovan is not the tour guide he claims to be and becomes this crazy man who is meeting with these big-shot government types. He chases me with absolute cold hatred in his eyes and then his 'wife' who also isn't (wasn't?) using her real name ends up dead. Dead at Lake Tekapo with myself as the prime suspect. The newspaper story stated she drowned and considering she was found in only a couple feet of water, foul play was suspected. She was fully clothed and was wearing the same severely cut suit.

That stopped me cold and I felt bad for her. As the chase

replayed in my mind, her face was not filled with hate that was in Donovan's, but with something else — fear perhaps. I couldn't understand it but by replaying my memory it became clear she was not chasing me but Donovan. Insight flared in my brain and I knew Donovan had killed her. Of course, there was no proof but it was abundantly clear to me that for whatever reason, this David Street person had done in Mrs. Boers...Tracy...whomever she was. Had he done it because she screwed up or he lost his temper? Or did he do it simply to frame me? That last possibility chilled me. Anyone that cold blooded was someone to avoid.

These findings and thoughts flared my paranoia in the same way that gasoline flares a fire. I went around and double-checked the windows and the van. While outside, I noticed that dawn was not a long way off but the world remained quiet. There was nothing out of place anywhere. I rechecked all the police files I was monitoring. All was still quiet but my anxiety continued to climb. Damn it, Rick, wake up and check your email!

As if by providence, there was new mail. To my surprise, it was from Michele. She was happy to hear things were going well and was sorry I had missed her performance on TV the previous night. This meant to me that there would be something on tonight. She meandered in the way that young girls sometimes do. I smiled and resolved to keep her out of this as much as possible. She had enough to handle being a motherless teen without me adding grief. There was no way to know where I would be by nightfall, but would try to remember to watch the tube.

The next thing on my to-do list was to research those two government big shots. This was the easiest work of the night since politicos love to be in the news. I searched back far enough to get a feel for what their views might be and what they considered important.

The guy who had been on the phone was apparently a highly ambitious man. He was currently foreign secretary but was clearly aiming higher. The fat man, secretary of finance, was a genius with numbers but had no personal political agenda or much history. I delved deeper into the first guy's history and could not understand why he would in any way care about me — or wish me harm.

He was the prototypical politician: always in control, with no history of losing his temper or even allegations of wrongdoing — the typical Mr. Clean. He had been divorced a long time ago and at least in the US, that kind of history is passé. I invested more of my precious time on his behalf and then dug as hard and deep on everyone else that was even remotely involved in this case.

I was uncovering megabytes of information. The hard part in a search like this is to decide what is relevant and what is simply noise. Just at the time Rick should be waking up and getting his email (a forwarding subroutine that would send it to me), the screen again notified me:

FLASH! Police file being created with keywords hearse and grand theft auto.

My software was automatically connecting me to the file while inwardly I died. My time was running out sooner than I'd hoped. I restrained myself from dashing outside and ditching the van immediately. As good as the police may be down under, they still could not work miracles. The clock was definitely ticking, but it would take time to re-route the description to the various departments. On the positive side, I was now wide awake and ready for anything. Any thoughts about taking a little nap were history.

"...Mr. H.R. Thompson reports that his funeral van is missing and presumed stolen. He went to use it for a sudden death at the local hospital and could not locate it. Inquiries in the area were fruitless. Tire tracks were seen but could not be followed. A serendipitous report from a motorist places the van at the Conoco Station outside of the city. Computer records from the credit card bureau show the gas was paid for by a known fugitive Ms. Yolanda Prescott, also traveling using the alias Yvonne..."

I audibly gasped and stopped reading while I recovered my equanimity. In just a few sentences, the police had connected Kevin (or possibly the girls at the peak), the hearse and me. They were only half a step behind and I had not expected them to get anywhere until Monday. They may or may not be underestimating me but I sure was underestimating them. I forced my breathing to slow, waited for my pulse to drop below a hundred then went to all the windows. No one was there so I continued with the rest of the report.

"... Further inquiries reveal that suspect purchased a ticket on the bus to Dunedin but had a disagreement with the ticket agent and must have changed her mind. She then stole the hearse. We suspect that she arrived in Dunedin well ahead of the bus and that she is hiding out there."

So they weren't that close after all. And they had no idea I could see their cards. Or did they? The doubts could be merciless. I had to get out of here and away from that van. But it had to be hidden so they would not recover it anytime soon and realize I was not in Dunedin.

"...we have sent inquiries to Dunedin and all local constabularies. We expect to find the vehicle and suspect shortly..."

"I DON'T THINK SO, whoever you are," I said to no one. The final note was disturbing, "...Please pass this on to the secretary."

That was it then. The wolves were howling but I had enough lead time to plan my next move. They possessed enormous resources and were willing to use them. I could not expect to rely on luck anymore; luck and chance would be on their side. All I had on my side was a good head start, remarkable cunning and unparalleled guile. It was at that moment of introspection that the message from Rick came in.

We were able to communicate in real time and thanks to my scrambling software we could be direct.

"What is your current situation?" he came right to the point.

It took fifteen minutes of my nonstop typing to update him on everything. One piece of good news: my wrist no longer hurt when I typed.

"So there are no more cutouts between you and the police?" Rick remarked.

I knew what he meant by that. A cutout was a change in direction or mode of transport or a change in location. It was how many steps they had to travel to lead them to your current location.

"That's correct, Rick."

"That will become your second-highest priority. Your highest is, of course, to ditch that hearse."

"Where do you suggest I leave it?" I inquired.

"Give me a second, it needs to be somewhere they won't

readily discover it...yes, that will do. Find a hospital and park it in the area that the nurses and staff use. Place it as far from the building and behind some obstacle if possible. The parking lot will never empty and the hearse will not look out of place there. It may go undetected for days."

"How do I get back here?" I asked.

"You won't be coming back. When you leave that house you will never return. It will be your next cutout so even if they somehow locate the building you are currently occupying, they won't be able to pick up your trail until the next time you have to do something inconvenient." That concluding word was Rick's all-encompassing way of covering stealing cars, b&e, using a credit card, anything that could tag me.

"And where should I go once I dump it?" I asked with increasing concern.

There was a long pause before he responded. "I'm sorry, Yolanda, but I don't yet know enough about New Zealand, much less Queenstown. But I will next time we talk. Meanwhile, you are going to have to locate your next burrow by yourself. Keep in mind everything I taught you and let that right brain help out."

"Yes, master Yoda, I remember and will do as you recommend. After all, that's how I have managed this long. I suppose you don't want to go over my ideas right now."

"Yolanda, as much as I would love to chat and give you emotional support, you have seriously overstayed your welcome at that house and the hearse is a definite risk; they only have to find it to catch you. Consider leaving it there and just walking away."

"I don't know, Rick, I would be walking for hours and it would point them to where I hid out. They might be able to learn something from this place."

"That's right. Also, don't waste time wiping your prints. You don't have the time and you will inevitably miss one anyway. Do you have enough cash?" he asked.

I told him about the wire transfer.

"Great, blend in, speak little, and dress young. The establishment always ignores the young. You could pass for nineteen or twenty if you really tried."

"Thanks a lot," I interjected.

"Now go, and contact me as soon as you are safe."

"Bye Rick, tell Dad I love him."

With a tear crawling down my face, I disconnected my equipment and left. I did not bother with the window but simply walked out the back door, entered the van and drove.

I had no idea where the hospital was and had not seen it on Kevin's map (the fact that I had not looked for it may have had something to do with my lack of success). I drove to the 7-Eleven equivalent and asked for directions. The hospital turned out to be just around the corner — next door to the police station. I drove several blocks out of my way to approach the hospital from the opposite side. I avoided the visitors and doctors parking lot and found a spot between a pick up truck (no gun rack) and a minivan. I tokenly wiped it down, collected all my stuff, double-checked that nothing was left inside and locked it. Walking away, I did not look back but smiled; I had just increased my cutouts by one.

CHAPTER SIXTEEN

QUEENSTOWN ADVENTURES

It was a lovely sunny day and despite all of the recent events, I enjoyed the sensation of walking and noticing the little things we normally dismiss. The normal things: a man working in his yard, the postman delivering the mail (do they have as much junk mail here as we do?), a dog sniffing trees. It was my personal distance from this normalcy that made these things stand out.

I bought a map of Queenstown at the convenience store and was headed for a nearby park hoping the good weather would bring out loads of people in which I could get lost. As much as it grated me, I followed Rick's advice and did my best to look and act the part of a nineteen-year-old college student.

The park was much smaller than the map indicated. This was no Central or Hyde's park; nevertheless, there were a sufficient number of people enjoying the day. To my increased delight, the sunbathers had come out — I decided to hide in plain sight and selected a spot where I would blend in with the other sunbathers; I was just a local girl out for a bit of sun. The sun block claimed it had an SPF of 50 and I was too tired to worry about their truth in labeling laws. I was asleep as soon as my head hit my backpack.

I found myself chasing my father in a large, strange house. As soon as he was visible, he would step out of the room and into another. He did not seem to be aware of my need to reach him or even of my presence. In some ways, he looked as if he wanted to find me. My frustration was mounting and he kept getting further ahead. I tried to call his name and discovered I could not talk. My voice would not come out loud enough. In the end, he started to disappear into the distance.

"Hello, hello," a disembodied voice was repeating itself.

I couldn't locate its source. It was associated with this repeated pressure on my shoulder, as if a large bird kept landing on it.

"You'd better get going before the police come," he said.

That finally did it. The magic word: POLICE. As my mind cleared from the dream, I looked briefly about me.

Right in front of me was this tall skinny kid, of about seventeen, with dirty blonde shoulder-length hair, cute in a drab sort of way and with a stud in his left ear. He was clean-shaven and exactly the kind of guy I would have dated when I was younger. It would drive my father completely up a tree.

I can hear him say, "Why would such an intelligent and beautiful young lady want to be seen with someone who doesn't pay better attention to his own appearance?"

It took him years to understand that getting his goat was a large part of the attraction. Of course, as soon as he found that out, it stopped being fun — but I digress.

The guy seemed about to leave.

"Wait, please wait," I said but it did not come out right. The first word was shrill and the next two not loud enough. Still, he stopped and looked back at me. "What did you say about the police?"

"That you had better get moving before they make their rounds. They had a bit of trouble with drug dealers coming here at night, so they patrol in the late afternoon."

That's when it finally sunk in, it was late. Although it wasn't dark yet, it was getting there. How long had I slept? I felt achy and stiff. "What time do they start?" and quickly looked at my watch. I was shocked, "It's ten after six!"

"It sure is and they will be rounding the corner any minute. If they don't approve of how you look they stop and question you. It's a bloody nuisance. They stopped me yesterday and it took twenty minutes so we need to get going."

My mind cleared quickly. The last thing I needed was for a policeman on a routine check to ask for ID. I would be between the proverbial rock and hard place. If I showed it, they would arrest me and if I did not they would detain me. "Could we walk together? I mean, it might look better to them if the two of us were together." He paused a moment to think. I used the time to straighten my hair and pick up my backpack.

"Yeah, that would look better to them. Like a gal and her bloke out for a stroll."

"Sounds good to me," I said, worrying that my fear and desperation were being transmitted and would alarm him.

Instead, he smiled, "But will you respect me in the

morning?" The statement was such a non-sequitur and he smiled so devilishly that I burst out in a much-too-loud laugh. He laughed also and soon we were walking together arm in arm, just as two police officers rounded the corner and looked our way.

I kept my voice low and confidential and told him the joke about how many therapists it takes to change a light bulb (only one, but the bulb really has to want to change). He had not heard it before and liked it a lot. The police officers just waved as we walked by and I audibly sighed.

As soon as we were out of sight, this guy stopped and looked me right in the eyes, "Are you in trouble with the law?"

I tried a bluff, but it came out poorly because I was unprepared, "No, why do you say that?"

"I thought so, you were far more scared of the police than you should have been. What do they want you for?"

This guy was amazing, he could read right through me and did not bother with my evasions. I was completely out of ideas. Since there was nothing else to say, I used my method of last resort and told him the truth. "They think I killed someone." He looked at me closely and seemed to make a decision.

"Did you?" He asked without any judgment.

"No I most certainly did not. But I know who did."

"Then why don't you tell them?" he asked innocently.

"There is no proof, and more importantly, he knows many low people in high places."

He smiled at that one. He said, "Follow me." Since I didn't know where else to go, I followed.

It took nearly twenty minutes of fast walking and slow talking before he stopped in front of a garage. "My name is

Tim and I live in the house over there across the street. If you want a place to spend the night, you can sleep in this garage. I am the only one that uses it. It's kinda like my club house."

It was my turn to look at him directly in the eye. "Why are you doing this?"

"You mean, why should you trust me?" he said this with a grin.

"No! I haven't gotten to that yet. Why are you doing this?"

"I don't know."

"Bullshit!" I yelled at him, "Tell me!" He had jumped at this outburst and was looking more his age (what was his age?).

Finally, in a confessional tone, "I saw you come into the park and noticed how you looked around before you fell asleep. It seemed that you would never wake up and the afternoon passed while waiting for you to wake up. By the way, I believe you; what you said about the police being after you. Don't know how much to trust you, but feel that you are OK and I generally trust my feelings."

I was still not appeased and persisted, "Why were you waiting for me to wake up?" He looked down and shuffled his feet without saying anything. My ordeal deadened my brain and it took me several more seconds to put it together. "Oh I get it! You were going to hit on me." It wasn't a question, but a realization.

He responded, "I didn't mean anything bad by it; just thought you looked kinda cute. You didn't look all that much older than me and you carried what was clearly a laptop. I thought perhaps you were a college student. I didn't know you were a tourist until you began talking."

The next few moments do not have any explanation at all. If you pressed me I would have to say that after all of the day's stresses and worries, the hiding and having no one with me — that I was vulnerable to someone saying something nice about me. I went right up to him and hugged him. "Thank you, my guardian angel. By the way, you are cute too, even if you have an earring." He blushed. It felt so good to hold someone, that I did not let go of him for a long time.

"How old are you?" I asked, still holding onto him.

"Uh, twenty-one," he lied.

"How old are you. If I am to trust you, you need to be straight with me."

"Seventeen," he said it in almost a whisper. "I'll be eighteen in three weeks."

"Don't rush it, Tim! I think that seventeen is just fine."

A thought occurred to me. "Just how old do you think I am?"

"I couldn't tell, you looked about twenty or twenty-one, but you act much older."

"Thank you, twenty-one is close enough. Do you usually hit on girls my age?" He didn't answer right away. Instead, he looked around and verified we were alone.

"I don't get along with girls my age. Most have nothing interesting to say."

"I'm sorry if I was prying; by the way, my name is Yolanda, but my friends call me Yo." We sat down at the curb and continued our impromptu chat. After twenty minutes or so, it ended naturally. "Thanks again for getting me out of a tight spot with the police. However, it is getting late and I had better be on my way."

"You're leaving? Don't you need a place to stay? I promise it is safe. No one will find you." His tone was getting desperate.

I held his hand firmly and lifted his chin so he could see the sincerity in my eyes, "Tim, I like you and would say yes to your asking me out, but at this moment I am bad news and you don't need any part of this."

"But you said you were innocent," he pleaded.

It caused me to reflect. "Innocent — probably not, but I didn't kill the woman, and I need to hide out long enough to prove it."

He looked sad but there was no way at all that I was going to involve this boy in my troubles. As it was, there were a plateful of amends to make. This was one that would not happen. I lightened the tone by asking, "Tim, do you have an email address?"

This seemed to catch him by surprise, "Yes, why?"

"Why don't we trade addresses and that way we can keep in touch?"

He looked at me as if I had grown another head, "I don't know any girls that use e-mail, they use social networking." He said the last few words as if he was spitting.

"You do now." He seemed to like that and we exchanged addresses. I could barely make out his eyes, but it was clear his eyes were tearing up. Over me! I put my pack down, moved closer and kissed him. My kissing strange boys was becoming a habit with me.

I made sure he was not following and walked in a random direction. I felt good and had been sorely tempted to stay at his 'club house,' but it would not have worked. I would have been up all night waiting for either him or for the police to show up. I had no idea where I was or where I was going. This would prove embarrassing soon. I found a filing station with a phone booth and pulled out my map. Between the phone book and the map, I located a nearby church. I picked up something to eat from the station (chips, nuts, cookies that sort of thing) and walked over to the Queenstown Church of Christ.

They clearly did not have a crime problem in this country. There was no alarm system and several of the ground floor windows were not locked. I verified that the parsonage was not directly on the grounds and made myself at home. Having already eaten my supper, I decided to nap while it was dark. On waking, I would work into the dawn and be ready to leave before anyone came. My computer booted up and would beep me awake half an hour after midnight.

Please do not assume that this was easy. On the contrary, this required an extreme amount of discipline. I desperately wanted to contact Rick — as in NOW! However, my narrow escape at the park had sobered me (figuratively) and I was determined to be more careful. Having come so close to being in another New Zealand jail (probably with Louise still there) chastened me. I would be there this minute but for one sweet and cute seventeen-year-old boy, who thought I was cute.

It was important to take careful stock of my condition and situation: one, I was still tired, the nap on the grass had not made up for the loss of an entire night's sleep, not to mention the enormous emotional toll I had suffered (am still suffering); two, if there was a sudden need to vacate this place at dawn on a Monday morning, I better be rested and ready to innovate; three, my situation had not significantly changed in the last twelve hours. There was no burning issue that needed handling that wouldn't wait a few hours. The hunters were not having a strategy meeting in their war room on how to track me down. At least not at this very minute, late on a Sunday night. Perhaps on Monday morning they would do that but I would be taking care of it at that time. Lastly, although capable of pulling all-nighters and pushing myself to and past whatever physical limits there are, I function better and quicker when rested. If this was a job for a client, it might be worth pushing it, but with my own freedom at stake, something I place an unusually high value on, I would pace myself. This was not a fast one-mile race like the ones in high school, but a marathon that requires patience, persistence and fortitude.

CHAPTER SEVENTEEN

HISTORY LESSON

I remembered how good I was at running. I loved the feeling of the air whipping during my sprint of the 440, heavy in oxygen debt, legs and lungs burning as if on fire. My heart would be pumping hard as it revved up to almost two hundred. Through the entire five minutes of the race, my focus would be fixed on the runners in front of me.

My teammates called me the rabbit. They meant I would hang back for the first three laps, trying to keep the leaders close, then when the bell lap came I would turn on the afterburners. There was no one in the entire state that could match my last split time. I think it had something to do with my high threshold and tolerance to pain. I could just sort of ignore the pain. I could feel the pain but that would not stop me from running. I just had to get past them.

Sneaking up on the leaders was crucial so that by the time they heard me coming, it would be too late. The looks of disbelief when I would zip past them was what drove me. Just thinking of that made me smile. Winning wasn't the point; it was beating the other girls that was important. Oh how I missed that. (How I ever gave that up to take up my life of alcoholism will remain one of my life's enduring mysteries.)

I had to think of my messy vacation like a marathon. I had to play it smart, with planning and with adjustments for how the body is doing. This requires checking in periodically to make sure all systems are in good functioning order. Now, my body was telling me that it was not working anywhere near peak efficiency. There was no way to know when my next opportunity for rest would come and if I did not get some rest now, something important might be overlooked.

I worried that I would be too tense to sleep but needn't have bothered. I was out with no preamble. This time there was no dream and awoke refreshed and smiling. Having a sweet seventeen-year-old pining away for me had done wonders for my spirit (not to mention my battered ego).

I checked in with the police department. They were frustrated by not finding any trace of me in Dunedin. That would have to be remedied — in a little while. The name Yvonne surfaced from interviews of the girls at Fox Peak. Kevin's name was never mentioned (the kiss worked!) and the hearse was still missing. Checking the news reports, I was alternately said to be a material witness (JP) and a dangerous crazy person (Donovan, et al). The official police line was that I should turn myself in for questioning (yeah, right).

In my email inbox, there was a letter from Dad saying it was OK about the money. I emailed him back and told him how much I loved him and would call him as soon as circumstances allowed. My heart ached to be there with him and I allowed myself a short cry. I emailed my new young friend, Tim, and reiterated that I was not a dangerous criminal and deeply appreciated his help. (Just in case he was having second thoughts.)

Before it was time for Rick, I scanned the next day's headlines. (You don't need any special skills to do this, they upload them around midnight.) I had suspected as much, but it still shocked me. There I was on the front page, in living color. The police had obtained an old photo of me. It did not even resemble me all that much. This surprised me because the hotel had my passport and they could have used that photo. Was this JP at work? I couldn't think of why anyone else would go out of their way to find another picture, particularly one that was significantly inferior to the one they must have right in front of them. Is there some arcane rule that you can't use passport photos in a manhunt (womanhunt)? I DON'T THINK SO. Did this mean that JP was helping me to whatever extent he could? Damn how I hoped so, not realizing until this moment how much I wanted to believe in him.

A little further down the page was an interesting small article. 'Two wives for the Foreign Secretary?' The article related how the final papers for his divorce twenty-two years ago were never finalized. This made his current marriage null and void and I won't go on about what it said regarding the status of his kids with his current wife. He had met the story with the customary denials. The issue was further complicated since his first wife had married a member of the other political party and had kids of her own by her current husband. I smiled then started to laugh; I could not help myself. It is childish and immature to take delight at someone else's misfortune, but I did so anyway. Please forgive me but I actually did a little dance inside the church. What a wonderful story; maybe, just maybe, it would keep his mind off me for a little while.

I finally could call Rick. He was waiting and apparently worried. He told me it was six AM and he had been up all night waiting for my call. I filled him in on the recent events. He was angry at me for the park incident, but calmed down quickly (probably because it all worked out OK). He had been thinking and had several ideas for me. As usual, he had unusual approaches to the problem. Having done his homework, all of his ideas would probably work here. I would let them percolate inside my brain and would use whichever one my right brain felt was best. I already knew which one felt the best, but I kept this to myself.

He had researched Soltex (Peter Osbourne's and Donovan's most recent employer). For the past year, ever since their new president was installed, they had acquired a variety of companies. Lately, they had bought some mining rights in Malaysia as well as a papaya processing plant in the same country. He felt that maybe Donovan was an advance man to explore possible mergers, which would explain the need for secrecy but not the violence.

Donovan's history of problems controlling his temper could explain a lot. He might lose his job if he blew this assignment and maybe he had finally broken under the pressure. It did not explain anything about the dead guy in my bed, or who Marc was, but Rick had an idea.

After he went through it with me, I agreed that it did explain a lot. The motives were still not entirely clear, but at least the players were out in the open. Next, we discussed strategy. My focus was entirely on clearing my name. We needed to discover why they (whoever 'they' were) were doing this to me; I would then be able to continue with my life, without having to look over my shoulder all the time. Rick insisted on getting me out of New Zealand first, then focusing on the rest. I countered that we could not effectively accomplish all of it if I ran away. He stated that it was not running away but making a strategic repositioning to escape the reach of the apparently corrupt local government — this would level the playing field. I told him there were allies here helping me. He said that we couldn't be sure of them and the alliance might not last.

We went at it for a long time, like we usually do when we disagree (which is rather more frequent than either one of us would like to admit). It ended predictably; he relented and told me to do whatever I felt was best. I thanked him for all of the input and his obvious concern for my safety and added that under no circumstances was he even to think of coming down here. I could not imagine having him out of reach for the day-and-a-half that the trip would take to get here. We finished up by making a list of all the things to do and we prioritized them. High on the list was to leave a false trail for the hounds to find. That would be fun. Low on the list was getting hot food and a shower.

I started with my first task as soon as he hung up. Using my own credit card, I purchased a one-way ticket from Dunedin to Wellington (capital of New Zealand and where my two nemeses live). I purchased it for someone named Holly Talbot. The purchase was made minutes before the plane was to leave. Once the plane left, I toyed with the airlines computer and changed the entry to read that Ms. Talbot did, in fact, board the plane and arrived in Wellington as scheduled. By the time their computers could tell them of the purchase and they deduced that another name had been used, the plane would have landed and they would assume they had missed me.

The next part was to leave a trail of appropriate purchases scattered throughout Wellington and vicinity. The materials would initially be innocuous but eventually someone would piece it together that a bomb was being constructed (what else do you make with some pipe, ammonia, sulfuric acid and glycerin?). In fact, I don't have the foggiest idea how to make a bomb — but they needed to think I did. All their efforts should be spent way over there in Wellington, so as to leave me alone here in Queenstown. I could then get on with my other assignments: finding a permanent home, figuring out what the hell was going on, and most importantly, making them pay; oh, how I was going to make them pay.

CHAPTER EIGHTEEN

RICK'S PLAN

I looked over the pastor's schedule. His first appointment on Monday morning was not until ten AM. Considering that Sundays are his busiest day, he probably would not be coming through the door any earlier. The secretary, however, might come early to get a head start on the week. I decided to be out by seven, maybe seven-thirty, but on further reflection, I decided not to push my luck and would be long gone by seven AM. That still allowed me over three hours for sleep. Packing everything but the computer, I set it to wake me at six-thirty and also left my early warning program on. The early time was because I noticed a shower and was anxious to use it. Not being able to risk turning on a light, it would have to wait for daylight and even then would have to rush through it. It would not do for the police to find me once again without clothes. Alas, the inconveniences of being a fugitive.

The morning went as planned and I was up, showered,

186

packed and out of there by seven. The only traces of my presence in the church were the wet shower and a few food wrappers in the trash. Neither one could be connected to me and I left feeling great. My first stop was the Western Union office to pick up my cash. The reason for the cash was obvious. I could not use my own credit card and not having my dad's card with me, everything would have to be bought with cash. I looked over my list and realized how much stuff I needed to buy. After the initial transfer, I'd worried it would be insufficient and had wired another thousand dollars, this time to a different office. Collecting the money would pose another problem, but it was not insurmountable.

I thought of ways of stretching my limited cash supply. One way was to order things electronically using my dad's charge card and then leave instructions that a messenger (fitting my description) would pick it up. This would work as long as they did not require identification, which, unless the purchase price was exorbitant, they would be unlikely to do.

While walking I decided I might as well enjoy myself. After all, I reasoned, it was supposed to be a vacation, and it had been a long time since the last one. (The way this one was going, it would probably be a much longer time before the next one.) There is something cool about a crisis. It focuses your attention and you end up noticing things that you would have taken for granted before. Now, routine, normal everyday things were beyond my reach. With no identity papers and with my photo (albeit a bad one) plastered all over the newspaper and (presumably) TV, my actions were limited. Despite all of this, the walk left me invigorated. There was so much here in Queenstown that was reminiscent of home and at the same time, so much to see that wasn't.

I went through the various plans Rick had dreamed up. The first one was to log on to a realtor's computer and search for just the right house. Unoccupied, for sale/rent, out of sight of neighbors. It would have to be one that had been on the market for some time and was stale. That way it would not have a lot of showings, and even if it did, not until the weekend. I would have to be ingenious to get in the house, but that promised to be easy. Since these would be large estate-like homes, there would be service people coming and going, mostly for the lawn care. There would probably be some access. The big insurmountable problem was my lack of wheels. These houses would not be close to either my present location or to each other. To try more than one or two would require transport. We felt that if it came down to it he could rent a car over the phone, however, they require a driver's license and other nonsense, so at least for now — on to plan B.

Plan B was Rick's favorite and he exerted all his powers encouraging me to accept this option. I can't understand him sometimes (I don't know if that is simply because he is a man or because of the man he is). He studied the local area and noticed it had an active airport and marina. He could teach me to identify the boats at the marina that had not had anyone on board and further would not have anyone soon. He knows the typical locks on boats are laughable, and with a pocketknife I could be in the cabin safe and secure within minutes of arriving at the marina.

His second favorite plan was the airport. Apparently, a huge percentage of hangars remain undisturbed for months at a time, and the only trick is identifying them. He was confident that I could do that. That's Rick, always so confident and optimistic. Maybe that is why we connect so well. My cynicism and paranoia seem to mesh with his optimism and security. I did not hesitate in discarding this plan as totally out of the question. It just did not seem workable, at least by me at this time. I would reluctantly have to accept the bugs idea, which leads us to his third and final, most disgusting idea.

This option remained the least attractive but unfortunately was the easiest to implement and in my estimation had the most promise at keeping me out of the authorities' clutches. Something important about me that you may already suspect is my predisposition to athletics. Despite tolerating heat, cold and pain and the general discomforts of extreme physical effort while exercising, I do very much enjoy my comforts when indoors. After an intense game of racquetball or whatever, I am passionate about my hot steamy shower and my air conditioning. Accordingly, I hate bugs with unrestrained intensity. I absolutely, positively despise them and their tiny little legs crawling over me.

Oh, I suppose they are an integral part of the earth's ecosystem. They probably form an indispensable link somewhere, somehow. If it was left up to me, I would chance it and eliminate the nasty things. Perhaps we could spare the honeybees and spiders (they are both cute) but those nasty flying critters that either bite, sting or buzz — good riddance. I don't even care if birds die out from lack of a food supply. There are enough pictures of birds to last me a lifetime.

The reason this is of any current significance whatsoever is that Rick was taking my comforts away (I love blaming him whenever I can) and trying to make me a luscious meal for the bugs. The plan I decided on is as follows: I would shop at various stores and purchase (with cash) the necessary supplies for an extended camping trip — food, shelter, supplies, whatever. With one of those huge backpacks on my back, I would become virtually invisible to regular people. Who would think a fugitive would go camping in the open?

I bought one of those super expensive satellite phones that do not require a land link. I could thereby remain in constant contact with Rick or anyone or, in fact, any computer I chose. It would free my movements significantly and even in the unimaginable event they discovered how I was communicating, they would be unable to trace my signal. It would make intercepting my letters nearly impossible (unless they had access to the NSA). In so many ways, this plan was perfect (except, of course, for those bloody bugs). There was nothing for it but to enact plan C.

I arrived at the Western Union office and had my cover story rehearsed and ready. I need not have concerned myself because in fact they handle this kind of problem regularly. A tourist loses her purse, it not only has all her money and credit cards, but it also has her ID. So how is she supposed to identify herself as the person to whom the wired money belongs? In my case, I specified a code word. I talked to the nice teller who handled the transaction quickly and efficiently. By the way, all the people on this island have been nice — with three notable exceptions.

So…what's the deal, do they all take 'nice' lessons? How do we import that to the US? I gave the teller my code word, "Happy campers," and the money was mine and walked out of there with nearly NZ$2000. A hefty sum that was going to be spent very fast. It did not warrant thinking how long it would take me to pay that back. The visit to the second office was just as easy. With a grand total of NZ$4000, plan C was ready for execution. In retrospect, we should have thought of some cute code word like the military does for its covert operations; like 'operation Kiwi,' or some such thing.

It took me the better part of the day to collect everything on the list. The guys at the store (particularly Bryon) were immensely helpful in adjusting the pack and making sure it would not rub me, and thus the backpack fit me perfectly. Perhaps I overdid the helpless female role a touch too much. I wore a floppy hat like Gilligan used to wear, sunglasses, loads of sun block and most important of all, I had many different brands of bug repellent. I simply couldn't help myself; every time I saw a different brand I just had to have it. The tent would fit one standard-size person (me) and had mosquito netting. I was set to go camping.

After walking all day, I was so tired that I took a small calculated risk. I inquired at several shops and identified which bus would take me close to the nearby mountains and reached them just before dinnertime, but my stomach would have to wait. It was crucial to find a spot and set up camp before my light failed. After some comfortable hiking up the mountain, an open area had a few tents pitched and occupied. I took that as a good omen and plunked down all my stuff.

Before long it was clear I should have allowed Bryon, the salesman, demonstrate how to set up the tent. Initially, it looked to be a two-person job. How could a one-person tent require two people to put it up? Eventually, I broke down and read the directions. Within minutes, it was ready and I was eating my cold supper. Fortunately, food has never been a big issue for me. I know some people live to eat, somewhat in the same way I used to live to drink. But I eat to live and generally find it an unrelenting chore to have to eat so often. I enjoy the social aspect of dinnertime, and trying new foods has some appeal, but overall I would rather have my nourishment in IV form.

Night approached and I readied for bed. Not wanting to drain my batteries, I did not set my alarm. I would wake up with the sun, which at this time of year would be early enough. It was a cool but comfortable night and I slept on top of my sleeping bag, relaxed for the first time since Friday night. God, had it only been two-and-a-half days since all of this started? It felt like I had been hiding for a month or more. How much longer could this go on — emotionally? I wasn't sure, but I knew it wasn't much longer. I would have to crack this case soon or I would crash and burn.

The remarkable thing of plan C was that there were no bugs! There just weren't any around me. This was amazing! With all of the nice people and no bugs, this country could grow on me. With bizarre thoughts of what I would do if things went back to normal, I fell into a sound and dreamless sleep.

The sun did not wake me; it was the sheep that woke me. A herd of undulating wool was moving a few hundred yards from me and the incessant bleating did the job. It startled me to realize it was eight-twenty. Then I remembered I did not have a clock to punch, and took my time getting up.

Eventually, I rose and after a cold breakfast continued my escape. On my hike up along the mountain, I slowly gained altitude and the viewpoint that comes with it. The city could be seen as well as the approach up the mountain. At least if they sent a cavalry regiment after me I would be able to see them coming.

By early afternoon, I found the place; it was slightly secluded and the searchers would have to be right on top of it to see the tent. There was a stream nearby, a thick blanket of pine needles was already laid out, and within a few meters, I could see the approach up the mountainside. I set up camp for an indefinite period of time. When my food ran low, I could go down and restock. Without all the heavy stuff, the round trip would only take two or three hours. As it was, there were enough supplies to last me the rest of the week. I might make a vacation out of it after all.

Being up there alone and with no one to remind me that I was wanted and hunted made it possible to ignore all of it. This included talking to anyone. It was nearly lunchtime on Tuesday before I set up my phone link and called Rick.

"Thank goodness you are all right, Yolanda." These were Rick's first words to me. He was supportive and attentive. I wondered how he was perceiving me. "You have done well and I am proud of you. It is very hard to keep going all alone."

"Thanks, Rick, I have felt depressed and alone. That's why I didn't call sooner, I needed some down time."

"That is completely understandable, just get in touch whenever you can. You must also consider that you are running your laptop on battery power and you have no way to recharge. You will have to monitor it carefully."

"Yes, mother, and I promise to brush my teeth every morning before I put the cat out."

It felt so good to banter back and forth with Rick. I almost did not feel alone. I briefed him quickly on the news I scanned prior to calling him. The police were coming under greater pressure to find me, but the stories were now appearing on page three or later. I no longer rated the front page.

To my chagrin, the police were getting dozens of calls from every part of the country responding to my picture in the paper. Apparently, I had been spotted from the ninety-mile beach district at the northernmost tip of the North Island, to Invercargill at the southernmost end of South Island. There were several reports from Wellington and that added to the false trail I laid out so meticulously.

Mr. Foreign Secretary was being harassed mercilessly by the story of his apparent bigamy. He insisted that he was completely innocent and that he would produce his final divorce decree to prove it. Unfortunately for him, he had 'temporarily' misplaced it. Rick hooted over that part; he felt it was such a wonderfully fortuitous event and it could not have come at a better time. Donovan punched a reporter who asked unwelcomed questions and after being arraigned, had been released on his own recognizance. The hearse had yet to be found and there were no police reports from either Tim or Kevin.

Rick had done some digging himself. As I have mentioned before, he does this much differently than I do. He relies on people and their connections. In his circle of esoteric friends, there is usually someone who can give him significant background information on any given subject. If not, they can usually get him in touch with someone who can. After significant digging (and a phone bill that would be astronomical), he found that Levox and Soltex were both aggressively competing against each other in many parts of the world. Evidently, the two CEOs disliked each other intensely. They were constantly competing and undercutting the other. Donovan and Peter (the dead guy) had clashed before with the last time Peter getting the best of Donovan.

This was starting to fit together and I was getting a rough outline of the situation. It had a few key pieces missing but the general outline was there. Rick concurred, but he still could not understand how I ever fell into this mess. I smiled to myself because I had a growing suspicion, but wasn't telling — it seemed too crazy; too silly.

Marc Roberts turned out to be an ex-CIA field agent. (How he found this out, I do not know and knew better than to ask.) He is a freelance agent now and Rick thinks he has worked for Soltex before. He could, however, not confirm that he currently was working for them. If he was working with Peter, then we may have been completely wrong in supposing he killed him. He may have panicked when he found out. Do Ex-CIA agents panic? Was he called back to home base when he reported Peter's death? Did Donovan kill Peter? Who had been in my room? If I could figure that last question, the rest would fall together. Rick and I batted it around for a short while and then we set future times to check in.

After Rick was gone, it occurred to me that I had never heard what Peter had actually died of, or Tracy for that matter. It was a now routine thing for me to get into the police computer so I located JP's files and there was a copy of the autopsy reports.

"...a small puncture hole at the base of the occiput, just over the lower part of the brain stem was found. It had been made immediately prior to death. (They can tell this by the fact that he bled from the hole but not for long.) There was no poison found in any of the tissues examined. However, extensive damage to vital parts of the brain stem was evident and significant hemorrhage occurred. Death was most likely instantaneous. (The brain stem among other things controls respiration and heart function; if it stops working, so do you). The placement of the needle had to be extremely precise. It had to go between the second and third vertebrae to a specified depth and then the needle had to be vigorously agitated. There is no way this could have been an accident, the gap between the vertebrae is minute. It had to be performed by a highly trained individual who was able to approach the victim from the back and get extremely close to him. Therefore, it is assumed that the victim knew his assailant and trusted him..."

I remained analytical and distant.

Just like my dad says, "When you are with a patient, you need to remain in control. You may show emotion and sentiment — in fact, it is important that you do — but it must be under your control. The patient does not need someone out of control when he is trying to deal with his own issues. After your role as physician is over you can do all the falling apart that you want."

So I had learned to listen to difficult things and compartmentalize them, study them, make decisions, etc. Nevertheless, it soon started caving in on me. All that the report stated had happened in the same room I was in, probably within a few feet of me. My heart started racing and despite the cool night, I broke into a light sweat. I allowed the feelings to come. If I tried to push them away, I would simply have to deal with them later. It took almost thirty minutes before the worst was over; by then, my first battery was nearly used up.

I used what was left to get the report on Tracy. Her autopsy was straightforward. She had drowned in Lake

Tekapo. There were signs that she had fought and that someone had held her down. I am strong but not that strong. I felt much better. If those government types were not involved, I would feel pretty comfortable about turning myself in...a message flashed.

"You have a priority letter from Rick."

I had just talked to him, what else did he want?

"Dear Yolanda, I did not want to argue with you but I sent you a package that will arrive tomorrow in Queenstown. It is of the utmost importance you retrieve it. It will help you immensely through your ordeal. Please be at the Hastings' Street UPS office at or about seven AM. Use the same code word as before. Love, Rick."

As I was digesting this unexpected message, the battery ran out and the screen went blank.

I alternated from being mad to being excited. What could Rick have sent? Something that would help me that he sent via UPS. My stuffed bear? Nala, my cat? (Probably neither.) A transporter ring that would instantly zap me to my home? A time machine that would allow me to travel back to the start of this so-called vacation? My thinking was clearly deteriorating and fast. I relaxed and savored the feeling that tomorrow would be a good day. Rick had said so and thus it would be so, and I desperately needed a good day.

I decided to explore my neighborhood. I couldn't bear to part with my powerbook so I placed it in my pack with my dinner (peanuts, canned ham and canned tomatoes). On my climb, I was pretty much alone. The path up the mountain was several hundred feet away, around a rock outcropping. No one was being adventuresome enough to find me.

I am not usually interested in fauna and such, but I did not have much else to occupy me, so what the hell. The trees were interesting and clearly they were somewhat similar to those at home, with bark (worse than its bite), leaves and limbs. But when I looked closely at them, they had a distinct character. Elegant, independent, and many of them easy to climb. The rocks were similar to the ones around Madrid. Huge granite boulders peeking out of the ground with some moss around the cracks.

About an hour's easy walk up the mountain, I found a wonderful little pond with what must have been a ski lodge in the winter. There was an unused ski lift that descended on the other side of the mountain so it had been hidden from view. Although it was a comfortable day for hiking, there were actually moderate-sized 'icebergs' in the pond. These had formed in the shaded part and it indicated cold nights indeed. There was no one in sight: no cars, no people noises. Suddenly, I had an great idea — a typical Rick idea. I walked quickly to the chalet to check it out. Yes indeed, I was right, things were going my way now. This was wonderful news indeed. Rick would love it. After this, we could talk things over at length. I settled down for a leisurely dinner and by the time the last morsel was gone, the sun was setting over the taller western mountains. Somewhere over to the west was Cook's Peak, the tallest in the country, reaching 12,314 ft. From this angle, it could be any of them, or none of them. I imagined myself climbing up one of those peaks with a group. What an adventure that would be. I sighed; with all the trouble I had in this country, that was one adventure that would never happen. I just had barely enough light to make it back to my humble abode and arrived excited and ready to work. I spent the next five hours or so on the laptop, checking things, exploring and snooping, pretty much par for the course for Yolanda Yvonne Prescott.

I learned many things. The press was having a fun time roasting my favorite cabinet member. Even though it was now generally accepted that it may have been a mistake in the record department, and that he did indeed get a final decree, they don't call politics a blood sport for nothing. I rarely listen to such drivel; I made an exception in this case because of my deep personal interest. It was also highly educational; I obtained insight on how the Romans felt when they watched the Christians vs. the Lions.

Donovan had been interviewed and had then disappeared. The police did not yet have a dragnet out for him. It wouldn't be long; the autopsy report indicated a struggle with someone stronger than her and the preliminary inquiries in the United States revealed her use of an alias. The police were interested in finding him and asking him questions that he would undoubtedly find awkward (to say the least; most likely it would be incriminating). How was Mr. Foreign Secretary taking these developments?

The police still did not know where I was, but they were suspecting it might not be Wellington. There was also a note of concern on their part that I might be leading them on a goose (wild or otherwise) chase. Fortunately, they still didn't suspect how this might be accomplished and thus continued to use email with abandon. It would not be much longer before they dug deep enough into my background and found out what my true skills were. Then I would stop getting any information at all.

I have been through this exercise before. The first thing they would do is go to paper and put nothing online. Then they call in the bloodhounds (hackers gone bad) to skulk around and find a trail, set a trap or make a goat sacrifice, whatever they think best. Unless the police were unusually smart, it would be obvious the second they knew I was in their system.

Their first reaction would be to shut down all correspondence. Only later would it would occur to them that they should not have done that but should have used the opportunity to set a trap and the reports start up again, this time with misleading information. Unless they had a world-class person working there, I had nothing to worry about. I would be cut off, but they would not be able to trace me.

I sent innocuous letters to Michele and JP informing them that all was well. I further told them not to worry and that all the recent events notwithstanding, my time in New Zealand had been worth it — especially meeting them. I might have to leave in a hurry and hoped they would understand. To Michele, I added that we would be in touch, that I would return to visit her and that she would be welcome at my home any time.

I desperately hoped she would be OK. She had so many losses to deal with and hated giving her one more, but she did not need the kind of trouble I was offering at this moment. I projected my own feelings onto her; how could she handle the loss, the guilt, the emotional roller coaster of seeing your friends have mothers when she didn't? Whom would she talk to in the next few years as she matured into a young lady? Would JP be able to handle it? Would he remarry? I went down this line of thought for a few minutes more and then out of necessity let it go.

To my amazement, the hearse was still undiscovered.

This was a real break! When the second battery was halfway drained, I switched it off and went to sleep. It had been fortuitous to find an outdoor plug at the chalet. I had been able to recharge my spent battery through my dinner. It could get recharged again in the morning and once again (if needed) prior to the trip into Queenstown to pick up Rick's package. If Rick knew what was good for him it better not be too big or heavy. (Was I in for a surprise!)

Wednesday morning was cloudy and drizzly. Not nearly as warm as it had been, so I layered my clothing and deemed it to be a good omen. People would be in too much of a hurry to notice what this scruffy hiker looked like, which would be difficult in any case with my hood over my head. I rose with the dawn so even with the detour to the chalet, I reached the UPS office by seven-fifteen. I felt great this morning despite missing my coffee. The lack of worrying about my every move plus my anticipation about the package was charging me up. The package had to be something Rick felt invaluable and worth my risking a trip into the city.

All of my planning and guessing did nothing to prepare me for the shock I was about to receive. All of my efforts to deduce the nature of the essential package turned out to be completely futile. In addition, all of my years of learning to remain composed and to control my emotions would not help me in this situation.

The UPS office was on a side street off the main thoroughfare of the city. I concentrated on walking like I belonged there and tried not to show my fear every time a police officer walked by. Once when one of them tipped his cap to me, I almost had a stroke and nearly used my best weapon: my feet. I do not suppose that any one of them could keep up with me, particularly since I had left all of my stuff on the mountain (I had not wanted to, but had no choice). If I had run, it would have tipped my hand. So as I approached the street I was looking for, I was distracted by my attempts to calm myself.

"Hi, sweetheart," I heard a familiar voice say.

I spun around not believing my ears. It just couldn't be, it must be a trick. When I turned and finally saw him, I ran, yelling, "Daddy!" and jumped into his arms and held onto him as if for my very existence. I could not let go.

I was immediately transported to another place and another time. Saint Dorothy's school for girls in Boulder, Colorado. During recess I had been beaten up in a schoolyard by some of the older girls (mostly for being Latina). I was twelve at the time and it had shaken me to my core. I had been trying to retain my composure while the teachers were helping me clean up. Daddy had come in and swept me into his arms. He had made everything all right by holding me tight and reassuring me that I was still his precious. He reassured me that nothing anyone else did or said could ever change that. From that moment on, until my mother died, my father and I had a special bond. Now I felt the same way; a twelve-year-old being beat up by strangers for no good reason. He kept saying that everything was all right, that he would take care of everything. I loved hearing it.

We must have made a beautiful sight. An immaculately dressed middle-aged man, slightly balding but physically fit (in a linebacker sort of way) and a disheveled, sullied young lady hugging in the middle of the sidewalk in the rain. He was six feet two inches, so despite my height, he still towered over me.

He enjoyed working out and would have had no trouble carrying me. But alas, I was no longer twelve and needed to carry my own weight. This reminded me of playing basketball with him (among other sports). We were evenly matched. He had the superior skill and patience; I had fitness on my side. Initially, he would win a game or two then we would play evenly and finally when he was worn down, I would win consistently. I wondered if we could find a court and a ball. Do they even know what basketball is down here?

There were a million questions buzzing through my head, but instinctively knew he would not answer them now. Besides, I was truly enjoying just being with him. I realized that he and Rick had connived and conspired to get him here and thanked both of them. If they had asked me, I would have fought them. I would not have wanted to show any weakness and would want to prove that I could handle anything. I would have refused to meet him, etc. Now Dad was here with me. And he was going to take care of me and make all of the bad guys go away.

We started walking toward his car; he parked it around the corner opposite a fire hydrant. My father never learns; he feels that his MD degree gives him the right and privilege to park wherever he wants. (It doesn't help that the city of Boulder generally lets him get away with it.)

He filled me in on his call from Rick on Sunday morning my time, and the plan for Rick to stay there to help as much as he could while Dad flew over immediately to help me here. He had arrived last night at Invercargill and driven up from there. We reached his car, a Mercedes rental in a nice raisin color. I had a hard time getting in because it was so incongruent with the subsistence existence I had been living.

He drove as close to the tent as we could and then hiked up and carried everything down to the car. We drove back to Invercargill, a drive of 180 kilometers (about one-and-a-half hours the way my dad drives). During the trip, I filled him in on everything, but mostly we talked about Mom. I told him how I wanted to let go of my anger about it. He said that he wanted that more than anything. We spent that ninety-three minutes getting reconnected to each other.

We arrived at the best hotel the city has to offer. It was wonderful. My dad likes to travel in style but almost never does. He must have chosen this hotel for me and I wasn't objecting. I could certainly use some pampering. It helps that a hotel like this usually is more discreet about its guests. I did not have to talk to or see anyone. We just went up to his (our) room. He had rented a suite that had a central meeting area with a kitchenette. It was nicely done with a burgundy motif and some seascapes on the wall. The chairs were the nice ones that you can sit at and work for hours without getting sore. The suite had two small bedrooms off to the side. They were not big but each fit a full-size bed. I looked at the bed longingly.

Many things did not sink in for some time. Things would be so much easier with Dad here. He would be able to function completely normally; after all, no one was looking for him. The name Prescott was common enough in this British land so as not to attract attention. Things were definitely looking up. I could feel this chapter of my life coming to an abrupt end.

When the door was closed and locked, Dad and I held each other some more. It was so good to have him here. I sat next to him and we spent a long time talking about our old wounds. We talked about how much we had missed the way it had been before Mom's death. I let him know how sorry I was for being so stubborn. I should have let go of my anger long before now. He talked about how much it had torn him up to be pulled in two directions by the two women he loved most. Regarding Mom's prognosis, he had chosen to be optimistic and hoped she would survive until the next school vacation. Then when she deteriorated so fast, he froze and couldn't act fast enough.

We both cried over Mom, but this time it was a healing cry. Neither one of us, of course, would ever forget her, and a place in our hearts would always remain unhealed, but we both felt we could now go on with our lives, with our relationship intact and maybe even stronger. Maybe I could even learn to let others into my heart and run the risk of losing them.

After my mother's death, I slipped into a prolonged persistent pattern of keeping everyone at a distance. As soon as someone started to get close, I would distance myself from them. It caused havoc with my love life. Typically, I would be attracted to someone, then when we would become emotionally closer, I would create a reason why I could not pursue the relationship. Unfortunately, this behavior spread to friends as well. The only exceptions were Dad and Rick — especially Rick.

"How long can you stay?" I asked.

He looked surprised, "Long enough to get you off this island. Rick and I came up with a plan."

"Leave? How can I possibly leave, I can't use my passport. They will be watching for that. They are also looking for me. They have circulated my picture..."

He waved my concerns aside, "Rick is a smart and conniving man and I am learning to like him much more. I have never been entirely comfortable with the kind of influence he had on you, but..."

"But what?" I blurted out defensively. I was ready to defend Rick even from my dad.

He smiled knowingly, "But I should have been more concerned about what terrible influence you were having on him; the poor sod." He smiled wickedly.

I realized he was pulling my hair (or is it leg, I can never remember which culture pulls which part). I laughed and punched him in the arm. "Now cut that out!" I demanded. "I have enough problems without you two yahoos ganging up on me."

"Yes, ma'am, right away, ma'am," he said through his laughter.

I knew I needed to hear their plan despite my unwillingness to leave the island. "Tell me all about it."

"What about?" he asked.

"The plan, Dad, whatever the two of you cooked up while I was fighting off the dragons here," I said petulantly.

"Ah, yes, the ultimate plan. Would you like to go to dinner and discuss it?" I looked at him with my mouth hanging open. He clearly was not totally up to speed with my circumstances. I decided to give him slack since he had not personally been successfully avoiding an entire police force plus a crazy company executive for four-and-a-half consecutive days.

I placed my hand gently on his shoulder, "Time to talk about the facts of life." He flushed a bit. I think more from surprise than from the implied subject.

"Now, Yolanda, I don't think that..."

I interrupted with a forceful but caring tone. "They are still looking for me and they will lock me up if they find me. I don't want to be locked up. You can roam about freely, but every time I show my face, or I hear steps or see a police officer my heart races, my stomach churns, my muscles tighten and my entire body instinctively gets ready to flee and hide..."

He stopped my lecture by coming over and hugging me. "I am so sorry, Yolanda; please forgive your thoughtless old dad. Of course you are right and we can't go out; we will order room service. Anything you want, the sky's the limit."

I looked at him and saw the tears forming. "Since you put it that way, I am game. Just order me two of whatever is the most expensive thing on the menu." He knew I was kidding, of course, but it broke the tension and we were once again able to relax.

Despite his protests, I ordered the chopped sirloin. I told him it was my favorite food and when done right, it is superior to the lobster he was having. I have always hated fighting with my food. Why people get something and then have to wrestle with metal tools just to carve it into bite-sized pieces is truly beyond my comprehension. I suppose it goes back to our hunting/gathering roots when wrestling with our food was probably commonplace. I can see Joe and Jane Caveperson around the fire tugging and pulling at whatever their dinner was that night. Between fur, hide, scales, bones and feathers, they probably spent most of their dinnertime finding the edible parts. Not me, I firmly believe that if I am going to take the time to eat, then it should not require my having to separate it from inedible parts.

The hotel chef was exceptional and my steak was exactly medium rare just as requested with a thick creamy mushroom sauce that I mopped up with the whole wheat bread. A big slab of cheesecake finished the meal. Four days of catching whatever cold stale meals I could, whenever I could, had increased my appreciation for food in general and well-cooked food in particular. Dad concurred that the chef had true talent. Apparently, his lobster, like my steak, had been perfectly prepared.

The plan that Rick and Dad cooked up was ingenious. It was predicated on the concept of misdirection; a concept with which by now I was familiar. They, of course, had somehow managed to obtain a fake passport. (It can't be legal and I still cannot get over my dad being part of something illegal.) It had an age of thirty-eight, which hopefully would be outside the age range for which they were looking. However, for it to work, I would have to improve my disguise by an order of magnitude. I would have to cut my hair and change the color more. He brought glasses that had clear glass in them. This would change my appearance without distorting my eyesight. I would need new clothes; they wanted me to wear something that would make a peacock blush, something very Hawaiian.

The coup de grace was the casting material Dad brought with him. They planned to put me in a walking cast. They also planned to put some highly conspicuous bandaging about my head. I would then wear a big hat to hide the bandages. The story would be that I had been involved in a car accident and suffered a broken leg and severe facial burns. He was even going to go as far as placing poison ivy extract on some exposed parts since if applied right they could pass for second-degree burns.

I sat horrified when he was finished. They fully intended to go through with it. We were past the fun and games, and they actually intended to go through with this. "Dad, this is illegal — the fake passport is illegal in both countries."

"Yes, Yolanda, we are acutely aware of that, now what is the problem?" I just looked at him in amazement for the longest time.

"Nothing, it is a wonderful plan; I suppose we would be halfway to Hawaii before they even catch on."

"Maybe not even then or indeed ever. First of all, we are not going to tell them, and second, we will use your genuine passport to enter the States."

"How? I don't have it." He looked at me and smiled.

"Not to worry, my sweet daughter, Rick managed to get a duplicate claiming you lost yours. He FedEx'd it and it should arrive tomorrow or Friday at the latest."

"You guys, I can't believe the two of you and I have never in my life seen you so conniving."

Dad suddenly looked sheepish. "Well, Yolanda, you have never seen me deal with insurance companies, and you certainly have not needed my help like this before."

It was enough for one day. I kissed him goodnight and went to shower and crash. To my amazement and delight, I found the dresser and closet full of new clothes, shoes and accessories. They were definitely not my style but they were my size. Dad had been a busy man.

CHAPTER NINETEEN

SURPRISE PACKAGE

Despite the wonderful day and the improved future outlook, I slept fitfully. In my dream, I kept trying to find something, but strangers continued getting in the way. I awoke un-rested, irritable and not suitable for human company (in fact, I didn't think a dog would want me this way). When this happens, I have learned to immediately, without uttering a word, start writing. It is just stream-of-consciousness writing and allows the right brain to discharge itself of all the nasty stuff clogged up in there. That is why it's important not to speak since that is a left-brain function and will interfere with the exercise.

It usually works; after one page of writing, the scribbling starts making sense and by the end of the second page, I usually start writing things of which I wasn't aware I was feeling. By the end of the third page, whatever is going on inside of me is at least identified. It certainly does not solve my problems, but knowing what's gnawing at me is a big step. I then have to take responsibility for things, and on this particular day, my job was not going to be easy.

I made coffee and tried to plan what I would say to Dad and Rick. Rick would be the easier one since he was eight thousand miles away. (He was back home, right?) It had not occurred to ask if Rick was also on his way. After reflection, that would not make sense, and their plan did not need him here. Dad would be much more difficult; he simply would not understand.

The beep from the coffee maker indicated that the life-restoring coffee was ready, which brought me back to the present. With the very first sip, I relaxed and enjoyed the rather subtle taste of the Colombian Supremo Dad bought for me. It was the first time in many years I had gone four days without coffee. That I actually survived the experience is attributed solely to my supreme fortitude and fabulous strength of character. You may not believe me but at no point in the last four days had I seriously considered turning myself in for a cup of steaming Columbian (really).

By the time Dad was up, my radical plan was finished. It would be best to be direct and honest with him. This was decidedly a novel approach for me and I was queasy with the anticipation.

"Hi, Yolanda, did you sleep well?" Dad was alert and energetic this morning. "As far as I am concerned, I haven't slept this well in a long time. I feel great."

"No, Dad, I had a fitful night. Too many things on my mind." He stopped in the middle of pouring his coffee (my love of the stuff is from him) and looked me over carefully.

"Yes, that is evident, you also have a look I haven't seen since high school. Let's see, don't tell me." He finished making his coffee while he tried to recall something (he could always read right through me). "I have it, this is the look when you want to ask me something that you don't think I will approve of," he said triumphantly. "How close am I?" he said as he kissed my head and sat down next to me.

"Very close as usual, Dad. However, in this case, I am not asking for something but telling you something you won't like."

That certainly captured his attention. Except for the cup of coffee, it was entirely focused on me. "I certainly hope it is not as bad as the time you told me about your alcohol problem. How I did not notice that still escapes me...but that is not relevant here, is it? I guess I am as ready as is possible, shoot." With this, he brought his cup up to his lips but did not take his eyes off me for a second. He was going to listen to me and he was also going to evaluate how I told it. Sometimes he could act like a grand inquisitor. Luckily, not this time.

"It's that I can't go through with your plan. It's a great plan, and it took a lot of effort and thought but I can't go through with it."

"I don't think there is anything to be scared of, t..."

"No, that's not the problem. It's that running away won't work for me. I have to face this situation and clear this up. I don't want this to follow me back home, to worry about the next phone call and be afraid of opening my mail, or of thinking that every knock on the door is the police ready to extradite me. I can't live that way and most certainly cannot maintain my sobriety that way." Wow, I had gotten it all out in one breath and felt relieved. I looked up at him and set myself to defend my position.

"I hear you, Yolanda, and am certainly not happy with what you say, but that does not mean I am unhappy with you." He paused to sip and think, "In fact, what you say is well thought out and has a lot of merit; a lot of merit. I should have thought of that myself and will not make this anymore difficult than it is. I know that you realize better than I the dangers and risks involved. That you still choose this difficult road is a strong statement about your character. It makes me proud to be your father." With that, he put his coffee cup down and held my hand between his.

"You're kidding? That's all? I worked myself up for nothing? I was ready with all kinds of arguments, examples of you doing the same thing, and that's it?"

"Don't sound so disappointed, Yolanda, if it makes you feel better I can make a fuss," he said this with a grin. After all these years, I still could not figure him out.

"Yolanda, you are a grown woman. That you let me into your world and allow me to help is a gift I will not ignore, BUT...you are the one that has to live with the consequences of your decisions. It is not my place, as much as I might like to at times, to take those decisions away from you...or make them harder than they have to be."

I remained quiet for some time, just sipping my coffee and relishing the moment. We had come a long way. He was telling me that I was out of the nest and could come home to visit, but had to live my own life, not his. It was my turn to choose what path I would go down. When I looked back on my life, for good or for bad, I would know that I hadn't deferred the choices to others.

"And when, dear child, have I ever done anything remotely similar to this?" he asked with a touch of defiance.

I looked him straight in the eye and with a smile told him, "When the AIDS epidemic broke out in the mid-eighties, we weren't sure how it was spread. Yet you remained adamant that you had to continue treating your patients regardless of their disease. Mom was not happy with your decision."

Dad sipped his coffee to give himself some time to think this over, "I didn't even think you were paying any attention back then. You continue to surprise me, Yolanda; pleasantly though. And yes, you are right, it was the same thing."

He added, "Since we are going to stay here, can I play too? I want to help you, if you don't mind."

Tears welled up, "I can't see how it would put you in any danger, and it would make things so much easier for me."

He smiled at me, "Just tell me what you need and it will be done. I will start saluting you while we are on this mission. Maybe even get a trench coat and a fedora."

"Daddy, now cut that out; this is serious stuff."

"Yes, Mon Capitan, your wish is my command." He faked a salute in my direction.

He was enjoying himself immensely. I took this opportunity to get myself ready. At times like this, I wonder why Mom ever married him. He just refuses to grow up.

When I was ready and in my new clothes, I felt great and showed off for Dad. He made all of the necessary noises of approval that I needed. "So do you have a plan? Or do we need to come up with one?"

This was his subtle way of getting me back on track. "First we should meet with Chief Inspector Yves of the Christchurch Police Department," I said.

"You mean JP, of course," Dad said.

I gasped. "What hasn't Rick told you?"

"I wouldn't know, but would suspect not much. Rick and I developed a rapport, you know. Nice guy, too bad he is so much older than..."

"Dad, stop digressing, we have serious work here." We reviewed our options and determined which ones would allow us any measure of control or input into the process. We decided that we could trust JP and that by meeting we could pool our information and perhaps resources. Dad would make the first contact and we would let JP decide where to meet.

We decided that Dad should use the satellite phone I had recently bought. He would not be at the hotel but walking about town while he talked to him. We felt reasonably secure with that arrangement. I hadn't been on my powerbook for two hours when Dad came back with all of it arranged. He said JP was excited about the idea and had implied there were many forces at play but he wouldn't say more on the phone because he was not sure that his phone was not being monitored.

The problem with security is that there is never enough. The only true security is not to have a secret at all. The moment anyone has something they need to keep secret but still allow access to select people, then there is a security problem. Sure, IT guys can erect all kinds of barriers (even call them firewalls for all the good it will do you) to either keep out the riff-raff or at to least catch them when they enter. You can even catch the brilliant ones that want to be caught.

You have seen them in the papers; they are more interested in the publicity than anything else. They give themselves a code name, they drop hints and eventually someone like me will hunt them down and their pictures will be in the paper. More importantly, among hacker circles their names will attain the status of master hacker.

"Did you hear that so and so got into such and such computer?"

"I heard they would never have known it if he hadn't left clues all over the place," and so on.

The hackers that security people rightly fear are the rest of us. We are the ones that have a significant amount of skill and use every bit of it to keep our intrusion from even being detected. There is no way for them even to know how big a problem this is. Of the many computers I have 'entered,' I would say that the vast majority do not even know I was there (or if they are beyond stupid, that it is even possible). Of the rest, the ones that know someone had their way with their data; if I did my job right, they won't be entirely sure what was done and certainly not who did it or how it was done.

To keep out someone like me (I'll try not to be unduly modest or too full of myself) is a real challenge. I am pretty sure that if pushed, I could probably make it so frustrating to obtain access that someone like me would look elsewhere. But even for me, that would be a significant endeavor. Particularly since passwords are so easy to find. The one good thing is that up to this point, the people who have these skills are either self-destructive (see above) or are reasonably socialized and thus do not cause any significant harm. With all these thoughts of security, I was ready to meet JP one more time.

The meeting was set for tonight. We had an address in the south part of the city where he would show up by about seven. This would allow us to stake it out and make sure no one was going to crash the party. I looked forward to seeing him again, although it was not entirely clear why. I was sorry that Michele would not be there.

What alarmed us was that JP mentioned he was no longer in charge of the investigation. They had put someone more 'tame' in charge. He had given my father a strict warning not to get caught. It would be outside his ability to help us. This revelation came as a severe blow. Being holed up in this luxury hotel, I had relaxed for the last twenty hours. It was hard to be awakened to the reality that nothing in fact had changed. The wolves were still after me, hot as ever and just as intent on doing me harm.

While waiting for the appointed time, I paced around the hotel room probably the way a tiger paces in captivity, finally admitting to myself that I was not as sanguine to clear this mess up as I had felt when we were in the planning stage. The escape plan started looking better and better — at least the anxiety would be over. I tried writing down my apprehensions and tried repeating the serenity prayer ad nauseam. I tried nearly everything but was desperate not to return to my previous existence of looking over my shoulder every minute; of expecting the other shoe to drop at any second; of worrying that something had been overlooked, or I made a mistake somewhere and right now at this moment in time the forces of darkness were gathering themselves to overwhelm and destroy me. It was clearly beyond Dad's ability to help me.

I finally broke down and called my sponsor. Her name is Sallie and if wisdom is any guide, she must be a thousand years old. Physically, she looks a young seventy. I heard her tell her own story many times, before mustering up the courage to ask her to be my sponsor. Her only requirement had been that I work hard at my sobriety. She did not have the time to waste on people that weren't even trying. It was early evening when I called and although she wasn't quite done with her dinner of huevos con chorizo, she heard the urgency in my voice and deduced the importance of the call.

I summarized my dilemma, not needing to tell her the gory details. She was understanding and expressed real concern for all I had already been through. After a moment of reflection, she answered my concerns with just one question. It wasn't what I wanted to hear, but knew immediately that she was right. I had hoped she would say that it would be OK to leave, that the situation was out of control and that our higher power did not expect me to slay these dragons. What I received instead was a question to answer. I had already known the answer to it. The challenge was in accepting the answer.

The question was, "What amount of effort and risk is your continued sobriety worth?"

I filled Dad in on Sallie's comments and her question. He has come to several of my meetings and he always left wondering what they are all about. Like most people not in the program, he doesn't get it. Despite this, he tries to understand and is supportive of the entire process. He felt that Sallie had only reiterated what I told him that morning. I explained that she placed enough additional emphasis on the crucial issue so that I could feel its importance despite the fears that were currently paralyzing me.

We spent the afternoon going over what were facts and what was conjecture. We also tried to come up with a timeline of all of the events to make it easier to track the characters. Some of them like Marc hardly entered at all and others like

Donovan entered late but had prominent roles. After several hours, we realized that we knew a lot but still had some key pieces missing. The big picture was still tantalizingly out of reach. Both of us felt strongly that the murder in my room, (man, did Dad grill me on that. Was I OK? Did it give me nightmares? How was my wrist healing? Yada, yada, yada) had to be connected but it wasn't obvious how. It just seemed such an astonishing coincidence that two murders within three days both involving yours truly could be completely separate and unrelated events. The involvement of the government officials was also a puzzler. Were they just dupes? Was Donovan deceiving them into chasing me all over New Zealand?

We gave up trying to make sense out of it and played chess for a while. Dad is an avid player and never goes anywhere without a board. If he finds himself having to wait, he will recreate the moves of some championship. Today we played speed chess. He gave me ten minutes to his five. With this advantage, I could almost beat him. A couple of times I scared him, but he knows the game too well for me to fool him. When I would get ahead, he would make several confusing moves that would require me to take my time, and then he would nail me. In speed chess, it is important to remember that your opponent is able to plan during the time you yourself are using. So the ten minutes I had gave him a lot of time to plan his moves. Only by moving extremely fast myself could I force him to react rather than plan, but I just wasn't up to that amount of concentration. After losing the sixth game, it was time to go and look the site over.

It was a nice part of town — nice, hell, it was opulent. There were large estates with well-cared-for lawns and large but distant houses. Most had detached garages and what we took to be servants' quarters. We drove by the address and we both gaped. It couldn't be right. If it wasn't the grandest of all the houses on that street it was a close second. There were large iron gates with a crest of some sort. A long windy road led to what could only be called a mansion. The grounds were wonderfully creative. They were filled with unique and distinct specimen tress and flowers. It was not your typical garden. This required someone with taste and the self-assurance to deviate from the normal and expected. What had caused both Dad and I to do a double take was the large sign on the gates with the family name on it. It was large and clear, no possibility of confusion. Four letters that would shake me to my core: 'YVES.'

We drove past and around for a while before finding a place to stop and talk it over. It just did not make sense. What was a police detective doing with a place like this? If it wasn't his place (an uncle perhaps?) why was the meeting here? Had he asked them to leave for the evening because he had a highly secret and confidential meeting? And what of the dozen or more servants that must inhabit the place? This was not boding well.

We decided that I would hold onto my portable phone while Dad went in alone. If all was well, he would call and not use the word 'OK.' If he did use it, I was on my own again and I should promptly get lost. To facilitate this possibility, we went back and I put everything I might need in my backpack. It took extra time, but by working together, Dad and I were bonding even closer.

We needn't have bothered. Dad called me almost immediately after entering and everything was on the up and up. The servants were in their quarters in another building and JP was not the only one there; Michele was also there. I was confident that he would not have brought his daughter if this were some sort of trap.

When I first laid eyes on JP, it shook me to see how tired he was. It would seem he'd slept less than me.

"Hi, JP," and I went over to hug him.

"Hello, Yolanda, good to see you are well. You've led us on a merry chase if I may say so."

"Thank you, I will take that as a compliment. There was a tremendous amount of help from the person that chose the picture for the paper. Where in the world did you get that?"

JP laughed, even so it was muted. "You liked that, did you? Michele found it somewhere in the newspapers in the US. She is a bright lass that one."

I quickly changed topics; I did not want to go there. "How is Michele? I missed her."

"You can ask her yourself, she is upstairs unpacking." I looked up and around. This place was enormous. How did they find each other in this place?

"Really?" I asked with anticipation.

He showed me where her room was. We spent the best part of an hour getting reconnected. It was as if the last four days had not intervened. We caught up with events and talked girl talk. We then went downstairs and joined the men.

JP had brought dinner in the form of Chinese takeout. We used paper plates and basically ate just like we would have at home. The only difference was the real crystal candelabra, the fifteen-foot real mahogany table and the priceless works of art on the wall.

"A detective must make more money here than in the

States," I said without looking up. I knew Dad was giving me his look. He hates it when I embarrass him.

It was Michele that answered. "Daddy inherited all this from Gramps. It is much too pretentious, but it has so much family history that we can't sell it. Mom used to say that it cost more to keep it up than it was worth."

JP looked up and added, "You know the story, one of my ancestors happened to be already here when the gold was found. He realized that the real killing was in selling stuff to the miners and Yves Supplies Inc. was born; it made him fabulously wealthy.

Since then, the Yves men have had a talent for turning money into even more money. I just chose the right parents."

Even my dad snickered. "But why are you a police detective?" I queried.

"Yolanda, being born into this kind of wealth is not the picnic it might seem. There are expectations and responsibilities beyond your imagination. When my time came to rebel, becoming a police officer was about as far as possible from my planned life. My dad almost disowned me over it. I was more surprised than he, when it turned out that I liked it and also had a tremendous aptitude for the job."

"I told you he was the best detective in the island," Michele interjected.

JP ignored the remark, "So here I am, completely exposed. Do you still trust me?"

"More than ever, JP, more than you will ever know," I said with moist eyes.

We cleared the table and convened in one of the many rooms. He called it the library, or was it the study? It could also have been the smoking room but I did not see any ashtrays or cigars. I insisted that Michele stay with us throughout the discussions. She had already contributed significantly and deserved to be in on it. JP acquiesced and the two of us sat next to each other on the couch.

We proceeded to compare notes and attempt to put it all together. When JP had left me on Fox Peak, he checked in with his answering service and found out that indeed his immediate superior wanted him immediately. The story he received was what we suspected. I had been seen with the victim just before she was found dead (according to Donovan). I had then run away and was their prime suspect. This was a high-profile case because it was of personal importance to several cabinet members.

He had just barely had enough time to get my computer out of my room, put a message on it (thanks to Michele), and send it to me — prior to being inundated by the publicity. No one wanted to listen to him. They all wanted to sensationalize the story. There were leaks from the cabinet most of which were untrue. They were clearly trying to pin this on me without bothering to find out anything.

This injustice had made JP furious and he started digging. Eventually, he found it was the foreign secretary that was the driving force behind this. JP became convinced that if I were caught, the truth might never come out. They would have their scapegoat. Therefore, he came up with the old photo.

To my chagrin, he suspected right away that I had not gone to Dunedin. He felt that yours truly was far too clever to leave such a glaring trail. However, he encouraged their speculation and placed most of his resources where he thought I wasn't. It was not until Monday that he realized my hiding hole had to be in Queenstown. He then sent one of his most trusted men (Officer Bentley as it turned out) to search for the hearse in all of the likely places. He found it Tuesday. He had a key and drove it to the impound lot where it sits today.

I must have looked disappointed because he quickly added what a remarkable job of disappearing it was. He still did not know how I avoided detection or where I'd stayed during any part of the four days. When I told him, he looked at me the way one might look at a shark, full of suspicion.

Then he looked at my father and asked, "Did you raise a spy?"

Dad said, "Don't look at me, I am as amazed as you are."

"Now cut it out, you two, a gal has to do what a gal has to do, and back then I had to disappear."

"And what a talent you seem to have for that," JP said.

He went back to his story. He started suspecting that Donovan was the murderer about the same time I did. By then, Donovan had disappeared and even now they were still looking for him.

The big stroke of luck had been the story regarding this big shot's prior divorce not being final. It took most of the heat off the investigation and it certainly distracted Mr. Big Shot. Unfortunately, his immediate superior had not been happy with JP's continuing efforts at finding out the real story. They wanted someone just to do as he was told. Therefore, they had taken the investigation out of his hands and assigned it to his deputy, a much more subservient person who was not in the position to make any waves.

JP had been trying to find me when Dad called him. He suspected they were desperately trying to cover up a big scandal. He wasn't sure who was involved or what it was about and he was frustrated that he didn't have anyone in power he could trust with this. He heard rumors that there might be a huge platinum find in the mountains of the Cook National Park and that several companies were bidding for the rights. Since this would be a sensitive ecological issue, they might be trying to make the deal before the press got wind of it and public opinion crushed it.

Dad said that it was hard to reconcile two murders with the mineral rights to a national park. To him it seemed out of proportion for the cabinet members, it just wasn't big enough for them to go through all of this trouble.

"Unless there are significant kickbacks," I added. Always a cynic in the crowd.

We discussed it into the evening before JP brought up his plan to ferret out the truth. He wanted me to be the goat. Like the one they put in a field to catch a lion. The kind that half the time gets eaten before they catch the lion (if they catch the lion). To my surprise, I was not all that upset by the idea. But boy was Dad upset.

"I won't let you do that to my daughter! She is not a pawn that you can move willy nilly and risk so that you can find out what you want." He ranted and stomped around for a while. He said that there had to be another way. Eventually, we calmed him down. I would at no point be in any danger. We needed to catch Donovan and get him to squeal. JP checked out Donovan's past and found what his name and background actually were. JP felt that Donovan would be easy to pressure. He was not the kind of guy to take the entire fall by himself.

The trap went as follows: a different location for me would

be given to several of the likely accomplices. They would also be told that I was ready to spill everything that I knew about Donovan's involvement and that the preliminary take on my testimony was that it placed Donovan at the scene of the crime with the strength to carry out the murder.

I had also apparently overheard some of the conversation in the cabin prior to being seen. This should get their attention. It would force them to try to intervene prior to my deposition. We could then wait to see which location received any action and if lucky, follow the person back to their hideout. We would then know who leaked the location and could pressure him to squeal in order to save himself.

JP was well liked and well connected. He had several detectives willing to stake out the different locations on their free time. All in all, it seemed a pretty safe plan. Although I did not have to be at those locations, I might have to show my face so that they would believe I had been caught. The only part left to work out was how to get the various locations to the various cabinet members in a believable manner.

While we were brainstorming, there was a knock at the front door. We all froze and stopped talking. We were expecting no one. The gate had been locked behind us. This could not be anything but bad news. I quickly put on my shoes and kissed Michele's head before dashing upstairs to her room. On my way there, I saw the flashing lights of several police cars through the windows in the front of the house. My mind became extremely clear, much in the way that most people report when confronted with a crisis. People tend to fall apart later, after the danger has passed.

Earlier while I talked to Michele in her room, I noticed that her window had a tree nearby. I'd even remarked that someone reasonably agile could get out that way. She apparently had done just that — several times. It was my turn and couldn't worry that I had nothing with me, no money, no phone, no coat. Just what I wore. Reaching the limb was easily accomplished. The climb down would have been easy in daylight. In the dark, it took a little longer but I had no difficulty. I landed on my feet ready to run when a strong person grabbed my arm and put a hand across my mouth.

"I have been waiting a long time for you." It was Donovan.

CHAPTER TWENTY

TRAPPED

He was far too strong to fight him, and anyway the shock of seeing him was too much for the necessary effort. He half led me, half dragged me to the front courtyard. He stayed out of sight of the front door and to my dismay, he did not take me to the police cars. Instead, we skirted them and he forced me into what initially looked to be an unmarked car. I became even more alarmed (if such a thing were possible) when I realized it was actually a rental. He handcuffed my hands behind me and bound my feet with tape. I wasn't going anywhere and was in the back seat trying to remain calm and focus on the situation. He jumped into the driver's side and took off. My entire focus for the past days had been on avoiding the police and he had taken me so suddenly that it had not occurred to me to yell for help. Now I was in much deeper trouble than being in a New Zealand jail with someone like Louise as a cellmate.

Donovan started jabbering about how much trouble I'd

caused him (my heart bled for him); how he would make me pay, and now that I was neutralized how he was going to straighten everything out.

He appeared to be talking to himself more than to me. He was completely unaware that the cat was pretty much out of the bag and that he could not expect to keep everything hidden for much longer. As we say in the program, he was navigating the longest river in the world: 'The Nile' (denial). He just wasn't in touch with any reality whatsoever.

Whatever it was he was involved with, it had pushed him over the edge into madness. For me this was not good news. He might do anything; it wouldn't even have to make sense. I was in deep kimchi indeed.

We had a saying at Kalamazoo College, which we attributed to Nietzsche: "Beware: when you look over the edge into the abyss — the abyss looks back." Boy was the abyss looking back at me now. I tried to involve him in conversation, anything at all, but he was totally lost in himself. I began taking note of where he was taking me. He didn't seem to care that I could tell we were going to Dunedin (or perhaps passing it on the way to Christchurch). An hour later, Donovan turned north toward a town named Momona and just past the town turned into a lane that led to what looked like a farmhouse.

"We're home," he said in a mocking tone and then proceeded to laugh hysterically.

After freeing my legs, he shoved me inside. There was at least one other person in the house but I did not get a good look at him. All I saw was how disheveled the house was. I could smell stale cigarette smoke (I guess I needn't worry about second-hand smoke at this point). It was the kind of mess men make when they are holed up for several days without anyone to clean after them.

He led me down to the cellar. There was a heavy door that had not only a lock on the handle but a recently placed sliding dead bolt on it. It was firmly anchored from what I could see. He changed the handcuffs from behind my back to in front and pushed me in. I will never know why he did this kindness, maybe out of habit or maybe without even thinking. Or maybe he felt it would never matter; for whatever reason, I was grateful (and would be even more grateful later, much to his dismay).

The room was dark, damp and smelled of rodents. There was only the light of an outside floodlight shining through a barred window. I stumbled along until I found a place to sit. That is when I started to fall apart emotionally.

"Who's there?" I heard in a whisper.

I screamed, jumped up, and nearly fell down; it isn't easy to retain one's balance with both hands secured in front of you. I was not alone.

"Calm down, lady, I am in no position to hurt you. If the light was on you could see that I am somewhat inconvenienced." His words plus his relaxed tone calmed me down and regained a thread of control.

"My name is Yolanda, what is yours?" My voice came out in a high-pitched screech that revealed the great strain I was under and made my own skin tingle. There was a troubling silence and I began looking for some sort of light. It did not take me long to find a string dangling from the ceiling, the kind that usually is connected to a bare bulb.

Before pulling it, he said, "So they finally caught you. You sure gave them a big scare. I hoped they would have a stroke because of you. My name is Marc Roberts."

He said his name just as I pulled the string and the light showed me his face. I stood there paralyzed, realizing the person in front of me had killed the man in my bed.

I wanted desperately to run from him, to run far and fast so that he could not hurt me. It did not take much time to realize that not only was it impractical, but it was not necessary. Marc had a calm expression. This was hard to notice, however, because of all the swelling and bruising he had over his face, arms...actually, everywhere I could see. Marc looked to be my height with an unremarkable build, plain features that would be easy to forget and hard to describe. His clothes had spots of clotted oxidized blood covering them. It did not take a medical degree to know he had recently suffered severely.

Marc propped himself up on his cot to see me better. It was evident that it cost him dearly to move and I must have reacted to his pain.

"Oh, it's not so bad, just getting to be a wimp in my old age." He looked only about forty-five.

"How did you..." I didn't know how to ask him how he became so bruised. I didn't want to know.

"Our friends upstairs decided to try some persuasion on me. It worked pretty well. I told them anything and everything they wanted to hear except..." He paused, looking at me closely.

"Except what?" I wanted to know what in the world was so important to merit such torture.

"Except why you were spying on them and where you were. They wanted you badly. And the only reason I didn't tell them that was because I bloody well did not know."

This revelation caught me off guard. To be the one responsible for this kind of physical damage shook me and opened several doors to my soul that up to now had managed to keep closed. My only response was, "I'm so sorry."

There was a laundry tub with a faucet and some rags. I went over and found a small Tupperware container and started to clean him up. He did not protest. I suspected that he had been alone for a long time and appreciated the company of someone that wasn't trying to hurt him.

We chatted about unimportant things while we scoped each other out. I wanted to know if he would rat on me (the second he had a chance) in exchange for better treatment. I suspect he wanted to know if I was going to fall apart when things started getting rough. In fact, I wanted to know the same thing about myself.

I discovered Marc was not the gruff, uncaring person he pretended to be. There was a family back home in Australia with small children. He started his family late in life and that remained his only real regret (I could think of others). He remarked how I did not look much like the picture in the paper. I had no trouble agreeing with that, since it was so obvious.

I usually don't open up to strangers, but this was not 'usually' and it felt good to talk and connect with someone. It kept the paralyzing fear at bay; the drenching, soul-destroying, agonizing fear that was now sniffing at the periphery of my life.

"I was arrested a few years back and they had some pictures in the local rag. That was one of them." He hid his surprise well (whether it was at the news or that I shared it

232

with him, I will never know).

"My, my, my, are you ever a constant source of inspiration; please, dear Yolanda, tell me more."

I told him about how the police picked me up for a DWI and being the only daughter of a respected doctor in the town, and because the town is not a huge metropolis, my picture made the news. Never in my wildest dreams would I ever have believed I would someday be grateful that picture was in the public domain. It just goes to show how difficult it is to know how things will eventually turn out. This was a thought I hung onto for dear life.

It was my turn to ask questions. "What is this all about? What is all the fuss? I take a bloody G---D---holiday for the first time in years and the entire world goes nuts." He was startled at my intensity and looked at me curiously; finally, he shook his head chuckling.

"You mean you don't know? You are not in on it? You aren't with The Company?"

"In on what? One minute I am walking along a lakeshore, the next I am the most wanted woman on this bloody island… what company?"

He abruptly sat up, evidently not as badly hurt as he let on. Although he couldn't be feeling in top form with all of the damage I had seen, there were no obvious disabling injuries.

"I think we should have a talk, and we had better make it quick. Why don't you summarize your last week for me. Start the morning you woke up with Peter dead in your bed. 'The company,' by the way, refers to my former employer, the CIA."

He said it so matter of fact that I didn't initially realize he had tacitly admitted to being his murderer, as well as a spy.

"Don't worry about Mr. Peter Osbourne, he was a world-class jerk and won't be bothering you anymore. I'll explain when we have time."

I felt the urgency communicated and I did as asked. When I reached the part where I saw Donovan at the lake, Marc took notice and made me go over it in minute detail.

"I did not know that you had seen those blokes together. No wonder they wanted to shut you up." He chuckled at the way I had toyed with Donovan. "Even though he took out his anger on me, it is a great satisfaction to know you put that strutting peacock in his place."

Marc did not interrupt again until I related my series of hiding places in Queenstown. He was professionally interested in how I managed to evade capture and found places to stay. He liked the church the best but was pleased with the entire escapade.

"Are you sure you aren't with the company? I guess you wouldn't tell me if you were. It doesn't matter. You are in much deeper trouble than you can imagine."

This disturbed me. "You are making me nervous since I have a very creative imagination."

"It's OK, they won't try anything for a little while. They are just buying time.

"What will they eventually do?"

"Well, that depends on whether anyone comes over and reigns in that Mr. Donovan. You know what happened to his last minder, right?"

"You mean Tracy?" I said.

"God damn, how in the world did you find out her name? Even we had a hard time and we knew where to look."

I ignored his question, "It is your turn to start making

sense of this for me. I am tired of being in the dark while everyone is either chasing me or kidnapping me or threatening to kill me." It came out with far more anger than I intended. He did one of his, by now familiar, double takes and smiled.

"I suppose you should know, since it has surely changed your life a mite."

"Bloody right it has," I added.

He proceeded to disclose what 'all this' was about. His style of talking was circuitous. He would jump around, digressing every time he thought of something interesting. It took a good deal of patience and restraint to let him tell it his way.

As Dad likes to say, "You can't hurry a person telling a story about themselves, you can only slow them down. Believe me, I have tried getting my patients to tell me a two-minute story in two minutes instead of the ten they are intent on, though all I ever have managed to do is to turn it into a fifteen-minute story and then I don't even get all of it because I have upset their train of thought too much."

So I sat back with my hands interlaced behind my head trying to make myself as comfortable as possible while actively avoiding intrusive thoughts regarding my current predicament.

CHAPTER TWENTY-ONE

ANSWERS

His story without the digressions is as follows: Approximately three years ago (about the time my mother died), a mining geologist was vacationing on the Cook Islands (a group of small islands that are politically part of New Zealand but at least twelve hundred miles to the northeast, mostly populated by natives that eke out a subsistence living). He liked to rock climb and he noticed that the rock layers on that particular slope did not conform to expected island formation and while looking further afield kept finding discrepancies. Eventually, he brought over more sophisticated equipment from his office to do soundings. (Typically, you set off an explosive charge at the surface and you analyze the sound echoes from deep inside the earth.) What he found startled him. He had found an oil-bearing rock formation in one of the most unlikely places on earth.

The geologist decided to skip his supervisor and report directly to the president of the company. He was and is still being richly rewarded. The quid pro quo was to keep it a secret. Next, the president of the local mining company involved Levox to get better equipment and better people. Once they saw the raw data, Levox jumped at the opportunity. Because they wanted to do this in total secrecy, it took them almost a year to complete the survey.

The results were so startling that no one would believe them for the longest time. It took a second independent analyst reviewing the data to convince them of what they had found — the largest oil field ever located. It even dwarfed the Saudi fields. In fact, to this day, for a lot of technical reasons, they cannot put a firm boundary on the size of the find. Not only that, but it's easily accessible and is not near other countries, plus it is in a politically stable part of the world. There would be no dispute regarding who owned it. This would transform New Zealand into a world-class country overnight. It would also change the balance of power away from the Middle East. With this much oil readily available, the price has nowhere to go but down. We could have a resetting to pre-1973 embargo oil prices. I could easily appreciate what an enormous find this was for the entire world's economic future (but perhaps not its ecological future) and the immeasurable riches waiting to be harvested. Then Soltex found out about the find.

"Now both Soltex and Levox want to be the company that rides this economic train into the next century?" I asked.

"Right, and for good reason, the company that does this would become the next Microsoft in size and scope. The losers become footnotes if they can even survive."

I chose to ignore that he was working for one of these two giants. "I still do not understand how the government is involved. One would think they are in the driver's seat and can just pick and choose."

"Except that it's not the New Zealand government that's meeting with them, it is certain members of the government who have their own agendas. The government is still unaware."

Suddenly, I had it, the veil had been lifted and I understood it all. Marc noticed and nodded, "That's right, lass, now you see the whole picture."

It was simple. The foreign secretary had ambitions to be the president. By setting the deal up by himself and getting the credit, he would be a shoe-in for the next election. He would not only be elected president, but of a country that would become one of the richest and most influential in the world for the foreseeable future. This must have been beyond his wildest fantasies. Everyone would be at his beck and call. All he had to do was deliver the oil exploitation rights to Levox who in turn would finance his run for office and give him glowing praise for his part in lifting New Zealand to its new status.

Another smaller reason for the secrecy was that New Zealanders are extremely sensitive about their environment. He did not want a public debate prior to a deal being set. The fact that any ecological damage would not affect the main islands would work in his favor: if only he could deliver a fait accompli. My seeing Levox and the foreign secretary together at Lake Tekapo threatened everyone's plans. Their paranoia led them to believe that it could not have been a coincidence and that I must be with the opposition.

I sat in the room with the weight of these revelations on my mind. "Wait a minute, this does not explain how or why your partner ended up dead in my bed." I glared at Marc, daring him to sidestep the question.

"I hoped you wouldn't ask but in your shoes I also would want to know," he said sadly.

"Please tell me he didn't miscount," I pleaded. He looked at me and shook his head, "He miscounted."

I swore and swore and kicked something before I could think again.

It was the most ridiculous stupid thing. I had started suspecting this when I found out that Donovan had the room beneath me. It percolated in my subconscious until just recently. Peter was supposed to climb into Donovan's balcony and search their room for any evidence relating to the oil find or the meeting or anything that Soltex could go public with. The idiot counted the balconies but did not adjust for the fact that here they count the ground floor as the first floor and he was one floor too high (my room). He was still searching my room when Marc climbed up to tell him of his mistake.

Unfortunately, I woke at that very moment. They then injected me immediately with the Versed to induce the amnesia. So far so good, but Peter noticed that I was still breathing. He had thought the drug would kill me and was angry that it would only knock me out. Peter insisted the project was too important to take any chances and the two of them argued at length. Eventually, Peter grabbed a pillow and went to put it over my face (I cringed as I heard this). Marc was sick of Peter, sick of the entire project and he now had a daughter of his own. Peter was a loose cannon with no morals whatsoever and furthermore had been the idiot who had entered the wrong room. Now an innocent bystander (yours truly) was going to pay the price and Peter would probably get away with it.

Marc told me that something inside just said no. He had been holding him back and blocking his access to me and suddenly let go of Peter. While I was being suffocated, Marc used the needle from the syringe to insert it precisely into the brainstem as taught years ago by the company. Peter never felt a thing; just slumped over on top of me (Yuck!). Much too heavy to carry out, Marc rolled him to the side and left. Then left an obvious trail to Australia to make things easier on me and came back to the island under a different identity.

I sat stunned and horrified and could have gone an entire lifetime without knowing this. When taken to the emergency room that morning, I'd noticed a small cut on the inside of my lower lip. Now I knew it was from Peter pressing the pillow against my face. I went limp with postponed anticipation of death and discovered I had to make an effort to breathe, as if a metaphorical pillow was being pressed against me.

I would not listen to anything Marc said. I told him to let me die and be done with it. The only thing needed now was to get plastered so all of this would go away. I could not face this reality; just couldn't handle it, I told myself. Why keep fighting anymore, I curled up into a ball and started to rock. If Marc said anything, I did not even hear it and also lost track of time and place. In a little while, my mom was coming for me. She was young and beautiful just like in her wedding pictures. She was smiling at me and trying to say something that I couldn't quite hear. Despite my attempts to get closer, her voice just would not reach me. When I finally reached her, she smiled and said, "I love you so much, my dear, take good care of yourself. I don't want to ever lose you."

I woke with a start. It had been so real that for a second I looked for her. When Marc noticed, he got up and was going to say something. Cutting him off, "So what do we need to do to get away from these bloody f@#$% assholes?"

He sat up, stunned, "I thought you had decided to curl up and die?" he said with an attitude.

I retorted with just as much attitude, "Been there, done that, seen the movie; now what can we do?"

He seemed energized by this. "For starters, we can get the hell out of here and see if we can raise the alarm."

"Do you think that is all it will take?" I said.

"Absolutely, after all that has happened, if anyone talks to the papers anywhere in the world and gives them the names of the people involved, it won't take them long to verify it. As soon as it is in print, they are all washed up. The trick is to get us out of here and over there."

My mind was so clear now, I could think faster and better than ever and after a minute, I looked straight at Marc and made him an offer, "If you can get us out of this house I can get us to Christchurch."

Another double take, "I don't know how you plan to do that, young lady, but you have demonstrated the ability to do whatever you set your mind to. It's a deal." With that, I shook hands with the man that had, unbeknownst to me, saved my life once and hopefully would do so one more time; we had sealed our bargain.

I discovered that he had been planning an escape for some time. His biggest hurdle had been that he was by himself and he could not accomplish a distraction by himself. Further, they knew him to be a resourceful ex-company man and they did not underestimate him one bit.

We had at our disposal a small array of utensils. Under his cot was a small wooden board he'd pried loose from a shelf. He had managed to place a nail at one end protruding in a menacing way and rub the other end against the wall so that it was easier to grab. It was a little over a foot long so it would only be good for close work.

Next was a small, nearly empty can of turpentine. I could only imagine what his plan was for this. We discussed many ideas but his main emphasis was discovering how squeamish I was and what amount of mayhem I would be capable of inflicting. The breakout would have to be my doing since they were watching him too closely. Marc was supremely confident he could provide the distraction. I would have to be explosively vicious, brutal and decisive. We would get no second chance.

There were only two of them. One of them would have a gun, the other would use his hands to change the cuffs around to our backs. It was my job to irreversibly disable the gun wielder (most likely Donovan) immediately. Then it would be the two of us against the remaining asshole. He would try to hold him still enough and long enough for me to incapacitate him. Their car was there for the taking and we would be on our merry way. We talked late into the night, still trying to uncover what my emotional capacity for inflicting pain onto a stranger was.

There had been a time during my drinking days when I might have been capable of just about anything. In one specific instance, I'd even fired a gun at someone I was mad at (another time, another story and missed anyway). However, since my sobriety started nine years ago, I have pointedly avoided violence, mayhem, and all associated behaviors.

I needed to focus my energy into my higher self, the one that could be called our conscience. The one that usually keeps me trudging on the road to happy destiny. As you are probably perfectly aware, most situations we find ourselves in are truly hopeless: your height, intelligence, parents, etc., are all predetermined. But fortunately they aren't usually all that serious. We learn to adapt and get on with our lives. In a reversal of this, our situation was not hopeless, Marc and I were making certain of that; but by dear God was it ever serious.

Don't get me wrong, I was not under any illusions regarding what was in store for us. However, that still does not enable one to give up a lifetime of socialization. It is hard to hit someone on the head with a nail wielding board hard enough to incapacitate. Some people are never able to overcome that early life training. Most people never have to find out.

I evaluated my life, my family, my goals and my values, and visualized myself doing a variety of things with those items and searched for what it felt like to do them. After what had seemed like hours, though Marc insisted was only twenty or thirty minutes, I was clear on what mayhem was within my capacity to accomplish. We used that information to plan for all the possible contingencies. We would have to be ready and would receive no warning. If we tried to lure them down with some trick, they would be vigilant and would allow no opportunity whatsoever to surprise them.

Before going to my cot for some well-earned rest, I bent over Marc and kissed him. Not too brazen but not too sisterly either. "Thanks — for the other night," continuing the habit of kissing strange men. I would have to seriously evaluate this new behavior of mine — some other time.

It was dark and I wondered what time it was. It felt like I had been in this stinking basement for hours. Marc was certain that it was only about one (AM) or so. He claimed that he could tell by the position of the moon. Trying hard not to giggle, I could just visualize it at the CIA training school: Moontime 101 followed by advanced graduate courses in telling moontime, such as Moontime 202: cloudy days and Moontime 303: moonless nights.

I made him laugh with this monologue. We went on to exchange whatever jokes we could remember, and it turned out to be a great way of relaxing. I liked it that he had a sense of humor; it helped me unwind and not think about how I was going to put this nail deep in someone's skull, in a very specific place in someone's head. Marc had shown me the vulnerable areas; the ones that have thin bone. I knew my anatomy pretty well and had no problem knowing where to aim. Being athletic, I did not doubt my ability to hit the target. Whether I would be able to go through with it, that was another matter entirely.

The only 'facility' was a large pail over in the corner. When I could hold it no longer, Marc turned the other way and I tried it on for size. Wouldn't you know it, halfway finished is when we heard footsteps coming down the stairs. I wet myself trying to stop midstream and hurried to my battle station (laying down in the most dispirited and least threatening manner manageable). The door opened quickly and both Donovan and the other guy were there.

It was the other guy who had the gun. He was a tiny person of about five feet seven with a thin but muscular frame; someone used to large doses of heavy physical work. Despite my size advantage, I doubted that I could take him in a 'fair' fight.

One of them smelled of beer, or maybe it was both. I could hope that they would be slowed down by it, not emboldened by it.

Donovan spoke, "Up and at 'em. We are going to have ourselves an important visitor in just a little while. We have to get you two looking respectable for him."

I made small jerky movements somewhat like what I imagined a scared rabbit would make. They didn't seem to be paying too much attention to me. They were clearly being careful with my partner, Marc. He was toying with them, complaining about how he hurt all over and he couldn't move well. He moved fast enough to keep them from getting too angry but slow enough to keep their attention off me.

I was in place, the ratty blanket covered the board and could grab the handle easily and quickly (hadn't we practiced dozens of times?). Finally, Marc got onto his feet and I tried not to tense up, but to remain slouched, just like he taught me. He had made a strong point that most people telegraph their intentions and anyone paying any attention can see it clearly. I had to telegraph the opposite.

So here I was trying to have my body say how much of a scared little mouse I was and couldn't hurt anyone with this one big tooth...Marc sprang. He had planned it to look like he was going to jump the guy with the gun. That way his attention would be completely off me. He would then fake that something hurt too much and fall to the ground. He had to time this so that the guy would be initially startled but quickly relax when he fell to the floor. That way he wouldn't end up shot. His leap would be my cue. Donovan (without the gun) might see me act but it would be too late. By that time, Marc's full attention and his truly remarkable skills (or so he assured me) would be upon him.

It began just like we planned it. Marc was perfect, my weapon came out just like he taught me and I had the drop on him. Then while swinging my makeshift club, I just couldn't hit him in the temporal bone (where it thins out to little more than strong tissue paper) as the planned called for. I altered the swing and aimed for his gun hand. I hit it squarely enough and the nail stuck, but the bastard would not let go of the gun.

I became enraged (mostly at myself for being such a weenie) that as I yanked out the nail from his hand, my intention was to use the back swing to hit him right in the face and hopefully stun him. Somehow, as he moved his hand and I yanked, the club rotated and the nail went right into and through his left eye. Time stood still as I saw where the nail was going to enter. This time I did nothing to stop its trajectory.

The soft almost musical squish heard as the eye enucleated and the crispy orbital bone crunch that was transmitted to my hand will never leave me. Neither will the sight of the bloody vitreous fluid squirting and splattering all over my face and neck. Although the fluid had just a slight salty taste, there was an urgent message from my stomach that it needed to empty and now.

Fortunately, it was easily overridden by more important messages, like the image of the guy flopping on the floor as if he had been disconnected from his power supply. After his initial unbelievable scream, he was remarkably quiet, just writhing on the floor cradling his lost eye.

I let go of the club as if it had been electrified. Despite the illusion of time stretching out, our little conflict had taken but six or seven seconds. I wheeled around and saw the struggle on the floor. Donovan was on top of Marc trying to choke him. Marc was defending his throat. I grabbed the turpentine and poured it on the rag. From behind, my hand forcibly jammed the cloth into Donovan's face. That's right, I didn't just place it on his face, but attempted to push it into his brain through his eyes, nose and mouth.

He leaped backwards while screaming in agony. All I could feel was sheer joy and did not want to move. He became a bronco trying to throw me off, with his hands clawing at the cloth. After some long seconds, I let go and watched as he stumbled around — blinded. Finally, Marc's screams penetrated through the blood haze.

"Let's go, Yolanda, we have no time!"

Marc had grabbed the gun and had picked up the keys for the handcuffs (good training, I would have forgotten that). I was right behind him, then changed my mind, turned around and without much thought, grabbed the club still dripping with aqueous humor (eye juice) and with a sense of violence not ever felt in my life before, slammed the nail into the exposed lateral ligaments of Donovan's right knee.

"That's for Tracy, you miserable piece of male trash." Only then did I run out and joined Marc.

When I reached him, he was at the front door. He told me there was no one else here, but we had to hurry and leave. There were no arguments with that, I didn't have anything to pack and had definitively overstayed my welcome. We ran out to the car and told him I could jump it, but he was already looking for the ignition wire (more of that company training). It was then that I saw them.

Initially, the road must be at right angles with trees in the way, because I had not noticed the lights, but when they turned toward the house, the lights were blazing. They could not have been more than 150 meters away.

"We have company," I screamed but he did not respond. "Marc! They are right here, we have to go, like now!"

Only then did he look up. I heard him swear, "Not enough bloody time! Run for the shadow of the house! [I was already on my way.] With any luck, they won't have seen us yet."

Once on the backside of the house, we heard the car come to a stop. There had been no racing of the engine, no screeching of tires, and now no excited voices. As far as they knew, everything was as it should be. I sneaked a look and saw Mr. Foreign Secretary himself getting out of the car. There was the short, fat guy with him and a driver.

Marc muttered, "Damn, they have a driver, we won't be able to get anywhere near the car without being seen." That is when Marc discovered that the gun he had picked up was gone. It most likely fell out of his belt when he attempted to hotwire the car. Marc despaired and went on a binge of self-deprecation. I, on the other hand, felt a sense of calm and control come over me.

"That's OK, it is my turn now, you got us out of the house, I will now get us to Christchurch."

CHAPTER TWENTY-TWO

ESCAPE

I actually saw his jaw drop for a second, just before taking the lead and scurrying west by southwest (a heading of 250°). The country was flat and mostly composed of fields and the going was easy. When I arrived, there had been no fencing. At night on the run, we could only hope I had not missed it.

Once we were out of hearing range, I asked him, "You *can* still run?"

"Sure, anything you can do I can do."

But his face belied that claim. He was paying dearly for his exertion. We might have to deviate from my plan to run directly to the airport I'd seen when Donovan brought me here. It was only five or six kilometers, but Marc would not make it more than the first two. That was OK, I told myself, our first priority had been to get far enough away so we could buy some time and we had already done that.

In one sense, the timing had been horrible. Five more

minutes and we'd be cruising down the road. Marc would be grinning from ear to ear and I would be happily puking my guts out. But in another sense, the timing had been propitious; had they arrived any sooner, we'd both be dead. So I let go of all the what ifs and focused on letting my right brain work on this puzzle: *How do we get ourselves transportation and remain undetected?* It wasn't long before there was a disturbance behind us. Lights were going on and being waved everywhere, and I was sure the car screeched out of the driveway.

I grabbed hold of Marc's arm and helped him along. It slowed me down but it eased the amount of work he had to do. When the house had not been visible for at least a half mile, I turned our course to the more southerly heading of two hundred degrees. We went another ten minutes before I called for a rest.

"I can keep going," Marc insisted.

"No you can't! And I can't carry you. Relax, they can't track us while it is still dark. They may try but they will never catch us that way." (I also desperately still needed to pee.) He just slumped on the ground and probably would never get back up.

I counted fifteen minutes and helped him up. He was a remarkable man. Most people would have quit. Not him though, his body had received such abuse the last few days and he'd used pretty much the last of his remaining strength fighting Donovan. His ability to keep going greatly encouraged me.

Was this more of that remarkable training or a sign of the man that took the training? We began with a fast walk, and then began a slow trot, estimating we were making about fifteen-minute miles. After twenty minutes or so, we had to stop again. We had to be very close and not wanting to miss the airport, I hid him well and went for a quick run to scout things out, making sure to get my bearings so as to be able to find him again. He promised to keep an eye out for me.

I ran a standard search pattern learned from dad and his flying buddies. I went straight for five minutes then turned right for five minutes then left for one and left again for five minutes. If my pace was steady, it would be six minutes straight back to Marc. The taxi lights were visible on the fourth leg. Our course was only a few degrees too southerly. If we had kept going straight, we would have missed it. As it was, it was only about seven or eight minutes at my current pace (eight-minute miles) or twenty at Marc's pace. Hell, we could easily crawl there by dawn.

Marc had indeed stayed awake and was excited by the news. He said he was feeling better, but there was time so we rested some more. We talked in whispers and alerted at any sound that seemed out of place.

"I'd like to ask you something," he said.

"Sure, anything," without taking note of how serious he had become.

He paused while I fiddled with my shoes, "Why did you go back and ruin his knee?"

"Oh, so you saw that," this was not a question, just a statement.

We sat in silence for a long time then I finally told him, "While laying there in that cellar trying to decide what I could and could not do, the chase scene at the lake kept playing over and over in my mind. You had just had me go over it in detail and something had bothered me about it. I was able to see it differently. Tracy's face and her efforts became clearer. I was wrong about her. She had not been trying to catch me. She had been trying to stop Donovan. She was his minder, like you said, and he had gone out of control. She was trying to rein him in. And he killed her for it. I have had it up to my eyebrows with men taking out their frustrations on whatever woman happens to be close at hand." When I had finished my monologue, Marc had fallen asleep.

I planned out our next moves and hoped that the airport would have everything we needed. Once a car raced by and I could imagine how desperate they would be to find us. With all the adrenalin surging through my body, my mind began to wonder how many of them were there and I was unable to get much sleep. The night was cool and we huddled together, which helped a little. He was sleeping deeply and that continued to worry me. If he could not move on his own with minimal help, we would be stuck.

At the first hint of dawn, I woke him. He seemed eager to get going and did not complain once. We started by walking slowly. It allowed us to warm up our muscles. I briefed him on the first part of the plan (he probably would not like the second part). He had awakened refreshed, stronger and he could manage by himself if he took it slowly. When we were close and he would not miss the airport, I went ahead to set everything up; he was to get there as soon as possible.

Dawn was minutes away and it was much easier to find my way. Arriving at the FBO (fixed base operator), I broke a window to get in. There were many planes to chose from. (No chance of alarms, FBO's around the world are too poor to afford them.) All the keys for the rental airplanes were neatly hung up by their N numbers. Before doing so, I rummaged around and was able to find only one of the necessary items for part two of my plan — we would have to improvise.

This FBO, to my undying gratitude, filled the tanks at night so all of them had full tanks. The Cessna 182 was my choice because it was the biggest of the make I was familiar with. It also had doors on both sides. I had to check the plane quickly and carefully since I could be seen from a long distance. When it was all ready, I sat on the left side and waited for Marc to arrive.

He had pushed hard and he was limping at the end of the runway. It would only take him a few more minutes, however, looking around, the lights went on in the FBO office, "Damn," I muttered, "We're out of time."

I turned the engine over and without any of the regular checks, fast-taxied to where Marc was. There is no rearview mirror on these things so it was not possible to keep track of what the person at the office was doing; we had to get airborne, until then we were sitting ducks.

Marc started running the second he heard the engine; he was a smart man. Slowing, he jumped in and we turned around to taxi back to the runway. We were downwind and would need to taxi back for a proper takeoff. One look and that was out of the question. They were waiting for me to do just that. A big black car and several people on foot had materialized. Marc finished strapping himself in; we were going to either take off with a tail wind or crash trying.

Tail winds are great if you are at altitude. They help you get where you are going faster and with less gas. However, on takeoffs and landings, they are not just inconvenient, they can be deadly. The reason is simple: airplanes rely on airspeed, not ground speed. At sixty knots (sixty-nine mph to you groundlings), most light planes will takeoff — just barely. With a ten-knot headwind, your ground speed is only fifty knots (trust me). With a tailwind of ten knots, your ground speed will be seventy before you can lift off. The difference in runway requirements is tremendous; as much as fifty percent more. Because runways are expensive, they are made just as long as needed and a bit more. They count on the pilot choosing the end of the runway that gives her a headwind or no wind. Runways are definitely not designed with tailwind takeoffs in mind. I was flagrantly violating one of the cardinal rules of flying. You don't live a long life by breaking these rules often.

He held up his thumb and smiled. That was all the encouragement I needed. I tightened my belt and opened the throttle to full. I initially forgot to set the prop to the correct pitch, but once I dialed that in, the plane accelerated well. When they realized what I was planning to do, they started running to the car. It would take them a few seconds to intervene because they had blocked the runway and I was taking off from the taxiway (perfectly safe, it's just narrower). I hoped that the extra few seconds it would take them to adjust would be all I needed. When we reached sixty knots (just above stall speed — see above), I lifted it into ground effect and forcibly kept her there (about three or four feet off the ground). In practice, this requires a tremendous amount of effort. The plane wants to keep climbing.

I was having a difficult time controlling her and couldn't remember what I was doing wrong. Then it hit me, TRIM! Use the trim. It made it a lot easier. Unfortunately, one of the guys on the ground was making it harder by shooting at us. I steered from side to side but did not have much success.

Still...they hadn't hit us yet. We were now going at over eighty knots and closing on them fast. I aimed for the shooter and made him kiss the concrete as the plane jump right over the car, and once cleared, went as close as I dared to the ground so they would have no target. Within ten seconds, it wouldn't matter; we would be well out of range.

Once clear, I climbed fast, wanting as much altitude as this bird could give us. A change in course was necessary for we were headed south and we needed to head north. Over the airfield, the car was next to a plane that had just started to move.

"They are going to try and chase us," I told Marc.

"Can't we outrun them?" he asked.

"Don't know, depends on the plane and the pilot. Our destination is obvious to anyone with a brain. There simply aren't many places for us to go without money or ID and with the government still tacitly allied with them. We have to try for Christchurch or Wellington."

Marc beamed, "So they won't know which one we are aiming for, it has to give us at least a fifty-fifty chance."

My silent look deflated his spirits. "Studying the chart before we left, both cities are on the exact same course. There is hardly one degree of difference between them."

"Oh," was all he said. He had barely held himself together and was on the ragged edge of losing it. So I reached over and slapped him. Not mean, not malicious, but pretty hard. My hand sure hurt enough afterward.

"What in hell was that for?" he yelled.

"You broke my hand," I retorted.

"I asked you a GD question. Why did you just hit me like that?" He was getting more animated by the minute.

"You also broke one of my nails, that hurts." With that retort, he finally got it. He started laughing, which got him to coughing — either way he was alive and energized.

"I can't bloody believe that some amateur is treating me this way. By all rights, it should be me carrying you around. If anyone ever finds out I will be washed up in this line of work."

I turned the plane left thirty degrees to a course of 360 degrees and looked behind us. It did not take long. There was a tiny speck coming our way and it pretty much had to be them.

"We are fortunate that you know how to fly one of these things. How long have you been flying, Yolanda?"

"Not long. They are behind us, and will catch up soon." So far, Marc was being helpful, but I could just make out the seed of disquiet coming from him. He probably had the fear of small single-engine airplanes that many people do.

"Please define 'not long' — a year, perhaps?"

"No, not that long. I am going to gain altitude; maybe we can out climb them."

His sense of urgency was much clearer now. "Stay with me for a second, you do have a pilot's license, right?"

I did not like where this was going and if I'd had my druthers I wouldn't have gone there at all — but I could see Marc would not be easily mollified. "A license is just a piece of paper. Please check that you are belted in."

"OK, that's fine, but you have been taking lessons for a while, right?"

"Not exactly…they are keeping up with our climb and I am almost at the plane's ceiling. Are all these questions important right now?"

"You bloody better believe they are important, Ms.

Yolanda Prescott. What do you mean by 'not exactly'?"

"OK, OK, you should know, after all it kind of affects you somewhat."

"Somewhat? Somewhat?"

My, but he was getting on my nerves, with all the negative karma; support was called for, not questions. "If you must know, my father is the pilot in the family. I have flown with him many times and he has let me fly it occasionally; I took a few lessons and meant to get my license but just never got round to it. Now are you happy?"

I kept close track of the pursuit plane and eventually could make out its silhouette. It became crystal clear why it was able to catch us — it was a Mooney. It had at least twenty to thirty knots on us and would have a higher service ceiling than we had. We were quickly running out of options.

Marc's response was hardly audible — "Happy as a 'roo in a zoo."

I don't know why it was a surprise when they started shooting at us, but it was. It seemed so ridiculous to try to aim a gun out the tiny side window from a moving plane at a moving plane that it had simply not occurred to me. To make their chances better, they were attempting to get very close. Although the shots could not be heard over the engine, the flash was visible followed by the briefest of puffs before the slipstream dispersed it. I yanked the controls in the most random way, attempting to make the plane follow the trajectory of a knuckle ball. It helped for a while but it was just a delay; I couldn't do this all the way there (wherever there was). I also had not had time to navigate and might be seriously off course.

"But you can land this thing, right?"

"Not really." His attention became even more focused on me but he nevertheless started helping me look back and track their progress.

"You mean you took off in this thing without being able to land it?"

His voice was getting shrill, I would have to speak to his trainers, he didn't seem to hold up well in certain stressful situations. "Calm down, Marc. Of course I can land it. If we weren't being shot at, I could have my full attention on landing and had help from the airport tower. They do that all the time. I just didn't plan on playing target practice across the sky, that's all."

I had Marc take the controls and do some of the maneuvering. He was so nervous he over-controlled the plane wonderfully. Trying to keep from throwing up, I attempted to locate us on the 'borrowed' chart. A few minutes with the GPS (Global Positioning System — I do like toys) and we had our location to the nearest meter. It was not far until we would have to execute plan B. I would try to break it to Marc gently, so he would not get shrill with me again.

I took over and dove for a cloud. It was a tiny one but it was the only cover around. Once over the fear of not being able to see, it was great not to be shot at. I had to let the plane fly itself because it is so easy to become disoriented while in a cloud, and me without any training on instruments. As soon as we broke out of the cloud, they, of course, came for us. It went like that for a while — cloud to cloud. I would change our direction when in the cloud to confuse them. It was finally time for the second part of the plan.

"Marc, please can you hand me the pack in the back seat?"

"Pack? Uh, sure, no problem."

I held my breath. One, two, three, fo...

"Big problem. You are absolutely certifiable. No way, this ain't going to happen, not to this guy, no way, you are as crazy as a kookaburra, you are."

"I didn't think you would be too thrilled by it, but we have no choice. Unless, of course, you can land this thing." He looked hard at me and then at the chase plane. It was right at this moment that a bullet finally hit the plane. It wasn't anywhere near us but it made my point rather well. He seemed to draw some strength from deep inside and his entire demeanor changed, now the old Marc was back. The one that had come up with the escape plan, his training had kicked back in.

"We will be sitting ducks out there. They could shoot us or just ram the chute."

"Not really," and I told him the entirety of part two.

"He was visibly turning pale but he was making a strong effort to hold it together and I gave him a lot of credit for that. "It will be OK, I have done it several times. The only unfortunate part is that I only located one chute. We will have to buddy up." He was quiet for some time. I took the opportunity to pick my site. It wasn't too far.

I put the chute on and realized it was made for a bigger person than me. That was good since it would have to support two people. I'd found some duct tape and had Marc duct tape himself to my harness. I felt that he kind of overdid it with the tape — but didn't bother to mention it. The trick to this would be to get out of the plane together while we were in a cloud. We were still at well over eight thousand feet; this meant we would have a thirty-second freefall. Under other circumstances, this might be called exciting. Here we had a few other choice words.

A flying body falling out of the sky will reach terminal (poor choice of words here) velocity quickly. For a person, this can be anywhere from 120 MPH in a nice eagle position to over 200 MPH headfirst in a streamlined position. At any rate, you are virtually impossible to see. If they didn't see the door open they would not be the wiser. We could easily be on the ground and moving before they guessed what we had done and by then it would be too late — for them.

"Are we all set?" I asked.

"Yes, let's get this over with."

I was much happier with his new attitude. It allowed me to focus on our plan, not fight with him. I hadn't jumped in years and had only free fallen once (I didn't tell him this, it just didn't seem like the time or the place).

"See that cloud? As soon as we get into it, you have to push your door open enough to get both of us out. I will be right behind you. I slowed the plane down as much as possible to help out."

"Won't the plane just crash as soon as we leave?"

He watched as I let go of the controls. The plane liked to fly and it did it well. With the controls properly set, it would go until it ran out of fuel or ran into a mountain. On the way out the door, the scene from the movie 'The Fugitive' where the hero jumps off the dam into the river flashed in my head. At least I had a parachute.

There isn't much to say about the jump. It was cold, windy and it did take us some time to stop tumbling. The funny thing about freefall is that it is not free and that it actually takes practice in order not to tumble. If you tumble, not only do you tend to leave your lunch behind you, but the chute may not open well, and even if it does it may catch you in a poor position and strain something. Therefore, it was reassuring that we were able to manage to get into and maintain a reasonable facsimile of a spread-eagle position.

To my surprise, I actually enjoyed the ride and committed to take this up again when I got back home (did I say 'when'? I meant if — no sense in being overconfident). I had been worried about how to time the opening of the chute. There was no altitude watch so I had to fudge it and predictably I opened it a bit too soon (I may have been a little anxious). The glorious feeling of the chute opening up into the bright, beautiful colors of the New Zealand flag (a deep blue background with the southern cross and a Kiwi on it) was unforgettable.

From that point on, I knew we would make it and was so happy at that instant that I almost forgot to pick a good landing place. I picked a farm that was near Route One not too far from Christchurch where this entire misadventure had begun. There were haystacks but it was too much to ask for me to land on one. Instead, we plopped in a sheep pasture. We landed hard but didn't hurt anything too badly (Marc's ego was slightly injured because he landed in some soft sheep doo). Even so, Marc was ecstatic. He hugged and kissed me and jumped all around, laughing hysterically and making a complete fool of himself.

I didn't mind and joined him in the celebration.

CHAPTER TWENTY-THREE

PAYBACKS

It was no great feat to convince a passing motorist that we had drifted with the wind. He gave us a ride into Christchurch after which we walked toward the Square. I was headed for JP's house. I remembered the address from the first search I did on him a week ago. Marc was understandably not interested in meeting him so right when the two of us parted ways, two police officers turned up.

"Ms. Prescott, Chief Inspector Yves would like a word with you; and with your companion also." It did sound like a request.

"He has no part in this," I insisted. They did not bother to respond. They were courteous and polite and they had their orders. I was also emotionally exhausted and could not fight anymore. I just slumped into the back seat of their car. No handcuffs — a decidedly good sign. But how in the world had they found us so fast?

It had been simple. The TV and newspapers broadcast

my picture (a good one this time) for half a day by the time we jumped. The person giving us a lift recognized me and reported us as soon as he dropped us off.

Later, I found out that after the police showed up at JP's estate and I disappeared, JP pulled out all the stops and used his political influence to find me. Having Mr. Foreign Secretary otherwise occupied and not around to object made it much easier. Like I had planned but not dared hope, the secretary followed our plane for hours; way out into the ocean before turning back (I can still get hysterical with the giggles thinking about this). I was told that he did not realize what happened until well after he landed. He assumed that his bullets had done the trick and we would simply disappear into the world's largest ocean. Therefore, he was understandably dumbfounded when informed by the news media that we were safe and had been talking with the authorities for hours.

They debriefed Marc and me separately and I pointedly left out the part about Marc's involvement with Peter. Even so, JP had already deduced that part out and so he didn't press me on that issue. In a way, that was worrisome; it meant they did not need my testimony.

My reunion with Dad was wonderful, but before fully being able to appreciate the end of my 'adventure,' I desperately required a little time to myself (without having to constantly look over my shoulder). During this time, I luxuriated in an hour-long shower that was as hot as I could stand. We then went out to eat a huge hot meal. He had gone through the effort of locating the only genuine Mexican restaurant in Christchurch; it was called, 'MEXICO LINDO.' This was my first such meal out in the open in what seemed ages.

We then went over to visit Marc. They did not have any

hard evidence against him (yet) and he was set free on his own recognizance. To be sure, they assigned a policeman to further assure that he would not leave the country (under any name or passport). I suspected that JP had not yet understood him to be an ex-agent, otherwise he would not have been so cavalier as to let him run loose and decided not to upset him with such picky details.

The three of us went to the same coffee shop where I had said 'yes' to JP's invitation to tour the mountains. On reflection, it felt like it had been someone else entirely that had accepted that invitation; in many ways, someone else had. I was clearly a changed person. I had done things I had not thought myself capable of: both good and not so good. I would, in the coming days, have many difficulties with that. At the moment, however, we had something more important to worry about.

When Dad and Marc went to the men's room, I walked over to the policeman shadowing Marc and engaged him in conversation. I suddenly started to retch violently. Dad had timed it well. He had given me an emetic a few minutes earlier and it was working well. The policeman was so kind and helpful that he did not notice when a man and a woman walked by and disappeared.

The man was in his late fifties, distinguished (if I say so myself) and very American. The lady, poor woman, must have been in a dreadful accident because she had bandages all over her face. She also had a walking cast on her leg and had what looked like burns all over her face. I would bet anything that in the baggy women's clothes we had bought him, the customs agents would not even guess that it was a man underneath the bandages. They would undoubtedly allow Marc to board the next plane to Australia, which by the most amazing coincidence was due to leave within minutes of their arrival.

EPILOG

JP was not happy with Dad or with me. Initially, he refused to speak to me. He had even tried to keep Michele from talking to me but soon enough realized the folly of such a childish game. It took him days to get over it and realize that Marc was gone for good. He had held onto hope that he would be found on the big island of Australia.

I had rightly suspected that if a company man wanted to disappear, then you might as well write him off. After all, I have been told many times that they have what is some of the best training in the world (all trace had ended at the airport in Sydney). A few days later, I received a postcard. It had a picture of a Kangaroo with a joey (a baby 'roo).

On the back was a handwritten message that simply said, 'Kids and wife doing great, enjoying extended vacation. Thanks for all the laughs. M.'

The last several weeks have been a whirlwind. For a while, I was at the center of a press feeding frenzy. I needed and received a tremendous amount of support to get through it. Finally, my fifteen minutes of fame were over and it moved on to someone else. Donovan was found and arrested for the murder of Tracy (they also had to rebuild his knee). By all appearances, his touch with reality was not returning. The police assured me that they had him cold and I need not fret over him.

I was able to spend five wonderful days with Dad: touring, hiking and getting reacquainted. We made a fierce effort to make up for the last three years of semi-alienation. By the time he left, we were closer than ever. It hurt deeply to see him leave, but I had unfinished business to attend to and he needed to get back to his patients.

The President of New Zealand invited me over for lunch. An easy man to talk to, he was immensely grateful for everything done on New Zealand's behalf. I tried to inform him it was done on my own behalf, but he would have none of it. I had become the current media darling and he wanted some of that publicity. He kept saying that New Zealand owed me a debt of gratitude.

I did not feel they owed me anything, but he went ahead and reimbursed all of the people I had 'borrowed' things from. (I still sent notes of apology to them as part of my amends.) He further insisted that they cover any extra expenses incurred on their behalf. On this point, I did not object too strongly; after all, thousands of dollars (US dollars) went through my hands and it would take me a long time to recover from that.

Further, he wanted to know what he could do for me personally. I declined to mention anything in particular. Later that day, he had paid not only for my original trip but for an extension of my vacation also. His position was that I could get to know the country after having helped it out. I thought about it and decided to accept the offer and spent the extra time touring the islands (it did not take all that much arm-twisting).

I went to Michele's thirteenth birthday party and did my best to play the mother role. It was at that time that she elected herself to be my tour guide. We went on many trips during the extra two weeks. I took that mountain climbing trip that a few days ago had seemed so unattainable. Michele taught me about Mts. Cook and Aspiring, and the Franz Joseph and Fox Glaciers. I visited gold mines and even ran into Kevin while we were there. We saw giant Moa trees, ate local cuisine and visited the North Island. These were wonderful days and awful nights. Michele and I talked about many things and both continued the healing we had started at Lake Tekapo. JP would occasionally join us, but mostly he was too busy with the resulting investigation. He had been given wide-ranging powers to discover how extensive the conspiracy had been and to ferret out any other conspirators. He seemed to thrive on it. Unfortunately for us, ever since I helped Marc escape, we had been unable to connect at any close level.

I attended several AA meetings and talked with Sallie (my sponsor) and Michael (my initial AA contact in Christchurch) on a daily basis. I tried to reconcile the things I'd done with my self-image and it was not working. When Donovan placed me in that cellar and Marc told me he had been tortured because of me, I had felt an enormous rage; a rage I had not thought myself capable of attaining. That rage had scared me then and even more now. These were parts of me to which I had not previously allowed expression. Most notably, to that part of me that is usually termed the dark side. It was at this time that I found an entire category of literature regarding this phenomenon; it ranged from Star Wars to Star Trek to Nietzsche.

I had spent my entire adult life squelching it and now that it was out, I was having a difficult time living with it. There was no way to put the genie back in the bottle. I had become aware that it was a real part of me (it is present in everyone) and that my options were to ignore it or accept it. Acceptance sounds so nice, but ignoring it is so much easier. It was slow going and it quickly became obvious that I would be on this particular aspect of personal growth for some time.

I made a special trip to Queenstown and had my date with Tim. We had a picnic at the park where we met. To his credit, he did not try to show me off to his friends, but preferred that we spend our time getting acquainted. We found enough in common to pass the time quickly and to be sad when we parted.

There was going to be a referendum regarding the best use of the oil field. The entire world was being pulled into it. Not surprisingly, the Middle Eastern countries were suddenly expressing concern for the environmental impact of such a site. The Asian countries could not wait for ready access to cheap oil and were willing to invest heavily to get it moving quickly. The oil companies were predictably spending millions on public relations campaigns. Mr. Foreign Secretary was pushing for full and quick exploitation. As with most things political, he had enough powerful friends that he might actually avoid being indicted. At least his hopes for the presidency were now on indefinite hold. My interest waned; I just wanted to get back home and be left alone.

On the way to the airport, I asked JP and Michele to stop at the Foreign Secretary's office. He was astonished but saw me anyway. His office was large enough that we were able to talk in a corner without being overheard. I did most of the talking. JP and Michele were extremely curious, but I deflected their questions. They wanted to know why he had turned white after our talk. What had I said to him? Finally, after all the goodbyes and the tears were over, and after the first boarding call, I told them.

I had had time on my hands in the office building in Queenstown, and I had been snooping around in various public files. I simply told Mr. Secretary that if he did not want to spend the rest of his life proving every document and transaction in his life from his birth certificate to his current mortgage that he should make sure to leave me alone.

"You mean it was you who deleted his final divorce decree?" JP said with smiling amazement.

I winked at them, hugged Michele one more time and boarded the plane.

The End

ABOUT THE AUTHOR

Domingo Alexander Rocha was born in San Antonio, Texas the day after Thanksgiving 1955. His mother called him her little turkey for years (although she now denies it). After his first birthday, the family moved to Madrid, Spain to launch a restaurant business. On his turning ten they relocated to Jackson, Mississippi so he and his brother Richard could learn English and benefit from the educational system in place there. (Really!)

The late sixties and early seventies were a tumultuous time in Jackson and the author was thrown into the maelstrom of desegregation in the south. That experience pushed him to understand how people speak volumes without using words. This skill later became essential in his medical practice.

He attended college at delightful Kalamazoo College where he met his future wife Carolyn. The moment they met, each knew something special had come their way. He proceeded in his studies of Physics and Mathematics at the University of Maryland at College Park culminating in a master's degree in 1980.

Revisiting a youthful desire to become a doctor he entered the University of Maryland Medical School in 1982, graduating in 1986. He finished his Family Practice residency in 1989 and opened a family practice office in Hampstead, MD on November 1, 1989 and continues to care for his patients, some of twenty years.

He has been married to his wife Carolyn for 32 years. He has two daughters, Holly 19, a sophomore at St. Olaf College in Minnesota, and Allie 16 a junior at North Carroll High School. He has two cats, Tommy and Opus.

The author loves to write and also loves to race his 1996 Miata during track season. He lives with his family in Reisterstown, MD.

Made in the USA
Charleston, SC
03 November 2012